MORE PRAISE FOR ELAINE BARBIERI!

HAWK'S PASSION

Hawk's Passion "nicely furthers the Hawk Crest Saga and adds to the character of the villain....If you're a lover of Western romance, don't miss this series."

—Romance Reviews Today

TEXAS TRIUMPH

"For those who enjoy a good Western, *Texas Triumph* is an easy read that will hold their interest."

—Romance Reviews Today

TEXAS GLORY

"No one writes a Western saga better than Elaine Barbieri! The action, adventure, and passion of this volatile family continue at galloping speed with *Texas Glory*."

—A Romance Review

"I don't have to give you any explanations."

"You do if you locked me in a root cellar because of some crazy idea you manufactured in your head!"

"I'm a woman alone and you're a suspicious stranger. That should be reason enough for you to understand."

Ryder took a threatening step closer. She felt the maleness that radiated from him like the heat from the sun. A chill ran down her spine as he said, "I'm the fella you locked in the root cellar, remember? You owe me a better explanation than that."

"You got what you deserved."

"What I deserved? Lady, you may be good-looking, but you're crazy."

Closing the narrow distance between them so they stood nose to nose, Justine responded, "You didn't expect me to believe Pop's story that you were just wandering aimlessly, looking for temporary work, did you?"

"If I remember correctly, I told you that my wandering wasn't aimless."

"Right, but now I know why it isn't aimless."

"You do, huh?"

"You're married and you left your wife."

ELAINE BARBIERI

CRY OF THE WOLF

LEISURE BOOKS NEW YORK CITY

To my family, the true loves of my life.

A LEISURE BOOK®

June 2008

Published by

Dorchester Publishing Co., Inc.
200 Madison Avenue
New York, NY 10016

ISBN 10: 0-8439-6013-2
ISBN 13: 978-0-8439-6013-6

The name "Leisure Books" and the stylized "L" with design are trademarks of Dorchester Publishing Co., Inc.

Printed in the United States of America.

10 9 8 7 6 5 4 3 2 1

Visit us on the web at www.dorchesterpub.com.

CRY OF THE WOLF

Prologue

*L*etty paced her opulent bedroom in the darkness of night. The howlings that haunted her had grown increasingly louder. The mournful wails reverberated against the vaulted ceiling of her silent room. The insistent howls had jarred her from sleep—but *fear* had forced her to her feet.

Letty walked to the window overlooking New York City's Park Avenue and stared blindly out at the few, flickering lights below. Barefooted, clothed in a simple silk nightdress, her dark hair loose against her slender shoulders, she stood motionless as bleak memories assaulted her. She had learned the hard way that only she heard the howlings—and they were always warnings of dire circumstances to come.

She no longer attempted to deny that truth. For that reason, she had not bothered to light the lamp on her marble-topped nightstand when she had awakened to the familiar sound. She had been unable to bear the thought of light at that moment. The shadows of the room seemed to match the shadows that filled her life. However great her financial success might appear to be, *she had failed*.

Letty's brief smile was filled with irony. Her exquisite beauty, untouched by age, was renowned in the city. Considered one of New York's loveliest women, she was also believed to be one of the most clever, interesting, and intriguing. She was desired by many, admired by most men, and deemed an asset at any function she deigned to attend. She had married two men and had nearly married a third. She had taken an indeterminate number of lovers in the time since. She had borne three beautiful daughters who were now grown—but in spite of it all, she was alone.

Letty stared down at the gaslights that lit the street below. The thought crossed her mind that the empty streets had a fairy-tale quality in the silence of night.

But the night was not silent to her.

The howling grew louder and Letty clapped her hands over her ears, hoping to shut out the sound. Yet she knew the effort was useless. The lonely cries that had haunted her intermittently during her life had begun again in earnest when her daughters became old enough to declare themselves free of her influence and set off on their own.

Uncertain where her daughters had gone, she had hired Pinkerton detectives to find them. She had asked the detectives to tell her daughters she would reinstate them in her will if they would return before her fortieth birthday. Robert Pinkerton had assured her attorney that his detectives would locate her daughters.

She had refused to think about the hardships her daughters might encounter as they searched for their individual identities, just as she had refused to accept the possibility that her daughters might refuse to return. Yet two out of three—Meredith and Johanna—had already been located and had refused her offer, stating they wanted nothing to do with her.

She was grateful for the information the Pinkertons had provided: Meredith and Johanna were now safe. She was happy to learn that her daughters had found strong men who loved them.

Only Justine's whereabouts were still a mystery.

Only Justine's fate was as yet undetermined.

The howls rang louder and Letty's anxiety increased. Where was Justine? What was happening to her? Did the portent that had preceded every black moment of her life mean that Justine's safety was threatened?

No, that could not be! Not beautiful Justine, her youngest daughter. Not Justine, who was perhaps the most adventurous and idealistic of all three.

Why had she not nurtured Justine's idealism? Why had she ignored her daughters by putting them away in separate, private boarding schools while striving for the acceptance and security that had always seemed to elude her? Why had she given all three of them so little of her precious time— time that she now realized she had often squandered?

Anxiety surged anew, heightening the color that flushed Letty's perfect features. The glint of tears glowed in her fathomless gaze, heightening her timeless beauty as she straightened her trembling shoulders with a silent question: Was it too late to amend the mistakes of a lifetime?

Chapter One

Justine Fitzsimmons had been employed at the Savoy Saloon for only three days, but she had already decided she'd had enough. Her throat burned from the clouds of blue smoke that hung over the barroom as shrieks of drunken laughter grew louder. Dirty floors, chipped furniture, watered-down drinks, and marked cards were the standard of the evening. Scantily dressed women flirted outlandishly with men who smelled even worse than they looked.

Dressed in a cheap, spotted gown provided for her under duress by one of the other women working there, Justine faced the reality that she was expected to join those women in their pursuits and to allow intimate liberties in exchange for money.

It was a harsh realization indeed.

Justine's gaze tightened as she scrutinized her surroundings with open disdain. She had been onstage once that evening. She had sung her heart out to the audience of slobbering drunks, cowboys with more than music on their minds, and dance-hall women who appeared to despise the ground she walked on, but she had known from the outset that she was wasting her time. Her "talent" was the last thing on her audience's mind.

How had her life come to such a pass?

Everything had started out so well. She had responded to an advertisement in a New York City newspaper that offered a position with a troupe of touring actors. In retrospect, she supposed she should have been more careful, or perhaps suspicious of the fellow who interviewed her when she admitted her lack of experience. Instead, she had been blinded by the interest in the elegant Roger Worthington's eyes. He had openly admired her glowing brown hair, naturally highlighted with red and gold; her great, doe-shaped green eyes; her fine, perfectly sculpted features that hinted at the exotic; and her unusually tall, well-endowed figure.

"Do you sing?" he had inquired.

"I sing . . . and dance," Justine had added hastily. She had not bothered to say that she had not had professional training, and that she was relying on the musical talent she believed she had inherited from her father to carry her through. Nor had she added that that talent was her only connection to the shadowy figure who had sired her. Archibald Fitzsimmons had been a wealthy, older man who was killed shortly after she was born, and before he could marry her mother. She had always used his family name, but she remembered her shock when she realized how little right she had to it.

She had deliberately avoided mentioning to Roger Worthington that as soon as her sisters and she came of age, they had decided to separate themselves from the mother they barely knew—the mother who had diligently refused to discuss any of their fathers with them.

Justine absentmindedly coughed. It was hot and close in the crowded room. She was choking from the smoke, her eyes smarted, and she didn't like the way a few cowboys at the bar were looking at her. She knew what was expected of her. She also knew that she had run out of excuses.

It was an insult, that's what it was! She sang as sweetly as a lark. Her talent was undeniable. She should have been able to captivate any audience with her dulcet tones. Provided, of course, that her audience was *sober*.

"Howdy, ma'am. Are you looking for some company?"

Justine looked up coldly at a cowboy who swayed slightly as he stood in front of her. He was clean-shaven and had probably been well groomed when the night began, but he was presently looking at her with drooping eyes, a lopsided smile, and a shirt spotted from too liberal imbibing. He held a half-empty glass of whiskey in his unsteady hand, and appeared not to notice that it sloshed over the rim as he spoke.

She responded succinctly and without hesitation. "No."

If she'd been in a different frame of mind, she might have felt sorry for the fellow as he took a backward step and stammered politely, "I'm . . . I'm sorry to have bothered you, ma'am."

But her mood was foul.

She had not expected that the "actors" who had welcomed her so exuberantly into their troupe would abandon her just as easily. She had known their tour was not going well when attendance grew poorer at every stop, except for fellows who arrived at her door with a very different type of entertainment in mind. But never in a million years had she believed that she would wake up in a dingy boardinghouse room in the middle of nowhere to discover that the rest of the troupe had sneaked off in the middle of the night, leaving her with their unpaid debts. Faced with furious creditors, she had been forced to settle all accounts, which had brought her to her presently disastrous financial state.

She had taken the only job available to a young woman with questionable talent—and she was well aware that the bartender of the Savoy Saloon had his eye on her.

So, what was she supposed to do now?

"You don't look too happy."

Justine looked at the old man standing in front of her. He was short and balding, with a straggly gray beard. His bony shoulders and chest protruded awkwardly from his well-laundered shirt, and his trousers were gathered together at his waistline with a worn belt. He obviously had been lacking a few good meals of late; yet there was a wiry strength about him that could not be denied. She had seen him before and had heard some of the women talking about him. A regular weekend customer at the Savoy, he had a small, respectable ranch outside town and was considered a pleasant fellow.

She scrutinized him speculatively as she inquired, "Are you talking to me?"

"Sure am. I said you don't look happy."

"I didn't realize it showed."

"I don't figure you do much to hide it." The old man shrugged as he added, "I suppose there ain't much of an audience for your singing here."

"This town doesn't seem to be interested in my *voice*."

"Maybe not, but a good-looking woman like you could get by real well if she decided to do what comes naturally."

Justine smarted. "It just so happens that *doing what comes naturally* doesn't come *naturally* to me under these conditions."

"I figured as much."

Her patience short, Justine snapped, "Well, if that's all you have to say—"

The old fellow asked unexpectedly, "Can you cook?"

Justine squinted at the old man, assessing him more closely. She had overheard some of the women saying that the old man's housekeeper of five years had recently left to get married, and that things had been in chaos there ever since.

Frowning, she heard herself say, "Of course I can cook."

"How good are you about cleaning up after yourself?"

"What business is that of yours?"

The old man studied her more intently. He said abruptly, "I got room on my ranch for a woman who can cook and clean up a bit. The position don't pay much, but it's decent work. Do you want the job?"

Justine hesitated. An ear-splitting screech of female laughter pierced the raucous din at that moment, causing her frown to darken. This man was a virtual stranger, but her situation at the Savoy was dire.

The truth was, she had no choice.

She responded gruffly, "Yes."

"What's your name, anyways?"

"My name is Camille Marcel."

The old man frowned. "You don't look like no Camille Marcel to me."

Justine sniffed. Acutely aware that she had no right to the family name she had used most of her life, she had thought long and hard before adopting her stage name. She wasn't ready to abandon it any more than she was ready to abandon her temporarily aborted career. She said stiffly, "Like it or not, that's my name."

"All right, *Camille*. You can start tomorrow— cooking and cleaning up at my ranch, the Double Bar C. It's just outside town. I'll pick you up in the morning."

The heat of the bartender's stare was burning into her back. "What's wrong with starting right now?" Justine asked.

The old man appeared momentarily startled before responding bluntly, "I just got here. I ain't ready to leave yet."

"I am."

"Looks like you're more desperate than I thought."

Justine did not reply, and the old man nodded.

"All right, I'll tell the bartender you're going with me while you get your things together. He won't give you no trouble." He added in afterthought, "By the way, my name is Sydney Cooper. Everybody calls me Pop."

"I know what your name is."

The old man raised his wiry brows. "That so?"

Justine assessed him more closely. "You knew my name already, too, didn't you?"

"Maybe. Maybe not."

Suddenly wary, Justine said flatly, "Before I go any further, I need to make something perfectly clear. I may be desperate to get out of this place, but I don't intend to go from the frying pan into the fire." Her gaze intensified. "Do you get my drift?"

"I get it, all right." The old man turned away. He said over his shoulder as he started toward the bar, "We'll leave for the ranch in a half hour."

The Texas night was wet and miserable. Ryder Knowles scrutinized the dreary scene, aware that the relentless lightning storm and continuing deluge had turned the ranch-house yard and nearby corral into a quagmire of mud that would take days to dry up. He noted that the horses in the field beyond were gathered under a tree in an effort to escape the pounding rain. He had no doubt that his revitalized cattle herd was seeking similar shelter on the seventy-odd acres of his ranch.

Silently railing at the dampness, Ryder walked toward the fireplace. He easily threw another log on the fire with a muscular strength that he had earned the hard way. Tall and powerfully built, with dark hair, light eyes, and chiseled features, he had a stubborn cleft chin that bespoke the determination with which he had devoted hours of physical labor to the broken-down ranch he had bought years earlier. He ignored the general consensus of opinion that he was the most eligible bachelor in the area. He had no time for it.

The truth was that he had never been afraid of hard work. He'd grown up on a ranch where he had arrived destitute at the age of twelve after an epidemic took his family. He had known from the beginning he would have to work hard to make his place in life. He had been grateful for the many hours his mother had spent educating him before she succumbed. To honor her memory and his own natural curiosity, he had read every book that came into his hands in the time since. He had applied that knowledge and lessons learned the hard way to his life, and the Flying K was the result.

With the help of three loyal wranglers, he had achieved his goal.

Almost.

He had purposely avoided thinking about the fact that he had married young—a sweet girl with an unrelenting smile whom he had loved dearly—or that he became a widower after a year of marriage when his wife and newborn son died in childbirth.

Two of his wranglers had temporarily taken over the ranch then, while the oldest one, Bart, had taken on the duties of the household in Betty's place. In retrospect, he supposed he couldn't have gone on without them.

Five years had passed since then, and he had never met a woman who could match Betty's indefatigable smile and cheerful personality. He supposed he never would—but that was the least of his present concerns.

A strike of lightning was followed by a startling boom of thunder, and the deluge continued.

"If this keeps up, that corn we've been raising for the herd is going to be pounded into the ground, and the foundation we just set for the new barn is going to get washed away."

Ryder looked up at Bart's comment as the man emerged from the kitchen with dishcloth in hand. Shrugging, Ryden said, "So, we'll start all over again. It won't be the first time."

Bart shook his shaggy head with a half smile. "I suppose there ain't nothing that can make you give up once you set your mind to something."

Their conversation was interrupted by a heavy knock on the door. Ryder hesitated briefly before walking toward it. Both Joshua and Toby had retired to the bunkhouse for the night, and only a fool would venture out in this kind of weather.

Ryder opened the door and stopped short at the sight of the big man standing in the opening. Rain ran in rivulets from the brim of his worn Stetson, his clothing was drenched and clinging to his rounded shoulders, and his face—unnaturally red in color— was covered by a week's worth of whiskers, but Ryder's smile was instantaneous and sincere. Holding out his hand in greeting, he said, "Tom Monroe! Come on in. What are you doing in this neck of the woods?"

His expression blank, Tom took a step and then toppled forward into unconsciousness.

"Get those wet clothes off him."

"That's what I'm doing, boss."

Ryder struggled with the big man's wet shirt while Bart fumbled with his belt. Ryder remembered the last time he had seen Tom Monroe. Ryder had been not more than twenty, newly married with a pregnant wife, and in a dire financial state. Tom was a mature cattle buyer who was wearying of his job and who surprised him one day by showing up to work alongside him while his men and he were digging a new well. Tom had stayed on for a while, and had even gone as far as to supply needed funds in an emergency—funds that Ryder had made certain to repay. Tom had left the ranch suddenly, mumbling something about life being short. Ryder had heard that he'd quit his job as a cattle buyer and traveled north, but he hadn't seen or heard from him since. He would be forever grateful to the man—was glad to see him again—but he was also curious. What had brought Tom back to the Flying K, and with a raging fever, too?

"I ain't going to die, if that's what you're thinking."

Ryder looked at Tom's unnatural color, his fingers halting momentarily as he struggled with the buttons on his wet shirt. His friend's eyes were half lidded and his face red. Ryder replied, "Maybe not, but you made a hell of an entrance. I'm glad to see you, but I wasn't expecting to see you in this shape."

"I've got a fever that managed to get the best of me, but I—"

A bout of coughing interrupted Tom's response, causing Bart and Ryder to exchange glances before Ryder said, "It's more than that, and you know it."

"Maybe so, but I got a job to do, and no fever is going to stop me from doing it."

"A job—"

"I quit my job as a cattle buyer after I left here, you know." His eyes drooping wearily, Tom said, "I took a job up north in the city. The change suited me just fine. I got to move around the country a bit, and to use my brain a little differently."

"You've been traveling, and you only now stopped by?"

"Yeah, well . . ." Tom appeared suddenly disoriented. "It ain't been that long, has it?"

Ryder did not respond.

Tom continued, "Anyways, I figured I needed to stop off for a day or so when things started getting mixed up in my head. I need a rest before finishing my assignment."

"Your assignment?"

"Yeah." Tom's smile was halfhearted. "I'm a Pinkerton detective now."

Ryder closed the door behind Doc Martin and watched as the physician hotfooted it toward his buggy. It was still raining, a downpour that hadn't relented for days. The sky was overcast, the ground was saturated, and the situation inside the ranch house was almost as dreary.

He heard Tom call from the bedroom, "You're not going to listen to that old quack, are you?" Interrupted by a bout of heavy coughing, Tom continued breathlessly a few moments later, "I'll be fine tomorrow."

Ryder looked at Bart, silently agreeing when Bart shook his head. Standing in the spare bedroom doorway a few minutes later, Ryder gave his old friend as no-nonsense look. "You have pneumonia, and the doc still hasn't been able to get your fever under control. If you try getting up tomorrow, you won't last a day before you'll be off your feet again—and this time probably for good."

"Trying to scare me, are you, Ryder?"

"Maybe, but everything I said is true."

"I need to finish up the job I started."

"It can wait."

"No, it can't." Glancing away, Tom mumbled under his breath.

"What did you say?"

"I said, I ain't going to give them fellas a chance to say they was right."

"What fellas?"

"Them fellas that said I was too old for the job."

"What job is that?"

"I told you already. I'm a Pinkerton detective now."

"Right, but that's all you told me."

"It's complicated. Robert Pinkerton sent three Pinkertons out from New York to handle the case. Two of them have already finished their part of the job. Only mine is left. Robert went against a lot of advice by giving me this assignment. He believes in me." A new bout of coughing interrupted him, and then he continued breathlessly, "I'm not too old. Anybody can get sick."

"Right. Robert Pinkerton is in New York? I'll wire him and tell him—"

"Oh, no, you won't! I ain't about to let all them naysayers have the last word. They'll just say Robert should've realized I couldn't finish what I started."

"That's crazy!"

Coughing until he was breathless, Tom said hoarsely, "I figured this would be my last job for Pinkerton, anyways. I figured it was time—but I don't want to go out a failure."

"You're not a failure. Like you said, anybody can get sick."

Tom took an unsteady breath. "Not a Pinkerton. Not me."

"Tom—"

"That's the way it is, Ryder. I'm leaving tomorrow."

"And you'll probably be dead by the end of the week."

"I don't think so."

"I do."

"Look at me and listen hard," Tom said. "I'm not going out before I finish what I started. Robert put his trust in me. I won't let him down."

"I suppose you'd rather die first."

"That's right."

Ryder looked at his friend. His color was still high and he wasn't making much sense. There was more gray hair on his head than dark, the lines that the years had carved into his face were deeply pronounced, and judging from the heat emanating from his body and the sound of his cough, pneumonia had a strong hold on him. Tom was right. He wasn't old, but he wasn't young, either. If he did what he intended to do, it would be the death of him.

"We'll talk about it later," Ryder responded. "Doc Martin gave you a powder to make you sleep before he left. I figure the best thing you can do for yourself right now is to take advantage of it."

His eyelids heavy, Tom mumbled, "I'll be better tomorrow, you'll see. I'll be on my way then."

"Right." Ryder exchanged glances with Bart, who was standing behind him.

"Right," Bart repeated.

But Tom didn't hear him. He was already asleep.

Ryder looked at the runoff in the corral, where puddles had expanded into small ponds, and then at the soggy field beyond, where only a week earlier sturdy wildflowers had waved their bright heads in a pleasant breeze. The rain had slowed to a drizzle, but it was still damned wet. Joshua, Toby, and he had herded the horses into the barn for temporary shelter, but they hadn't been able to do much else. It was a waiting game.

Ryder glanced at the doorway to the spare room. It was a waiting game there, too, but Tom wasn't willing to wait. Unseen, Ryder had watched Tom trying to dress himself earlier. The stubborn bastard had been too weak to stay on his feet for more than a few minutes. It was then that Ryder made his decision.

His oilskins handy and his saddlebags packed, Ryder walked toward the spare bedroom. He heard Tom stirring again. He saw Tom's expression change the minute he spotted him.

"Going somewhere, Ryder?" Tom asked.

"I'm going to finish up the job you started."

"No, you're not!"

"Is that what I said to you when you slapped down your hard-earned cash to pay for the material I needed years ago?"

"I think you did."

Ryder shrugged. "Maybe I was stubborn at first, but it didn't take long for me to realize that if I didn't take advantage of what you offered, I'd lose the Flying K in a few months."

"That was different. I don't need your help."

"You're just as desperate now as I was then, and I'm in the same position to help you that you were in all those years ago. I figure it's tit for tat."

Tom frowned. "Don't go talking dirty."

Ryder held back a smile. "It's that old thing about casting your bread upon the waters—"

"Never heard of it."

"It means tit for tat."

Tom did not respond, and Ryder said, "Are you going to give me the background on this case and tell me where you left off, or am I going to have to rifle through your saddlebags to get it?"

"What makes you think you can finish up what I started?"

"You said you've done most of the work already."

"I have. I know where the person I was looking for is right now. It's just a matter of making contact."

"That sounds easy enough."

"It might not be."

"I can handle it."

"Ryder—"

"Don't worry. I'll take care of it."

"Ryder—"

His expression sober, Ryder said, "Are you going to give me the rest of the information or not?"

Tom shrugged. "I didn't write much down. I got most of it in my head."

And the fever had him all mixed up. Ryder was beginning to understand why Tom had said it might not be easy.

Tom studied Ryder's resolute expression a few moments longer. He began reluctantly, "The name of the woman I'm looking for is Justine Fitzsimmons."

Tom snapped out of a drugged sleep. He glanced at the clock ticking steadily on the nightstand beside his bed and briefly closed his eyes. Ryder had been gone for hours.

Damn! His mind must've been foggier than he realized. He had given Ryder as much detail as he could remember about the assignment, but he had forgotten to mention one very important thing.

He had forgotten to tell Ryder that Justine Fitzsimmons was presently using the name Camille Marcel.

Chapter Two

All right, so she didn't know how to cook.

Justine looked down at the huge, black stove in front of her. When she'd arrived at the Double Bar C several days earlier, she had met the three wranglers on the ranch, the mature Pete Williams and Harry Leeds, and the younger Josh Harter, who had all been temporarily speechless at the sight of her. She admitted to being briefly amused. She had long ago accepted the fact that she was beautiful. Her sisters and she had always been told they were. They resembled neither their ageless mother nor each other, but they accepted compliments with perfunctory gratitude and the realization that they could not take personal credit for heredity.

Justine was keenly aware, however, how far a young woman could advance on that attribute alone.

Her sisters and she had always been told that they were highly educated and accomplished. In her ignorance, she had agreed with that assessment. They all knew how to play the piano, could embroider beautifully, could quote the poets and classics alike, and could manage a household and easily plan a party for as many as a hundred people—in a household where a butler would do the coordination, a chef was a necessity, and maids did the dirty work.

It was unfortunate, however, that no one had ever thought to teach her sisters or her anything *practical*. She could not cook. She had no idea how to clean a house in an organized fashion. She was at a total loss as to how to maintain a fashionable appearance without someone to attend to her wardrobe and hair. Her present dishevelment attested to that fact. She was wearing a clean but stained cotton dress several sizes too large that had been left in the closet of her room. Her curls were haphazardly upswept, her fingers burned, and there was sweat on her patrician brow.

With the exception of Josh Harter, the wranglers were no longer stupefied into silence at the sight of her.

Yet she accepted it all as a phase of her transition—her room no larger than a closet, her humble attire, and the fact that working for a living wasn't what it was cracked up to be. For the life of her, however, she could not understand the pride with which old Pop had shown her the great black stove on which she was expected to cook. The horrendous contraption was scarred from former use and had been carelessly cleaned, which had necessitated long hours of hard labor on her part. To top it off, there was no way to regulate the heat that presently caused perspiration to trail from her temples.

Unconsciously wiping the sweat from her brow

with the back of her forearm, she reached for the oven door, burned her fingers again, and then mumbled a curse before wadding a dishcloth to pull the roast from the oven. Her eyes widened when the pan came into view.

The meat was burned black! How had that happened?

She frowned at the sound of Pop's voice as he called out from the informal dining room beyond, "What's the holdup? The boys and me are damned hungry."

Justine slapped the pan onto the table. Well, so was she!

The memory of the first supper she had cooked at the Double Bar C furrowed her brow. She had made a stew. She had expected it would be easy enough to make, but the gravy had been lumpy and tasteless, the potatoes soggy, and the meat stringy. To her further amazement, the precious vegetables that she had added had totally disintegrated.

In other words, a disaster.

She had attempted a tried-and-true Western menu for her second meal: steaks for everyone. What she hadn't realized was how difficult it would be to control the cooking heat on that great black monster.

Another calamity.

The third supper she had cooked at the Double Bar C—well, she preferred not to think about that.

Food had become her enemy.

"Camille."

Justine called back, "Supper's almost ready." Within the last three days, she had become an accomplished liar.

"Don't tell me—"

She looked up to see Pop standing in the kitchen doorway. His narrow shoulders rigid, he stared at the charred roast.

Justine heard herself say with a feigned air of confidence, "It's perfectly edible. It's just a trifle over-cooked."

"That's one way of putting it."

Ignoring Pop's response, she said, "I'll slice the meat up and pour some gravy over it. It'll be fine."

Pop looked at the great stove where a pan of gravy rested beside a bowl of "mashed" potatoes. They were both so watery as to be almost unrecognizable. His reply was spontaneous.

"There's a ham in the smokehouse."

"I said—"

"I'll get it."

Pop walked determinedly out into the yard, and Justine felt frustrated anger rise. Well, what did he expect with that awful stove, and with . . . with limited ingredients to cook with? Meat and potatoes, meat and potatoes, with a sprinkling of vegetables thrown in if she were lucky. She needed practice, that was all. With her natural intelligence and ability, she was bound to conquer the problems sooner or later.

Pop returned to the kitchen at that moment with the ham in hand. Raising her chin, Justine said, "I'll warm it up."

"No!" Pop managed a smile as he added, "The boys and me will be happy to eat it cold."

"All right, I'll serve the mashed potatoes and gravy with it." She added almost in afterthought, "I baked biscuits. They're black on the bottom, but they'll do."

Pop's expression said it all.

When she reacted with a frown, Pop managed, "Don't go getting all defensive on me now. Everybody makes mistakes sometimes. You just need some time to get used to things around here. The boys will be glad to gnaw on that ham. You can spiff up the place a little bit in your spare time, too, while I go into town tomorrow."

Justine glanced around her. Dirty dishes littered every surface, the floor was sticky, dried food was already collecting flies, and it was hot as hell.

She demanded suspiciously, "Why are you going into town? It's not the weekend yet."

"I got business there."

"Business—"

"I ain't going to look for somebody to replace you, if that's what you're thinking. I need to hire me another fella to work with the stock, is all. This place is growing too big for me and the boys to handle alone."

"Another fella."

"Right."

"Not another cook."

"I already told you that."

Justine nodded. Pop was a patient man. So were the other wranglers. They hardly complained at all, except for the growling of their empty stomachs, which they couldn't control.

She smiled and said sincerely, "Thank you, Pop. I know you haven't been entirely satisfied with what I've done here so far."

Justine was unaware that the glow in her eyes and the warmth of her smile enhanced her beauty to a breathtaking degree.

A momentary silence followed. It was broken when Pop said simply, "Let's eat."

Frustrated, Ryder leaned against an upright in front of the Savoy Saloon. Shielding his gaze from the unrelenting sunlight, he pulled the broad brim of his hat down further on his forehead, unconsciously accenting the dark line of his brows and the startlingly light eyes that scrutinized the main street of the small town. Deep in thought, he did not notice the attention he drew from the ladies of the saloon as they leaned out the windows and studied the breadth of his shoulders and chest, and the tight, muscular midsection clearly outlined by his cotton shirt. Nor did he see the way their eyes followed the line of his narrow, male hips, where a gun belt rested casually, or their brief smiles at the bulge beneath his belt buckle and the long, powerful legs that hinted at an intimate power. He did not note that the women inevitably glanced back up, their gazes lingering on the thick, stubby lashes bordering his intense gaze and the angular planes of his face, before returning to the full lips that hinted at a tender touch.

Their reaction to him was written on their faces. Yet one by one, they turned back to the saloon with a shake of their heads and the knowledge that Ryder Knowles had had only one thought upon arriving in town the previous day. Unfortunately, that thought had nothing to do with them.

The hard line of Ryder's lips twitched with growing frustration. Nobody in the small town of Wyatt, Oklahoma, had ever heard of Justine Fitzsimmons. How was that possible? Tom had told him that Justine was in Wyatt, Oklahoma. Could the detective have made a mistake? Admittedly, Tom's fever had mixed up his thought processes and some of his recollections, and possibly even some facts in the case, but he had been adamant about Wyatt.

After receiving only blank looks when mentioning the name Justine Fitzsimmons, Ryder had taken the young woman's folder from his saddlebags and read it again from beginning to end. It was unfortunate that Tom had not bothered with a written summary of his investigation so far. The information in the folder was sketchy, and the only photograph was of a child with brown hair and freckles, supposedly Justine at a young age.

Ryder inwardly groaned. He had not expected to be away from his ranch for an extended period of time. Unanticipated flooding on the trail had made the journey time-consuming, and his present difficulties were unexpected. He needed to get back to his ranch, where he knew there would be monumental work to do after the storm, but he also needed to take care of Tom's problem.

Momentarily stymied, Ryder reviewed in his mind the inquiries he had made the previous day. Justine Fitzsimmons was supposedly a beautiful brunette, but that didn't tell him much. When he first relayed that description in town, he was directed to the wife of a cattleman living on a nearby ranch.

Wrong.

Then had come the dark-haired spinster, the schoolteacher, the waitress in the local restaurant—all of whom had resided in the small town for more than a year. The only women who had come and gone in the last few months were part of a troupe of actors who had snuck away during the night, leaving behind a shocked singer named Camille Marcel, who'd been forced to pay their bills. The Marcel woman, who was also said to be beautiful, had taken a job in the saloon in the hope of replenishing her funds. He had gone there the previous night, only to discover that she had accepted a job as cook on a nearby ranch.

Cooking at a ranch? No, a young woman of privilege whose wealthy mother had pampered her from birth and had sent her to one of the most prestigious boarding schools on the East Coast would not lower herself to take such a job.

So, where was Justine Fitzsimmons?

"Hey, ain't you the fella who was asking about the whereabouts of a good-looking lady last night at the saloon?"

Ryder looked down at the young cowpoke who had come up beside him. Short and slim, with curly brown hair protruding from underneath his wide-brimmed hat, he appeared barely out of his teens, but Ryder knew looks were deceiving. He replied, "That's me, all right."

Holding out his hand, the young fellow said, "My name's Billy Trance. I just missed you at the Savoy last night, so I figured I'd tell you that you should talk to that fella riding into town right now." Pointing at an emaciated-looking old man riding down the street on a paint pony, he said, "Old Pop Cooper hired the woman that acting troupe left behind. She's dark-haired, and real good-looking. There wasn't a one of us at the Savoy who didn't try to get close to her, but she wasn't having none of it."

Ryder frowned. "You're talking about Camille Marcel?"

"That's right. She was good-looking, all right. I ain't never seen nobody her match."

"She took a job cooking at Pop Cooper's ranch, didn't she?"

"That's what old Pop said."

Ryder hesitated. "But you've got your doubts."

The young fellow laughed. "To tell you the truth, I would've hired her, too, if I thought it would make her look at me twice."

Ryder studied the young cowboy a moment longer. "But I'm looking for a woman named Justine Fitzsimmons."

"Yeah, I know, but that's one good thing about living out here. A person can take on any name that'll make her happy." Billy shrugged and tipped his hat as he said, "I just figured it was worth a thought."

The young fellow walked away as abruptly as he had appeared, and Ryder turned his attention to the old man, who had dismounted in front of the mercantile and was heading for the door. Ryder waited a moment, then pushed himself away from the upright and started in the same direction.

He had taken only two steps into the mercantile when he overheard the exchange of a whispered conversation. He paused to listen as the proprietor spoke.

"I'm only saying that don't make no sense, Pop. No wrangler is going to answer an ad like that."

"I know it don't sound right, but that's what I want."

"You just hired yourself a woman to do that, didn't you?"

"That's right, but . . . well . . . she ain't done too good so far."

"So fire her!"

"I can't do that."

"Why?"

"She was desperate, that's why. You know what that troupe did to her, abandoning her like they did and leaving her with all their bills. It's a lucky thing that she didn't sneak off in the middle of the night, too."

"She didn't stand a chance. Old Marge Heller at the boardinghouse was on her tail. She wasn't going to get cheated out of the money that troupe owed her."

"Old Marge wouldn't have pressed the poor girl if she wasn't what she is."

"What do you mean?"

"You know what Camille looks like."

"Well, you could be right."

Pop added, "I figure to give the poor girl some time to get her feet under her. It's only fair."

"I guess so."

"Me and the boys are agreed on that, especially if it gets them some help on the ranch."

"You really do need another wrangler then, huh?"

"Sure I do . . . temporarily. Weren't you listening to me?"

They continued whispering, and Ryder frowned.

Whispers . . . a beautiful, mysterious woman . . . a need that went beyond hiring a new cowhand . . .

Obeying sudden impulse, Ryder stepped into sight of the two fellows and said, "Did I hear one of you say he was wanting to hire a wrangler? I'm looking for a job."

Both heads snapped toward Ryder in unison, but it was the old fellow who spoke. Pausing only to look him up and down, Pop asked unexpectedly, "Can you cook?"

The afternoon sun shone brightly as Mason Little directed his carriage driver toward the seedy all-night club situated in a portion of town that he had previously avoided. He had known that his image as legal counselor might suffer if he were seen there, but now he had no choice.

"Driver, stop here."

It did not miss Mason's notice that the driver appeared nervous, as if he disliked halting his carriage in that part of town. He repeated, "Driver . . . stop!"

The carriage drew to a halt and Mason disembarked and paid the man carefully. He silently scoffed at the fellow's swift departure. Admittedly, he had felt the same way the first time he had come there to meet with Humphrey Dobbs. If he were to be honest, he still resented the fact that he needed to press Dobbs for details that the fellow had promised to provide when their association began.

The fact that Dobbs's men had already failed twice to accomplish the assignment Mason had given him did not seem to faze the rodent-like fellow. Dobbs insisted that although his men had failed to kill Letty

Wolf's two daughters, they had frightened the young women away from returning to the city to claim their inheritances. Mason believed otherwise. It was his opinion that his dear Aunt Letty's two elder daughters had their own reasons for turning her down, but he was not about to argue. Only one daughter had not yet been contacted, and if Justine Fitzsimmons declined her mother's offer also, his plan could go immediately forward.

Mason pulled open the door of the club and winced at the odor of stale beer and rancid food that struck his nostrils. He would never understand why Dobbs had chosen this club as his headquarters—but he supposed he should not be surprised. Dobbs, with his oversized clothing and large, pointed features, was probably perfectly at home in such sordid conditions. It was that fact, as well as Dobbs's connections in the underworld, which had initially convinced him Dobbs was the right man to contact for a bit of delicate business.

Mason's expression tightened. His dear, wealthy old uncle, Archibald Fitzsimmons, had all but ignored him in his will, but he supposed he couldn't complain. His uncle's mistress, "Aunt" Letty, had also been ignored. He could not be certain why he had bothered to maintain limited contact with Letty—a woman he secretly despised. He supposed there had been some part of him that had known it would be worth his while in the end—which it had. He had seen to it that his contacts with her increased along with her growing wealth and unexpected social acceptance. As a result, she began thinking of him as family. He had been elated when she named him her beneficiary after her daughters became estranged from her. Her change of mind shortly afterwards, contingent on her daughters' return, had been a blow from which he had not yet recovered. It was then that he had hired Dobbs to make sure Letty's children would *never* show up.

Yet it was Letty herself who had provided the perfect solution to his dilemma. In a weak moment, she had confided that she believed she was somehow cursed. She had said every man who truly loved her had been condemned to an early demise, and that a wolf's howling that only she could hear had warned her of every dark event in her life. She had whispered almost fearfully that the howling had grown louder since her daughters had left. She had even begged him to hire a detective to protect James Ferguson, one of her former lovers, from harm.

Mason remembered staring incredulously at Letty after that whispered revelation. Howls only she could hear . . . warnings that came in the night . . . an unknown predator stalking one of her former lovers. . . . She was insane!

The fact that James Ferguson had been attacked on the street shortly afterward had only served to strengthen her delusions, but Mason had seen the attack for what it was: merely a coincidence.

Letty's two elder daughters had already signed the paperwork declining a portion of her estate. Once Letty's youngest daughter was out of the way, he would be Letty's sole beneficiary. He would then use his legal connections, and Aunt Letty's unfailing trust in him, to obtain power of attorney so he could have her committed to a mental institution where she belonged. With free access to her fortune, the world would be his oyster!

Only Justine Fitzsimmons still stood in his way.

"What are you doing here?"

The unexpected question from a dark, shadowed corner of the club caused Mason to start with surprise. Squinting into the shadows, he replied tartly, "You always did enjoy catching me off guard, Dobbs."

Dobbs stepped out into the light. Appearing more rodent-like than ever as his small eyes narrowed into slits, Dobbs said flatly, "I asked you what you're doing here."

"My reason should be obvious."

"I told you I'd contact you when I had something to report."

"Which means your man hasn't found Justine Fitzsimmons yet."

"I didn't say that."

"You didn't have to!"

Dobbs hissed, "What's the rush, Little? That fortune you expect to inherit ain't going nowhere."

"That's right, it's just lying in a bank waiting to be spent, and I'm tired of waiting to spend it."

"Letty Wolf's life will have to end before that happens." Dobbs snickered. "No matter how you intend to make that happen, you're going to have to wait a reasonable amount of time or risk that someone will get suspicious about her death."

Mason almost laughed. Tempted to put Dobbs in his place by spelling out his plan, Mason repeated, "Which means that your man hasn't located Justine Fitzsimmons yet."

His lips tight, Dobbs responded, "My man is taking his time, but you can rest assured that Letty Wolf's youngest daughter won't be coming back to claim her inheritance."

"You must forgive me if I question your word on that."

Mason knew his sarcasm was a mistake the moment rage flashed in Dobbs's eyes.

"Nobody knows better then me that my men didn't do exactly what they was hired to do, but it all ended up fine for you, didn't it?" Dobbs whispered vehemently. "Letty Wolf's daughters ain't coming back. I'm the only loser. I lost two good men, and that's something I won't forget too easy."

"Which means?"

"Which means I won't let it happen again! I told my man to take his time doing this job—not to let anything or anyone push him into acting before he's ready."

"I'm not interested in your orders. I'm interested in results."

"My man knows what he was sent out to do, and he'll do it, but he'll do it in his own time." Dobbs took a threatening step forward. "My man will let me know when the job has been taken care of. Until then, I don't expect any more questions from you. Do we understand each other?"

Mason's expression grew rigid. The bastard! Dobbs knew he had the upper hand, and he wasn't afraid to use it.

"Do we understand each other?"

"I understand you, but I want to make sure you understand me, too," Mason said hotly. "I won't stand for any more slipups! I hired you to do a job, and I expect you to see that it gets done, even if I have to go over your head to make sure."

"Over my head . . ." Dobbs's expression darkened. "That could be dangerous for you."

"No, for *you*, not for me!" Mason added with growing heat, "Keep that in mind while you wait for your man to become comfortable enough to act. And remember, I expect to be informed the minute he reports to you. The very minute!"

"It looks like we understand each other very well." There was no warmth in his smile as Dobbs ordered, "Get out of here and don't come back. I'll let you know when there's something to report."

Holding back his retort with pure strength of will, Mason walked rigidly out onto the street. Whether Dobbs knew it or not, the slimy bastard had just made his last mistake. He would be sorry.

Chapter Three

She heard it again!

Justine glanced around her and then moved quickly to the window to search the horizon with a frown. Brilliant sunlight illuminated the midday scene of a muddy yard, a dilapidated barn, and several outbuildings that comprised Pop Cooper's small ranch. She saw an equally rickety corral where the ranch hands had put their horses overnight, a lopsided henhouse that sheltered chickens picking lazily at the few strands of grass visible to the eye, a barn cat stretched out motionless in the sun, and a wooden pen where a single pig was busy consuming the remains of the less than palatable breakfast that she had cooked.

Justine squinted, carefully studying the rolling, wooded hills beyond. She saw nothing—no sign of the animal whose howl reverberated in her mind.

She closed her eyes, her stomach clenching tight when the echoing howl rebounded again. She had almost forgotten that sound.

Justine opened her eyes, tight-lipped as she admitted to herself that wasn't really true. She had merely thrust the trauma of that first time to the back of her mind. She still trembled in retrospect. Five years old, she had awakened feeling content and secure that day. She had walked hand in hand with her sisters to the breakfast table. Her mother, who usually had little time for her daughters, had surprised them by appearing in the morning room. Justine supposed she should have been suspicious of that unusual circumstance, but she had been stunned into silence when her mother informed them that she had arranged for them to attend boarding schools—*separate* boarding schools—and that they would be leaving later that day.

The youngest of the three, Justine had burst into tears when her mother left the room to tend to her busy schedule. White-faced and quiet, Meredith had attempted to console her while Johanna had stood silently by, struggling against tears of her own. Her mother came to bid them a brief adieu when they were ready to depart for their schools, but Justine's nanny was left with the task of tearing her from her sisters' arms and seating her beside her escort in the carriage.

Justine had since asked Meredith, the eldest, why their mother had separated them. Meredith's solemn reply had been that they were too close to one another for their mother's liking—but most of all, they had become an unwanted distraction from the life their mother had chosen for herself.

Tearful and alone that night at her boarding school, Justine had heard that haunting howl for the first time. It seemed to express the loneliness deep inside her. It had reverberated against the walls of her solitary room, halting her sobs and consoling her somehow. It had reached out to her in a way that she could not quite define, and she had drifted to sleep to the sound of its bittersweet serenade.

It was then that she had first dreamed of *him*.

The old man had materialized out of the darkness and had whispered to her in a guttural language that was strange to her ears. His voice had been deep with a concern that had touched her heart. She had somehow understood him when he had promised her that she would see her sisters again. He had told her not to be afraid because she would never be alone, and she had believed him.

The old man had come to her whenever difficulties overwhelmed her in the years that followed. He had been her protector and her friend, and everything he had ever promised had come true.

She had never told anyone about him—not even her sisters. He did not visit her frequently once she had matured and become more confident, yet he had appeared in her dreams the previous night. His image had been clear as he approached. The setting sun was at his back, but she had been able to see that his face was older, more weathered. His long, unbound hair was almost totally white. A soft breeze lifted the ragged strands to brush his narrow, bare shoulders, but the dark, intense gaze she remembered so well had not changed. He spoke to her intently in the same guttural tongue that she mysteriously understood. But this time, he did not come in consolation. He came in warning.

Uncertainty gripped Justine's emotions as she reviewed in her mind the cryptic message he had brought her:

Take care.

Danger approaches.

Beware, but do not be afraid.

I will protect you.

The lonely call sounded again, and a chill ran down Justine's spine. She knew it was related somehow to the vision she had seen, but what did it all mean? Why had the old man chosen to come to her now? He had said she was in danger—but from whom, and why?

She walked back to the stove behind her. With a sense of responsibility beyond her years, Meredith had arranged for the sisters to keep in touch without their mother's knowledge in the years that followed their separation. When the sisters had gone their separate ways to discover what the future held for each of them, they had made plans to meet in a year's time. She was determined that she would not meet her sisters again as a failure.

Justine frowned at that thought. Her situation at Pop's ranch did not fit her definition of success, but her job there was just a temporary respite, a place for her to regroup before starting out again. Pop and his men had been patient through her many mishaps. They deserved better than she had given them, and she was resolved that when it came time for her to leave, they would say sincerely that she was the best cook they had ever had.

She reached for another piece of kindling to toss into the stove in preparation for the evening meal.

As for the warning howls, something was clearly wrong, even if she was uncertain what it was. But she needed to remember that he was her guide and her friend. The old man had told her not to be afraid because he would protect her.

The sad reality was that at present, he was the only thing she knew she could depend on.

Why don't you just fire Camille Marcel if she can't cook?

Pop had replied to Ryder enigmatically as they rode toward his ranch: *Ask me that again after you see her.*

Now that he was looking at the stunningly beautiful, though admittedly disheveled young woman standing in front of the massive black stove in Pop's stifling kitchen, Ryder realized how naive his question had been. Camille Marcel was the loveliest woman he had ever seen, and he had no doubt from Pop's response that she had learned to use her beauty well.

Camille scrutinized Ryder suspiciously as Pop continued, "I've hired Ryder to fill in the gaps on the ranch temporarily. I figure we needed somebody like him."

Camille's heavily lashed green eyes narrowed. Her gaze moved between them as she said, "You told me that. What you didn't tell me was what 'fill in the gaps' means."

"It means just what I said." His smile unconvincing, Pop continued, "Ryder will fill in wherever he's needed. Things fall behind on the ranch while the boys and me work with the stock. We don't never seem to catch up, neither. Ryder understands that, because he had a ranch of his own before he took to the trail. Since temporary work suits him fine right now, I figured he's the man for the job."

Ryder felt the full heat of Camille's exotic gaze as she studied him more intently. Finally nodding noncommittally, she turned back to the stove without comment. She looked up when Pop questioned offhandedly, "What are you cooking tonight?"

"Why?"

Her defensive tone caused Pop to respond weakly, "I was just asking."

Ryder looked at Pop with a frown. Damn if the old man wasn't all gurgle and no guts where this woman was concerned!

Hesitating only a moment, Camille responded, "I figure on making a roast again."

Ryder did not miss the responsive twitch of Pop's cheek. It was obvious to him from the way Camille had stuffed the great black stove with firewood that she had no idea what she was doing. Another situation became just as obvious when Pop replied, "Oh . . . good," and then added, "I'd appreciate it if you could take over for me and settle Ryder down on the ranch so I can ride out to work with the boys."

Resentment flushed hotly through Ryder as Camille nodded with obvious reluctance and Pop tipped his hat and made a fast exit. He didn't like having this particular problem tossed into his lap, especially when this beautiful woman appeared somehow suspicious of him.

Waiting until Pop had cleared the doorway, Camille confirmed Ryder's thoughts by asking abruptly, "Pop's gone, so you can tell me the truth. Why are you here? Unless I miss my guess, you're not the type of man to wander aimlessly around the country looking for temporary work."

Camille took a step closer. Her rounded breasts heaved with unexpected fervor, pressing revealingly against the oversized dress she was wearing as she ordered, "Come on, out with it. Why are you here?"

Ryder hesitated to reply. He had always considered himself a man who was unimpressed by a woman's physical beauty; but the woman standing in front of him, daring him to respond, was an exception, and she knew it. He had never seen hair the color of her gleaming brown, decidedly messy locks. Nor had he ever seen female features so delicate, or a form that was so . . . womanly. Yet the only things he had learned about Camille Marcel so far were that she wasn't French, she couldn't cook, and she had the men on the ranch under her thumb.

Was she the Justine Fitzsimmons he was looking for? Possibly, but an inner caution warned him not to ask her outright—not if he wanted the truth.

"Well, are you going to answer me?"

Ryder responded flatly, "Yes."

"Yes, what?"

"Yes to all your questions. Yes, I'm going to answer you. Yes, I'm not the kind of man to wander aimlessly around the country—my wandering isn't aimless. And yes, along with my duties on the ranch, Pop hired me to give you some pointers on cooking."

"Really?" Camille scrutinized him from head to toe in a demeaning manner as she continued,

"What makes him think you can teach me anything?"

"You tell me. You're the one who's been doing the cooking here for the past week."

Ryder noted the flush that suffused Camille's face when she responded, "Singing is my specialty, but there doesn't seem to be an audience for my talent in Oklahoma. Admittedly, cooking isn't my forte, but I've been doing all right."

"That isn't what Pop says."

"It's that blasted stove," Camille retorted with unexpected rancor. "Pop thinks any woman should be able to perform miracles on it."

"I guess that's why Pop wants me to show you how to use it. He said he and his men don't have the time to do it."

Camille's gaze was guarded. "Is that the only reason you're here?"

As determined to ignore her question as he was to ignore his unexpected reaction to her feminine appeal, Ryder said flatly, "Your first mistake is that you've put too much wood in that stove. It's so hot that it'll probably burn anything that takes more than a few minutes to cook."

He realized he had struck a nerve when Camille snapped, "You can take care of the contraption yourself if you know so much about it."

"No, thanks. That's your job."

"You said Pop hired you to—"

"I said he hired me to show *you* how to use it. He didn't hire me to do your job."

Camille replied with growing fervor, "All right,

but just remember that I'm not the one who invited you into this kitchen."

Anger flushed her perfect features, and her ample breasts heaved underneath the bodice of that damned baggy dress as Ryder said tightly, "If you'll tell me where the bunkhouse is, I'll put away my gear."

"It's out back."

Dismissing him with her turned back, Camille began peeling the potatoes on the table in front of her, and Ryder's lips ticced with annoyance. She wasn't even doing that right.

He turned toward the door. "I'll be back."

Silence was her only response, and Ryder slammed the door behind him. What had he gotten himself into?

The door slammed and Justine's frown deepened. Was he the one the old man in the vision had warned her about?

A howl sounded, sending a chill down her spine that effectively dismissed her former annoyance.

Danger approaches.

Beware.

Suddenly aware that she had allowed anger to displace the caution her mysterious nighttime visitor had suggested, Justine cursed under her breath. She had sensed the moment she saw Ryder Knowles that something wasn't right. Whoever he was, his gaze was too assessing to be casual. She felt as if he were scrutinizing her with an unspoken sense of purpose. There was nothing aimless about that rangy, long-legged cowboy stride. She wasn't fooled by that light-eyed glance that was meant to be offhanded. She sensed a coiled masculine power in him. She didn't like the look of him in any way, especially that unexpected cleft in his chin that women probably could not help commenting on in intimate situations.

The thought of their mewling sighs somehow nauseated her.

Oh, Ryder, you're so tall and handsome. I love dark-haired men.

Oh, Ryder, you're so muscular.

Oh, Ryder, your eyes send shivers down my spine.

Oh, Ryder, that cleft in your chin fascinates me. I want to taste it, to run my tongue—

Justine sniffed without finishing that thought.

She didn't like being forced to look up at him, either. Tall for a woman, she was accustomed to looking straight into the eyes of men who addressed her. It gave her a sense of power, of equality that wasn't usually afforded women, and she resented having it taken from her.

Beware, but do not be afraid.

That thought returned to sting her. She wasn't afraid of him! It would actually give her pleasure to bring that know-it-all down a peg or two, just so he'd know she wasn't as vulnerable to him as every other Western belle probably was.

Danger approaches.

A chill ran down Justine's spine despite herself. Her heart gave a nervous thump as questions without answers rang again in her mind. Was he truly the person the old man had warned her about? If he was, what was she supposed to beware of?

And, most unsettling of all, what was she supposed to do now?

Otto Tears rode slowly, his bloodshot eyes narrowed into slits as he scrutinized his surroundings. He sat his saddle effortlessly, his narrow shoulders hunched and his hawk-like nose protruding from underneath hairy eyebrows drawn in an intimidating frown. His thin, sweaty face was covered with more than a week's stubble, and the simple Western clothes that he had bought specifically for his present job looked as if he had slept in them— because he had. Except for a raging headache, an uncertain stomach, and a need to get back on the trail in order to complete the job, however, Otto did not truly regret the previous night's indulgences at the Red Slipper Saloon. He had craved the satisfaction that only a woman's body could grant him, as well as the pure pleasure of drinking himself unconscious. He had earned that much, even if he hadn't found the young and supposedly inexperienced Justine Fitzsimmons yet.

Damn it, the witch was just as cunning and determined as her mother, and not as inexperienced as everyone thought! Or she was just lucky, because she seemed to have disappeared into thin air. He had sent Humphrey Dobbs back a report on his lack of progress, only to receive a wire in return, warning him to be careful. He had destroyed the wire after memorizing the few lines:

BE CAUTIOUS STOP FINK AND SMART DID NOT RE-
TURN STOP IMPORTANT THAT YOU FINISH WHAT

YOU STARTED STOP WIRE ME AS SOON AS JOB IS
DONE STOP

He had not needed a signature to know who had
sent that wire. The cryptic message had been very
clear to him. Both Elias Fink and Percy Smart had
been killed on jobs that Dobbs had said would be
"the easiest they had ever handled." Obviously, it
had not turned out that way.

Otto unconsciously shook his head, then cursed
as a heavy pounding began anew in his temples. He
needed to accomplish what he had been hired to do
so he could return to New York City. Actually, the
fates of the two other men Dobbs had sent after
Justine Fitzsimmons's sisters did not faze him. They
had known what they were getting into, and he had
an advantage that they did not. Simply put, he was
Western born. He had worked on his father's ranch
as a boy, riding and doing all manner of chores until
the bastard's constant preaching and heavy-handed
punishments for imagined sins had become too
much for him. He had been barely nineteen years
old when he finally made his way to New York City
and met up with Humphrey Dobbs.

Doing Dobbs's dirty work wasn't dirty work at all
for Otto. It gave him a sense of power to render
punishments similar to those he had suffered as a
boy, and it mattered very little to him whom he was
asked to "take care of." He enjoyed the work—or
he had until Dobbs's orders sent him west to face
bitter memories and relentless demons that only
whiskey and a night with a woman could temporarily erase.

Damn Justine Fitzsimmons! He had followed the Pinkerton hired by her mother to find her, just as Dobbs had suggested, but the fellow hadn't cooperated. Otto was unsure whether Monroe had known he was being followed, whether he had simply lost track of Letty Wolf's youngest daughter, or whether he had just tired of the game—because the fellow had veered off in a different direction and disappeared. Forced into doing his own tracking without a picture of the Fitzsimmons woman to guide him, Otto had made slow progress in locating his quarry's trail. But he had a clue to her whereabouts now, and he was determined not to get off track again.

Otto paused to empty his convulsing stomach, and then continued slowly forward. He wouldn't make the mistake of overindulging to such an extent again. He wanted to go home to New York City, where harsh memories did not await him at every turn. He was acutely aware that he had Justine Fitzsimmons to thank for stirring up those dark recollections.

But . . . she would pay. He would make sure of it.

"The fire's too hot. Don't put any more fuel in that stove."

Camille halted only briefly before deliberately tossing another piece of firewood into the stove and slamming the door shut. She turned toward Ryder and said sharply, "Don't you have something better to do?"

"I haven't eaten since this morning. I've stored my gear, I'm hungry, and I don't like burned food."

"Neither do I."

"The roast is going to burn if you put it in that oven."

"No, it won't."

"You're obviously not the expert here."

"And you are?"

"From what I see, I couldn't do any worse than you."

Camille raised her chin and asked flatly, "Why exactly are you here?"

Ryder stared at the beautiful, furious woman in front of him. Her eyes sparked and her chest heaved. Silently cursing the heat that surged through his veins as a single drop of perspiration trickled down between her breasts, drawing his gaze, Ryder was momentarily tempted to tell her—but common sense returned. She was too angry to trust anything he had to say, and he needed to be sure that he—

"Well, are you going to answer me?"

She was beautiful, all right, but so damned irritating.

"I'm waiting."

Ryder replied pointedly, "Pop told you. He needed another hand, a fella who also knows enough about a stove like that so he can show you how to use it."

"And?"

"Were you expecting me to say something else?"

She did not reply.

Ryder paused to study Camille Marcel's tight expression. He had started out on the wrong foot with her, but the truth was that he wasn't sure how or why. Maybe he had resented the unexpected complications he had run into, or maybe he disliked the fact that Camille Marcel was a problem Pop had dumped into his lap—or maybe the truth was that this woman had somehow managed to get behind the defenses he had so carefully constructed around his emotions, and he didn't like it.

Her adverse reaction to him, however, was another mystery.

Wanting nothing more at that moment than to identify Justine Fitzsimmons, inform her of her mother's offer, and leave, Ryder looked at the defensive young woman standing in front of him. It wasn't going to be easy.

Deciding it was time to try another tactic, Ryder nodded toward the large roast on the table and asked, "Is that roast ready to go into the oven?"

"As ready as it will ever be."

Ryder inwardly winced at her terse response. He looked at the clock on the wall. Three hours till dinner. It was time to get started.

Ryder repeated, "The fire's too hot. We'll have to wait before putting the roast in."

Camille glared.

"In the meantime, we can get the potatoes ready." Ryder glanced around the kitchen. "Where are they?"

"They were rotten. I have to get more from the root cellar."

Rotten . . . right. Ryder responded levelly, "I'll get them. Where's the root cellar?"

"I'll show you."

"I can find it."

"You'll find it faster if I show you."

Ryder frowned at Camille's apparent about-face as she left the kitchen and walked beside him toward the rear of the yard. His frown darkened as her womanly scent wafted to him on the warm breeze, nudging at a spot deep inside him. He wasn't sure if she purposely brushed against him as they entered the small root cellar, and he attempted to ignore her as he crouched down and began filling the sack she provided.

He had been too long without a woman, that was his problem. Few women had held any appeal to him at all lately, and he—

Ryder snapped upright at the sound of the root-cellar door slamming shut behind him. He turned toward it in the sudden darkness and heard the scraping sound of a bolt being slipped closed. It was too late. He was locked in.

Anger flaring, Ryder called out, "All right, Camille, you proved you're in control. Now let me out."

"You're going to stay right where you are until I can talk to Pop again."

"What?"

"You heard what I said."

"Why?"

No answer.

Stunned, Ryder asked flatly, "Are you crazy?"

The only response to his question was the sound of Camille's departing footsteps.

This wasn't going to be as easy as he had thought. Mason Little stepped out onto the sidewalk of the prestigious medical building and paused to regain his composure. Damn that Dr. Bosworth! He had no doubt that Letty had spoken to her aging physician about the howlings she heard and the visions she saw, but the fellow had responded coldly that he took his Hippocratic oath too seriously to betray the confidence of one of his patients.

Rot! The man was just an anxious hypocrite who was afraid to take a stand—or he was simply too infatuated with Letty to take a step against her.

Mason turned to walk stiffly down the busy street without the customary smile he fabricated for well-connected shoppers passing by. In either case, Dr. Bosworth's reaction meant that he would have to find someone else to confirm his claim that Letty was unstable enough to be institutionalized.

But who?

Mason reviewed in his mind the copious legal volumes he had searched in an effort to determine the best procedure to follow in having Letty committed. He didn't like doing such tedious work, but there was no one else he could entrust it to. He knew the need for secrecy was paramount. He doubted that Dr. Bosworth would tell anyone about his visit. Mason had, after all, only expressed concern and a need to help his dear Aunt Letty.

Mason brushed past a smiling matron without a second look, his mind occupied as he glanced unconsciously up and down the busy street before crossing with his brow furrowed. Letty's many liaisons were legend, yet she had never remained intimate with any man for very long. The only exception was

James Ferguson. As a matter of fact, the revelation of Letty's instability had come about as a result of her concern for James—the only one of her lovers whom she claimed truly cared about her. When she'd asked Mason to hire someone to protect James from death, he had almost laughed out loud.

Yet after James managed to survive the attack on the street, and after Letty spent day and night at his bedside, she had perversely refused to see the fellow. She barred him from her apartment . . . from her soirees . . . from every facet of her life, a situation that undoubtedly did not sit well with Ferguson if the fellow still loved her as she claimed.

Mason halted abruptly as he reached the doorway of his office building. Pillow talk was a strange phenomenon. Letty had trusted James. She believed he still loved her. He was the most likely person she would have told about her hallucinations. Perhaps James would be angry enough with Letty to confirm claims that Letty was unstable. Or if James *loved* Letty too much to speak against her, maybe he would want to *help* her by making sure she was treated—in a mental institution, of course.

Mason took an optimistic breath. All he needed was another person to confirm that everything he said about Letty's instability was true. Of course, he would see to it afterwards that Letty's commitment was not temporary—but that was another matter.

His spirits rising, Mason entered the building with a smile and headed for the staircase. He pushed open the door to his outer office and walked through without speaking a word to the clerks who looked up at his entrance. He then slammed the door of his private office behind him, his smile broadening. He would appeal to James's love and concern for the health of dear Aunt Letty.

Yes, James could be the answer.

Dear, loving James.

Chapter Four

*P*op stared at Camille. His eyes wide, he gasped, "Are you crazy?"

The sun had begun to set, sending elongated shadows across the muddy yard when he and his men had ridden in from the day's work. Dismounting from his horse as his cowhands made their way to the bunkhouse, he had gone directly to the kitchen, so anxious had he been to know how his new ranch hand was faring with Camille.

He had hoped that Ryder had somehow solved the problem and that they would all have a good meal that evening. However, those hopes had been dashed the minute he walked into the kitchen to the scent of burning food. The weak smile he had managed had been wiped from his face the instant Camille spoke.

Incredulous, Pop gasped, "You locked Ryder in the root cellar?"

Camille nodded, and Pop's mouth opened another notch. He asked a single question. "Why?"

"Why? Because I needed time to think."

"Time to think . . ." Pop considered Camille's response and then inquired, "Did he offend you in some way, or take liberties with you? Is that it?"

"No."

"Did you think he was going to steal something?"

"No."

He swallowed. "Tell me . . . is he still in there?"

"Yes."

Pop groaned. His expression abruptly changing, he took an unexpected step toward her, put a conciliatory hand on her shoulder, and whispered, "I know that only drastic circumstances could have made you do such a crazy thing, Camille, and I want you to know that you can always tell me the truth. I need to know what the problem is." He hesitated, and then asked, "Are you in trouble?"

"Trouble?"

"You don't have to tell me if you don't want to. I know that whatever the law is chasing you for, you're not guilty."

"Pop—"

"Shhhh. You don't have to say nothing more if that's what you want. I said you don't have to explain to me, and you don't. But I need to tell you that you made a mistake if you think Ryder is the law. He's just a fella who's looking to find his way, is all."

"Pop, I don't want to mislead you. I—"

"Look, I know you were suspicious about a fella like Ryder looking for temporary work, and so was I at first. Then he said something about being married . . . and about leaving his ranch."

"He's married?"

"I figure that's why he took to the road, to make up his mind about going back to that ranch and his woman."

"Oh."

"So, you see? You don't have to worry about him. He's just a lost cowpoke." Pop added tentatively, "A lost cowpoke who can show you how to use that stove, among other things."

"That's what he told you?" she asked.

"I saw his face when he mentioned his wife and his ranch, Camille. I believe him."

Releasing a pent-up breath, Camille responded, "It's your ranch, so I guess I'll have to take your word for it. I'll let him out."

Pop tried to smile. "Maybe I should do it."

"No, I locked him up and I'll let him out." Camille raised her chin. "Besides, supper's almost ready."

"Supper." Pop glanced at the pans on the stove and his smile faded. "All right, if that's what you want to do."

As Camille started toward the door, Pop watched her with another thought in mind—a deadening realization that things had gotten even worse than he'd imagined.

Justine walked with head high toward the root cellar, her emotions mixed. Whether she believed what Pop had said or not, she had to let Ryder out. Yet she could not seem to explain her sudden sense of loss at Pop's revelations. Ryder was married? He had walked away from his wife and his ranch? Somehow, she did not envision him as a man who would do either of those things.

Justine paused in front of the root-cellar door, took a deep breath, and slid open the bolt. The door snapped open, so quickly that she was forced to step backward quickly to avoid being knocked down. Emerging with an expression as black as a storm cloud, Ryder towered threateningly over her and asked flatly, "Are you crazy?"

Facing him boldly despite the heavy hammering of her heart, she responded, "No, I'm just cautious."

Ryder breathed heavily in an obvious attempt to control his temper. His gaze never leaving her face, he growled, "What do you mean by that?"

"I don't have to give you any explanations."

"You do if you locked me in a root cellar because of some crazy idea you manufactured in your head!"

"I'm a woman alone and you're a suspicious stranger. That should be reason enough for you to understand."

Ryder took a threatening step closer. She felt the maleness that radiated from him like the heat from the sun. A chill ran down her spine as he said, "I'm the fella you locked in that root cellar, remember? You owe me a better explanation than that."

"You got what you deserved."

"What I deserved? Lady, you may be good-looking, but you're crazy."

Closing the narrow distance between them so they stood nose to nose, Justine responded, "You didn't expect me to believe Pop's story that you were just wandering aimlessly, looking for temporary work, did you?"

"If I remember correctly, I told you that my wandering wasn't aimless."

"Right, but now I know why it isn't aimless."

"You do, huh?"

"You're married and you left your wife."

Ryder went still. He took a step back.

"Which means—"

Ryder's eyes were cold. "Which means my personal affairs are none of your business."

"They are when they affect me."

"They don't affect you, but just for the record, I'm not married, I'm doing a favor for a friend."

Her smile acidic, Justine retorted, "That's as good an excuse as any, I suppose."

Ryder's face reddened. "I don't have to make excuses to you." Abruptly tired of the subterfuge, Ryder said unexpectedly, "Just tell me one thing. Is your name really Camille Marcel?"

Stunned into temporary silence by his question, Justine stared at Ryder. Why should he question her identity? More than ever, she believed he really *was* the man her nighttime visitor had warned her against!

"I'll answer that question if you'll answer mine," Justine said once she had her voice under control. "I don't believe that excuse about doing a favor for a friend. Why did you leave your wife?"

Ryder's face turned to stone.

At his silence, she retorted, "Then whether my name is really Camille Marcel is none of your business, either."

Turning back toward the house abruptly, she said over her shoulder, "Supper's almost ready."

James entered Letty's apartment building with a frown. Thinner since the attack, with more strands of gray in his well-groomed hair, he was still tall, virile, and handsome, a wealthy man of the world in his prime. Yet despite being considered one of the most eligible bachelors in their social circle and a man with much to offer a bride, he knew he would not be welcomed. Not that Letty didn't love him, or even that he didn't love her. It just appeared that their love was not of the same caliber. He loved Letty with a passion that filled his nights and days. He had loved her from the first moment he saw her. It didn't matter to him that she was considered the most beautiful, mysteriously alluring woman in the city, or that she just happened to have a past that matched her reputation. He had seen right through her facade to the woman underneath—a warm, loving woman with as much to offer as he; the woman he wanted to be with for the rest of his life.

For Letty, however, it appeared to be different. She had loved him intimately and passionately for too brief a time to suit him. She had then cast him aside, without explanation. He had been warned that would happen, but he'd been certain that he was not just another man in her life. When she casually dismissed him, the shock had been too great to immediately comprehend. After he made countless attempts to renew their relationship, she had finally told him she cared for him . . . as a friend. She had proved her friendship by remaining steadfastly at his side throughout his uncertain recuperation from the mysterious attack that had almost taken his life.

He would never forget the note she had left him when his convalescence was assured—apologizing for any misconceptions she might have caused, and telling him that his Aunt Ethel and Uncle George would take over his care from then on because she was returning to her busy life. When he was well again and refused to accept those words, she had responded by banning him from any contact with her.

James unconsciously shook his head. Strangely enough, he was certain that however misguided Letty's reasons, she had his best interests at heart. He had yet to discover a way to combat her faulty reasoning, but he knew he would never rest until he did—because he loved her still.

Just as he knew it was imperative that he warn her of a new threat.

After briefly pausing when he reached Letty's door, James knocked firmly. He smiled at Millie when the youthful maid responded. He noticed that her answering smile was sincere, but that she became distressed when she turned to inform her mistress of his presence.

"I'm not home to him, Millie. Please tell him to leave."

Letty's voice sounded in the parlor, setting James's heart pounding. Striding into the room where she stood facing her maid, he said, "It's too late for that, Letty. I know you're home, and I'm not leaving until you hear what I have to say."

"I don't think so, James."

Her face was sober and exquisitely beautiful, although she had yet to apply the makeup she wore for her thrice-weekly soirees. Letty faced him in an elaborate green gown that she had donned for the evening. But her complexion was pale and the shadows underneath her eyes revealed a vulnerability that touched his heart.

"Please leave so I may finish dressing," she repeated.

His desire for her never stronger, James said simply, "How are you, Letty?"

"I'm fine, but I want you to leave, James."

"You haven't asked me how I am."

Letty's dark eyes met his. Hesitating, she admitted, "I've been keeping up with your progress, you know. I understand you're doing very well."

"I'm thinner, perhaps a little more gray, but I'm fine, too."

"I'm glad." Letty paused, and then asked, "Aunt Ethel and Uncle George . . . ?"

"They've gone home. I think Uncle George was glad to be relieved of the responsibility for my welfare, but Aunt Ethel had to be persuaded."

"They are both dears. Their concern for your recovery was obviously sincere. You are fortunate to be so loved."

"I suppose." James frowned. "But I didn't come here today to discuss them . . . or us."

Letty tensed. "Did something happen? Is something wrong?"

"No, nothing happened and nothing is wrong. Why? Were you expecting a problem?" His gaze intensified as he asked, "Maybe you're afraid for my safety because every man who ever truly loved you has met an early death."

Letty's face whitened.

"Or maybe because you can't decipher the warning wolf's howls that only you can hear . . . or because 'Grandfather's' visits haven't provided the answers you're looking for."

Letty opened her mouth, but no sound emerged. She staggered backward and sat abruptly on the settee behind her.

"You're wondering how I know all this." James took a step toward her, his heart aching at the unexpected distress he'd caused her. "You're astonished that I know the secrets you've kept to yourself for so many years, and that I know about the howling that has haunted you since your daughters' departures."

Letty took a shuddering breath as James sat beside her. Clutching her hands in his, he whispered urgently, "I know all this because the person you confided in told me. He asked me to confirm his claims that you are unstable and should be committed to a mental institution."

Letty gasped, and James drew her closer. His voice was gentle as he continued, "Mason Little came to my office to see me, Letty. He acted so cordial that no one would have believed he barely acknowledged my existence previously. After some small talk, it became obvious that he had come for a reason. He told me everything you had confided in him, claiming that you stunned him with your 'excited ravings.' He said he was unable to believe the depth of your fears when you came to him and asked him to hire a detective to protect me. He said that the attack on me somehow aggravated your fears, that you were inconsolable when it happened, and that you blamed him. He said that was when the full extent of your instability became obvious to him."

"I'm sure he didn't mean—"

"He meant everything he said, Letty!" Drawing her so close that Letty's quivering lips were only inches from his, James continued, "I figured it was best to play along with him as long as I could, so I told him that I was astonished at his revelations because you had never mentioned any of those things to me. I said I wasn't sure what to do, except that I wanted the best for you, and I needed time to think it all over. He stressed then that you would receive the care you needed, that the best place for you was a facility where personnel were familiar with your type of problem. He insisted that I would be doing the right thing. He said the howls you hear are driving you crazier every day, that they were making your behavior erratic, and that your decision to ban me from any contact with you proved that your mental condition is severely challenged. He implored me to sign a statement that he had prepared, confirming that you need psychiatric care immediately. He claimed that time was of the essence since he couldn't be certain when you'd turn against him as well."

"You must have misunderstood him, James!"

"I didn't misunderstand him."

Letty shook her head. "But you must have! I knew Mason was worried about me. He said so many times, but he would never attempt to harm me in any way. He's my friend."

"*I'm* your friend, Letty." Letty looked away from him, and James turned her face back to his as he said more softly, "Don't dismiss what I'm telling you. Please listen to me, Letty. Mason is trying to have you committed."

"Why? For what reason? What would he gain?"

"I don't know. I thought long and hard about it before I came here, but I knew I couldn't afford to waste any more time. I needed to warn you first and tell you that you mustn't trust Mason. He betrayed you once that we know of. He'll betray you again if you let him. The only thing I can promise you now is that I will discover the answers to all your questions."

Suddenly struggling to free herself from his grip, Letty whispered, "No, I can't believe that what you say is true. There must be another explanation."

"Listen to me and stop struggling, Letty." Gripping her hands more tightly, James insisted, "You must believe that I'm telling you the truth. You may not want me in your bed any longer, but at least allow me to stand beside you as the friend you need right now."

"No, I can't do that."

At the fear that surged to life in Letty's eyes, James asked, "Is it because you don't believe me, or because you're afraid for me . . . because you know I love you and you think that means I'm in danger?"

"No . . . yes . . . this can't be true!" Ripping herself free of James's grip, Letty stood up, forcing him to his feet as well. "I knew you would resent me for refusing to see you, but I didn't think you would hate me enough to make up a story like this."

"I don't hate you, Letty. The truth is quite the opposite, and I didn't make any of this up."

"If you don't hate me, then why are you trying to alienate me from the only member of my family that I can depend on?"

"Mason isn't your family, and you can't depend on him."

Taking a backward step, her color fading to a ghastly white, Letty whispered, "Leave, James. Go, and don't come back."

"Letty—"

"Leave, or I'll tell Millie to call the police and have you thrown out of my apartment."

"Letty—"

Turning toward the door, Letty called shrilly, "Millie—"

"No, don't call Millie. The poor girl is upset enough. I'll go." His chest heaving with the realization that he had failed in his attempt to warn her, James looked at Letty and said determinedly, "Whether you believe me or not, I promise you that I'll find the answer to your questions, and I'll prove to you who your friends are."

"Get out."

"I love you, Letty."

"I don't want you to love me, don't you understand?" A sob escaping her throat, Letty demanded, "Leave now. Please."

That last, single plea was almost more than he could bear. James turned abruptly. His throat was too tight for response as he headed for the doorway.

He didn't like the way Josh Harter was looking at him.

Standing in the bunkhouse as the other cowpokes

busied themselves around him, Ryder turned away deliberately from the young man's heated gaze. When he turned back, Josh was still regarding him angrily.

It occurred to him that under other circumstances, meeting Pop's wranglers might have been the most pleasant part of his day. Pete Williams was a mature cowboy dressed typically in washed-out trousers, a faded cotton shirt, a ten-gallon hat banded with sweat, and boots much the worse for wear. Harry Leeds was similar to Pete in every way, except that he sported a long handlebar mustache that was beginning to turn gray. Both were likable men with considerable experience who seemed much the wiser for it; both had welcomed him warmly.

And then there was Josh. Young and excitable, Josh had seemed to resent Ryder from the first moment he saw him. His gaze had been suspicious when Ryder offered him his hand, and he had accepted it reluctantly. Yet the gloomy expressions on all the men's faces had been unanimous when Camille arrived at the table with the first platter of food.

Ryder wasn't certain which one of them had excused himself from the table first. He only knew that a mass exodus had followed. He'd looked back to see Camille sitting there alone with hardly touched platters in front of her. In retrospect, he supposed he should have felt sorry for her, but he just didn't have it in him. The dirt stains on the seat of his trousers from sitting on the damp ground of the root cellar were potent reminders of Camille's arrogance.

As for his own stupidity in asking her outright if

her name was really Camille Marcel, Ryder could only shake his head. It had been obvious that something had clicked in her mind at that moment. He had seen it in her eyes. He wasn't sure what it was, but he knew instinctively that it wasn't to his advantage.

"I want to talk to you, Knowles."

Ryder looked at Josh and said automatically, "Friends call me Ryder."

"Maybe so, but I ain't one of them." Josh's youthful face was florid. His thick, straight dark hair hung forward in his eyes despite his obvious attempts to sweep it back, his jaw was covered with the perpetual shadow of a beard, and what had at first appeared to be a stocky frame was solid muscle upon closer inspection. Josh's frown darkened as he said, "I got some things to say to you that need saying. First of all, to my mind Camille must have had good reason to lock you up in the root cellar all afternoon, whether the two of you want to admit it or not. I can't figure out why Pop is leaving you behind with her again tomorrow, but I figure Camille let you know how she feels about whatever you tried. As for myself, I wouldn't care how long it takes for Camille to get used to that stove and to start cooking up some good food, but Pop don't seem prepared to wait. So this is just a warning. Don't try taking advantage of her, because I'll be watching you. And you can bet that I'll pay you back for anything you try on her."

"Wait a minute," Ryder responded tightly. "First of all, the young woman that you're so concerned about didn't have any reason to lock me up—except for whatever she thought up in her mind. And second, your threats don't scare me one bit. I'll stay here and do the job Pop hired me to do for just as long as I need to, and not a minute longer. And you can bet that nothing you have to say will have anything to do with when I decide to leave."

"Is that right?" Bristling, Josh edged up to him, teeth bared as he said, "That don't sound like the tone of a man who's ready to—"

"Josh! That's enough!" Appearing unexpectedly in the doorway, Pop ordered, "Whatever your problem is with Ryder, I want you to forget it! He's got his job to do, and so do you. Remember that, and remember something else while you're at it. If either of you don't do your job, I'll be the one who takes care of things. *Comprende?*"

After waiting a few seconds for Josh to fully comprehend his warning, Pop turned to Ryder. "I need to talk to you about some things in private. I figure the best place to do that is outside."

Pop turned without waiting for Ryder's acquiescence, and Ryder followed him silently into the darkening ranch yard. It occurred to him, as a hen flapped across the pocked yard toward the dilapidated henhouse and horses milled lazily in a corral that had seen better days, that the Double Bar C bore startling resemblance to his own ranch when he first saw it. Years of neglect had been written in the condition of the fencing and outbuildings, as well as in the interior of the bunkhouse and ranch house itself—neglect that he had corrected with time and hard work. In Pop's case, the spanking new stove appeared to be his first attempt at making things right. It was obviously a mystery to Pop why Camille found it difficult to cook on the elaborate appliance, but the reason had never been a mystery to Ryder. The stove wasn't the problem. Camille was.

Pop turned toward Ryder when they were a few yards from the bunkhouse. Ryder noted the way in which the aging rancher looked around, making certain they couldn't be overheard when he said, "What I'm going to tell you is between you and me, you hear, Ryder? It's important. It's about Camille."

Ryder's cheek ticced. He should have known.

"Can I depend on you to keep quiet?"

Ryder nodded.

Pop's voice dropped a note softer. "I know the reason Camille reacted to you the way she did. The fact is, she's wanted by the law. I don't know why, mind you, but she don't have to tell me she's not guilty of whatever the law wants her for. Camille ain't the kind of girl to twist the law to her liking and expect to get away with it. She's too smart for that."

Wanted by the law? Ryder's jaw tightened.

"Anyways, she musta figured you was a lawman sent to bring her back. She locked you in the root cellar because she needed to talk things over with me first. She let you out when I assured her you wasn't the law come looking for her."

Ryder did not comment.

"So I want you to take it easy on her. The poor girl's had some trouble and she's got enough to worry about for a while. She's trying real hard to put a good meal on the table for us, too. She just needs a little help. I saw your face when you looked at that stove. It don't scare you none, so I figure you're the right man to do the job—along with other chores around the ranch."

Ryder did not reply.

"So what do you say?"

Inwardly amazed, Ryder barely restrained a shake of his head. Camille, or Justine, or whatever her name turned out to be—the woman had this whole bunch of men wrapped around her little finger.

"Ryder . . . ?"

But he'd be damned if he'd join them!

Pop prompted, "You'll take it easy on her?"

More certain by the minute that "Camille" was smarter than anyone thought, Ryder replied, "Just as easy as she takes it on me."

Appearing uncertain, Pop finally said, "Well, I guess I can't ask for more, just as long as you remember what I told you."

"That's what James said, Mason. I didn't believe him, of course, but I know he wouldn't have made all of it up. There has to be a particle of truth in what he said."

Letty walked stiffly at Mason's side, her expression rigid despite the warmth of the day and the sunlight that beamed through the trees swaying in the gentle breeze. Her frozen expression was in direct contrast with the warmth of the yellow frock and matching chapeau that she wore, drawing appreciative gazes from men strolling by, and annoyed glances from the women on their arms.

Letty awaited Mason's reply as they traversed the well-traveled path. She had purposely chosen the park as their meeting place, hoping to view Mason's reaction to her statement in the full light of day and in an atmosphere where the presence of others strolling nearby would act as a buffer between them. She somehow needed that protection.

Her heart pounding in anticipation of Mason's reply, Letty recalled the long evening past. She had forced herself to be vivacious and alluring at her soiree after James's visit. She had charmed and fascinated the men in attendance, and had elicited both admiration and jealousy from the women. Her responses had been quick and her banter light, yet, unable to get James's words out of her mind, she had fallen silent and morose the moment she stepped into her carriage for the ride back to her apartment. James . . . dear James. She could not bear to see him hurt again because of her! She had tried so hard to spare him by keeping him at a distance.

How could Mason have told anyone the secrets that she had confided in her moment of despair? Could it be true that he believed her insane and wanted to institutionalize her?

Letty had considered those questions over and again during a long, sleepless night. She wondered if she would have believed anyone who had confessed fears similar to hers.

It occurred to her that James had not questioned the truth of her confidences. She had looked directly into his eyes and had seen neither shock nor doubt there. She supposed his love for her was the reason for his acceptance—the same love that brought danger ever closer to him.

Danger that Mason doubted truly existed.

Mason hesitated in response to her question. Nervous perspiration appeared on his patrician forehead, and her heart fluttered. Was she wrong about Mason? Did he truly despise her enough to have her committed to a mental institution?

But . . . why?

Letty's heart fluttered again when Mason said, "It's true, Aunt Letty. I did go to see James."

"Oh—"

Letty closed her eyes at the pain his words caused, only to open them again when Mason led her to a bench and sat down beside her. "But I went to him because I didn't know what else to do. I knew that he loved you. I knew that you cared about him or you wouldn't have asked me to hire detectives to protect him. I was concerned about what you had told me. I couldn't hear the howls that you said you heard. The visions of an old man who spoke to you and who comforted you sounded strange to me. I didn't know what to think, and I was concerned about your health. I went to speak to the man you had nursed back to health, hoping he could shed some light on it all. But, Aunt Letty . . . dear Aunt Letty, I never thought to have you committed to a mental institution. No, never!"

Mason paused then, his fair skin flushed with emotion as he looked into her eyes and said, "James must have misunderstood me. He was as shocked as I was when I told him about the howlings that haunt you. I can only think that his shock may have caused him to misinterpret the things I said. All I can say to you now is that I'm sorry, Aunt Letty. I'm sorry to have brought you such grief, and to have caused you such worry, but I never sought to do you harm. On the contrary, I just wanted to do what was best for you when I asked James for advice. That was obviously a mistake, and I apologize for it." His eyes moist, Mason said, "I hope you can forgive me."

"This talk of a mental institution—"

"I suppose it was brought up in our conversation somewhere, but I don't remember when. I certainly never thought to put you in such a place."

"Your pressure on James to have him sign a letter of commitment that you had drawn up—"

"There is no letter."

"Your insistence on haste—"

"Haste was never an issue."

Letty looked at the young man she had trusted so completely. Would Archibald—Justine's father— have believed the claims of the nephew who was looking so sincerely into her eyes? Or would he have believed James?

"Aunt Letty—"

Letty interrupted him. "I don't know what to say except that I'm so sorry to have put you in this position, Mason. I never should have burdened you with my problems. I should have sought out a competent detective agency on my own."

"But I am your servant, Aunt Letty."

"You have been there for me to lean on over the years. I appreciate that more than you know, but I suppose I've taken advantage of you."

"It was my pleasure to have your confidence, Aunt Letty; yet I've spoiled it all now, haven't I?"

"No. Misunderstandings can always be overcome."

A trace of tension entered Mason's expression as

he said, "I'm sorry that James misunderstood my concern. I know the mistake wasn't malicious because he loves you, but"—Mason paused cautiously before continuing—"but it is possible that he resents our closeness, because it's a closeness that you and he no longer share."

Letty drew back. "I won't listen to anything against James, Mason."

"I didn't mean to speak against him. I was only speaking of possibilities."

"That possibility isn't plausible."

"If you say so, Aunt Letty."

Letty paused. "I'm not really your aunt, you know."

"Yes, you are . . . to me."

A tear slipped out of the corner of Letty's eye. She brushed it away and attempted a smile as she said, "I can't bear any more of this discussion. Let's forget this afternoon, shall we? You are my friend . . . as close to me as family." Letty stood up abruptly. "I shall pretend this whole day never happened, and I hope you will, too. For that reason I'll say good-bye to you now, Mason. My carriage is waiting around the bend in the path. I shall go straight home from here, dismiss this entire episode from my mind, and take a nap in preparation for the night's festivities."

Taking Mason's hand, Letty repeated, "Please . . . this conversation never happened."

Bidding him a quiet adieu, Letty turned and walked back up the path toward her carriage, leaving Mason standing silently behind her. She climbed into her carriage and waved the driver forward. She closed her eyes as the conveyance jerked into motion. She felt an almost overpowering need for James's arms around her, those strong arms that never faltered. She experienced an almost overwhelming hunger for that intensely honest gaze she could not forget. James loved her, and the problem was . . . she loved him.

Damn it all, she loved James!

Admitting it for the first time, Letty shivered. As for Mason, she had trusted him. She had relied on him. James said that Mason had betrayed her. She was unsure, but she was determined to dismiss the possibility from her mind.

Mason shook with rage. Standing beside the park bench where Letty had left him, he waited only until his dear aunt's carriage rode by before starting back toward the street. He had made a mistake in contacting James. The bastard had gone directly to Letty with everything he had said, hoping to save his damsel in distress. Well, he would not allow it! He had come too far to have James interfere now. *He* was his dear Aunt Letty's only heir, and *he* would remain her only heir. His future depended on it.

Mason smiled suddenly as a thought struck him. If James turned out to be a problem, he would just make sure that his dear aunt's greatest fear came true—that James met an early demise. It would be an accident, of course. Letty would blame only herself, and Mason would comfort her in her distress.

Mason's smile broadened. Letty would undoubtedly slip over the edge of sanity then, and it would be no problem at all to find someone to verify his claim that she was unstable. He would then be free to make his move, and he would win out in the end.

Yes . . . he would make it all happen if it were the last thing he ever did.

Chapter Five

You're in my way."

"No, I'm not."

"This is my kitchen. I'm the cook here, and I say you're in my way."

Ryder's jaw ticced with annoyance as he looked down at Camille in the silence of the kitchen.

The atmosphere in the bunkhouse had been tense that morning when he'd awakened. Josh had been his usual obnoxious self, with Pete and Harry appearing embarrassed at his behavior. Ryder had seen Harry attempting to talk to Josh quietly, but he had also seen the young fellow slap away the comradely hand Harry placed on his shoulder.

Breakfast had been silent and almost as difficult. Overcooked disks—supposedly flapjacks covered in honey—had been the morning fare, with eggs so runny they were almost raw or so dark they were almost black. The biscuits defied description, the ham had somehow been cooked into pink straw, and the coffee was so strong his hair stood up on end.

Pop's sickly smile had again been in evidence, but his expression had changed the moment he mounted up to ride off with the men. His glance at Ryder had said it all. Supper that night had better be good—or else.

So, he was supposed to accomplish the impossible and do his chores on the ranch, too!

Ryder's dark brows drew into an angry line. It had all sounded so easy when he had told Tom Monroe that he would find Justine Fitzsimmons and finish up the job for him. All he had to do was inform the woman of her mother's offer and get her to sign a paper if she refused the terms. There had been only one question in his mind at that time. What kind of a daughter would force her mother to such machinations just to see her again?

"I said, get out of my way!"

Ryder stared at Camille's tight expression. His question was answered.

Losing patience with the beautiful but obviously spoiled, hardheaded, demanding, and increasingly arrogant young woman in front of him, Ryder said flatly, "Pop hired me to teach you how to use that stove, and that's what I'm going to do. So watch and listen, and try to learn something . . . if that's possible."

Camille's exquisite features flushed as she said hotly, "Are you insinuating that I'm too ignorant to learn?"

"You said it, not me."

"Did it ever occur to you that I don't think there's anything you can teach me?"

"I doubt that."

"I don't."

"Look," Ryder began, holding on to his temper. "Do we agree that the meals you've been cooking here aren't exactly what they're supposed to be?"

Camille raised her chin. "I suppose you could say that."

"Do we agree that we both want to see you put a good meal on the table tonight?"

"Yes, but only if I cook it."

"Good. I'll just show you how to use the stove."

"No."

"Why not?"

"I've already figured it out."

"Oh, that accounts for the tasty breakfast you served this morning."

Camille flushed. "That was an accident. I know what I did wrong and I'll fix it."

"All right. I'll watch."

"No."

"Yes."

"I said, no!"

Ryder did not bother to respond.

Damn him, he was watching everything she did! Justine fumbled as she attempted to prepare the potatoes for boiling. She glanced back to see if Ryder was standing silently behind her. He was there, all right, as he had been most of the day—appearing intermittently behind her to watch as she muddled through the laundry, tried to put the house in order, and attempted to weed the herb garden. She was presently readying the supper meal in the stifling kitchen, yet it hadn't really been necessary to look behind her to know he was there. His presence was so strong that it was almost overwhelming. His masculine aura filled the room. He was so close that she could hear him breathing . . . could smell his intriguing male scent . . . could sense the awareness between them that was somehow expanding by the moment.

Her face flamed.

Distracted, Justine reached for a pot on the stove and jumped when she scorched her hand. Barely controlling her tears, she turned away, only to hear Ryder say, "Let me see that."

"No, I'm fine."

"Don't be so stubborn!"

Grasping her hand, Ryder pulled her closer. She felt his body heat as he looked at her hand and then drew her to the dry sink and submerged it in a bucket of water. "I know it's painful," he said, "but the burn isn't severe. The water will cool it down. I have some salve in my saddlebags that will lessen the pain."

"That isn't necessary." She attempted to draw back her hand.

Refusing to release it, he insisted, "Yes, it is."

Suddenly trembling, unsure why she was reacting with such hostility to his seemingly sincere attempt to help her, Justine said hotly, "Do you know everything, or do you just think you do?" Breathing heavily, she said, "I don't need your help. This isn't the first time I've been burned on this stove, and it won't be the last. I can take care of myself."

Her throat went dry when Ryder's eyes searched hers. After a moment's silence, he said, "Just let me tend to it . . . please."

Uncertain why, Justine snatched back her hand and dashed into the yard. Out in the sunlight, she suddenly began running toward the rear of the yard. She ignored the warning howls that began in her mind as she stumbled on the uncertain terrain.

She glanced furtively behind her. Ryder wasn't following her, and she was glad. She just wanted to get away, to have some respite from the awareness of him that had taunted her all day long, and to bring to an end what was turning out to be another disastrous episode in the kitchen. She wanted to be by herself for a while, to scream out her frustrations, to sort out her mistakes, to . . . to figure out why she reacted so strongly to Ryder Knowles. She needed—

The ground dropped away suddenly, thrusting her forward. Striking her head hard, she lay on the ground for a moment, stunned. Then she raised a hand to her forehead and felt a sticky substance there.

Blood.

She was almost amused. Her last conscious thought as the world darkened around her was that she had done it again.

Motionless, Ryder stared at the kitchen doorway through which Camille had disappeared a few minutes before. She had burned herself and she was upset, but he knew it wasn't the pain that really bothered her. He had been relentless throughout the day, returning again and again to watch her with the excuse that he was doing what Pop had hired him to do—but the truth was different.

Was Camille really Justine Fitzsimmons? And if she were, why was she hiding her true identity?

Or was she really Camille Marcel, a woman who was wanted by the law as Pop had confided? And if she were, what crime had she committed—and why didn't the question of her guilt or innocence make any difference to the way he felt about her?

And . . . how exactly *did* he feel about her?

Ryder resisted the urge to go after Camille. He knew that in the end, he was no better than the other men on Pop's ranch. Thoughts of her snuck into his mind no matter what task he was attempting. Although he was compelled to solve the mystery of her identity, his desire to do so had less and less to do with his promise to Tom. His final, silent admission was that part of his annoyance with Josh stemmed from jealousy because Camille was nice to the fellow while she obviously resented him.

He knew his feelings for Camille were complicated. When he had held Camille's hand after she was burned, he had felt her tremble, and he had known it was not from physical pain. He had looked into her eyes and glimpsed a vulnerability there that she struggled to conceal. He had realized then that she wasn't as sure of herself as she pretended to be, that for some reason it was important to her to conquer the tasks she'd undertaken at the ranch, and that part of her arrogance was a defense against the fear she wouldn't succeed. She needed help. She wanted it desperately, but she couldn't make herself accept it from him.

All he had wanted to do at that moment was to take her into his arms.

Ryder glanced again at the kitchen doorway, and then frowned. No, he wouldn't go after her and take advantage of her moment of weakness . . . or his own. Instead, he would do the only thing left for him to do.

Ryder took a deep breath and turned toward the stove.

Otto Tears woke up with an almost debilitating headache. It was painful to open his eyes. Payment for the debauchery of the previous evening, no doubt.

Otto closed his eyes with disgust. He had succumbed again to his baser instincts despite his former resolve. He could feel himself slipping more and more into the past—losing more and more of his self-control—but this time he'd had enough of the morning after. He needed to finish the job he had set out to do. He needed to leave this godforsaken country behind and go back to the city.

Squinting, Otto looked around the bright bedroom—at the handmade curtains filtering the sunlight, at the bedroom furniture that had been carefully polished, at the flowered coverlet that shielded his nakedness, and at the spotless sheets underneath him. His gaze came to rest on the clothing tossed haphazardly on the rug beside the bed. He scowled when he saw his own shirt, trousers, and boots lying intermingled with the worn finery of a saloon girl.

A snore beside him turned him sharply and he realized a heavily painted brunette was sharing his bed.

Oh, hell! What was her name? Dolores? Devina? Delia? It was something like that, but her name didn't matter.

Ignoring the pain in his temples, he shook the woman's arm roughly. When she opened her eyes, he grated, "Get out of here. Go home. I need some privacy."

The woman unexpectedly smiled. She pushed the coverlet down to her waist, revealing pendulous breasts as she asked seductively, "Are you sure? We had a good time last night in this little house. We could spend more time together before I go home if you want. It won't cost you much."

"Get out."

The woman shrugged. "If that's what you want."

Throwing the coverlet back the rest of the way, she stumbled to her feet, revealing without embarrassment a naked, more than ample body. Otto's scowl darkened. Her smudged makeup, disheveled hairdo, and sagging skin contrasted sharply with the pleasant, tidy room, and it disgusted him—but that was to be expected. He was done with the floozy, just as he was done with the countless women he had taken before her.

It was time to get back to work.

He said almost in afterthought, "Wait a minute."

The woman turned toward him, her expression brightening. "Changed your mind, did you?"

"No . . . not a chance of that." Otto swallowed his revulsion as he asked, "If I remember rightly, you mentioned a woman who worked for a little while in the saloon . . . a woman that most of the men made fools of themselves over. You said she turned them all down, and then left with one of the ranchers, supposedly to *cook* on his ranch."

"Yeah, that's right." The woman pulled her dress up onto her shoulders without bothering with underclothing. She shrugged again. "She thought she was better than the rest of us with her highfalutin ways, but she was only kidding herself. Taking up with old Pop Cooper wasn't a step up, that's for sure."

Otto forced himself to concentrate as he said, "She was left behind with the bills of a troupe of actors. She paid them and took a job at the saloon, but she left to go with the old fella."

"That's right, but that was a mistake. She won't make no money there."

"Did she say where she came from?"

"No. She didn't talk much."

"Did she say what she intended to do?"

"I said she didn't talk much." Obviously resenting his interest in another woman, the brunette said, "Why do you care?"

"That's none of your business."

She responded sharply, "It is if you're taking up my time with your questions."

Otto smirked. "Your time is so valuable, huh?"

The saloon woman's smile fell when she said, "My time is money."

Reaching for his trousers, which lay on the floor beside the bed, Otto withdrew his money pouch and counted out a few coins. Beckoning her toward him, he placed them in her hand and said, "Do you have time now?"

The brunette smiled at him and asked, "What do you want to know?"

Ryder slipped the roast into the oven and put the potatoes on to boil before mixing the biscuits. The simple routine took him back in time to his childhood when he had done similar work after his parents' deaths. His unconscious smile was bittersweet. He supposed he'd never forget those days he had spent earning his way in the kitchen of kindly Bart Richter before he grew old enough to take up other chores.

Ryder looked up, frowning. He had expected Camille to return by now. She'd had plenty of time to come to terms with her frustration.

Ryder went still as a wolf's howl startled him. He shook his head, uncertain. When he heard it again he walked to the window to look out at the horizon. Hearing a wolf howling at the moon was common enough, but hearing one during the bright light of day was a different story.

A strange anxiety came to life inside him when the howling sounded again, and Ryder searched the landscape. Camille was out there alone. He wasn't familiar with the territory. He wasn't certain what could be expected on this isolated ranch carved out of the wilderness, and he doubted if Camille was, either.

Ryder started slowly toward the doorway. His pace quickened when he reached the yard and the strange howling increased. He called out, "Camille, where are you?"

No reply.

"Answer me, Camille, please."

His only response was the twittering of the birds in the trees overhead.

His throat tightening, Ryder looked at the rear of the yard, where a narrow path led into the wilderness beyond. That strange howling . . . something was wrong.

His hand slid down to his hip, and Ryder cursed at the realization that he had left his sidearm in the bunkhouse. Deciding he didn't have time to go back for it, Ryder started forward at a cautious run. He stopped abruptly when the trail dropped off unexpectedly, his heart hammering at the sight of Camille lying motionless at the bottom of the awkward decline. The blood streaming from her temple was bright against her pale skin. A surge of panic started to propel him toward her, but he froze at the sight of a large gray wolf crouched a few yards away from her prone figure.

Ryder glanced at Camille again. Her eyes were closed. She was unconscious, and the wolf was so close to her. He felt the animal search his gaze, almost daring him forward as a growl rumbled in its throat. Swallowing, Ryder glanced cautiously around him. He spotted a broken branch on the ground nearby and reached slowly toward it. The wolf lunged at him, causing him to take a step back. He was about to make another attempt to pick up the branch when the animal turned and vanished into the foliage.

His heart racing, determined to take advantage of the animal's unanticipated disappearance, Ryder ran to Camille. He noted that her breathing was shallow as he knelt beside her and whispered, "Camille, are you all right? Answer me."

Panicking when Camille did not respond, Ryder paused only to scrutinize the foliage around him before sliding his arms gently underneath her and scooping her up against his chest. He felt her warmth against him; he clutched her tighter when her lips touched the spot where his heartbeat thundered underneath his shirt.

The unconscious thought *not again* drummed over and over in his mind as Ryder carried her back to the house. Minutes later he laid her on the narrow cot in her bedroom. He was bathing the blood from her forehead when he realized that the wolf had stopped baying at almost the exact moment he'd spotted Camille.

Had he frightened it, halting its attack? If so, why hadn't it run away as he approached? Why had it remained crouched beside Camille?

But he had no time for speculation.

Her head was throbbing. It hurt to open her eyes.

Raising her eyelids as little as possible, Justine glanced at the man beside the bed on which she lay. She felt a damp cloth against her forehead and heard him say, "How do you feel?"

It was Ryder, and he was frowning. Disoriented, she did not respond.

"Speak to me, Camille. I need to know you're all right."

The room whirled around her and Justine briefly closed her eyes. She opened them at the sound of panic in Ryder's voice.

"Speak to me, Camille," he said.

She managed, "I . . . I'm all right."

He said tentatively, "You fell and hit your head. You were unconscious for a while. Aside from the cut on your forehead, you seem to be all right—no broken bones. I don't want to leave you alone, but we'll get a doctor as soon as the men get back."

"No. I . . . I don't need a doctor."

"Yes, you do."

She did not respond.

Ryder's face drew closer as he whispered with sudden intensity, "I'm sorry, Camille. I didn't come after you sooner because I thought you wanted some time to yourself. I know now that was a mistake." When she remained silent, he inched closer. "Talk to me, Camille. I need to be sure you're all right."

Her head spinning, she muttered, "I'm just a little dizzy."

Ryder brushed a strand of hair from her forehead, his touch so gentle that he set her heart pounding as he said, "It was my fault. I should have come after you right away."

"No." Pain stirred when she shook her head, and she gasped. Ryder clutched her hand, and she said, "I acted childishly."

"I shouldn't have pushed so hard."

"I should have admitted my deficiencies."

"You don't have any deficiencies."

Justine was suddenly without a response.

Ryder held her hand tighter. "I wouldn't have come after you at all except for that wolf's howling."

Justine blinked. She deliberately closed her eyes

and then opened them again. No, Ryder was still there. She wasn't dreaming. She asked, "You heard a wolf howling?"

"When I went into the yard to find you, the howling became louder. I knew something was wrong. I took the chance that you had followed the trail at the rear of the yard because it led into the only place where the wolf was likely to be."

"I didn't see it."

"I did. It was crouching beside you." His hand tightened on hers. "If I hadn't gotten there when I did . . ." His voice trailed away. Then he whispered, "I'm sorry I made you feel that you had to run away from me."

"You didn't . . . not exactly."

Ryder's gaze intensified. "Then why *did* you run?" Why?

Justine's eyes fluttered closed against the throbbing that had begun in her head. Ryder . . . the wolf . . . she was so tired.

"Camille . . ."

She opened her eyes again.

Ryder pressed, "Tell me . . . I need to know once and for all. Is your name really Camille Marcel? You can tell me the truth, Camille—or whatever your name is. I promise you . . . I give you my word that I won't let the truth hurt you."

The brief silence between them was broken by an echoing howl and Ryder turned spontaneously toward it. "There the bastard goes again." He turned back toward her. "Don't worry. I'll get that damned beast tomorrow."

"No!"

"What are you saying?"

"I'm not afraid of it."

"You should be."

"No—"

"Camille, I don't know what you're used to, but out here a wolf is a dangerous wild animal."

"Not to me."

Ryder stared at her, momentarily silent. He then said, "You're confused. This isn't the time to talk, but we will talk, Camille. I promise you that, too." When she did not respond, he touched her cheek lightly and said, "Close your eyes and rest. Pop and the men will be back in a little while. I've already put the roast in the oven, and the potatoes and biscuits are ready to go, too."

She mumbled, "A good meal tonight . . ."

As she drifted off to sleep she whispered, "The wolf . . . my friend . . ."

She wasn't sure if Ryder heard those words, just as she wasn't sure that she felt his lips brush hers after her eyelids closed.

The door to Camille's room was closed tight while the doctor tended to her. Ryder waited outside with an agitated Pop, who had dismissed the other men with harsh commands.

"Tell me again," Pop demanded. "Why was Camille running away from you, and how did she fall?"

When Pop and the men had come home earlier, a panic had ensued as soon as they learned that Camille was injured. Pop had sent Pete immediately for the doctor and had spent the rest of the time beside Camille's bed, waiting for her to awaken. Old Doc Martin had finally arrived with his narrow spectacles and his large black bag, but it wasn't until Doc had closed Camille's bedroom door that Pop turned toward him accusingly.

Pop's question was forgotten when the sudden howling of a wolf broke the quiet. "There it goes again. I'm going to get that damned animal tomorrow if it's the last thing I ever do," Ryder said.

"I don't hear no wolf." Pop frowned. "I don't hear no wolf because there ain't none. A pack of wolves were preying on our herd a few years back, and me and the boys cleaned them out of the area."

Ryder returned coldly, "You only thought you did."

"I told you, I don't hear no wolf."

Just as adamant as he, Ryder responded, "Then you're more hard of hearing than you thought."

Pop's expression narrowed. "Maybe this is my fault. It looks like I made a mistake about you being the answer to my problem here. It looks to me like you only made things worse, because that story about a wolf just don't work."

Ryder replied vehemently, "I know what I hear, even if you don't. And I'm going to get that wolf tomorrow, just like I said."

Pop paused and then asked solemnly, "You saw a wolf?"

"Yes."

"You wouldn't lie to me, would you, Ryder?"

His anger suddenly deflating, Ryder replied quietly, "No, I wouldn't lie to you, Pop. Camille wants to make her own adjustment here. I made a mistake trying to force something she wasn't ready for. I knew that the minute she ran off. That's why I let her go. I know now that letting her go was a mistake, too." He added sincerely, "You can depend on me not to make that same mistake again. I'll watch out for her and I'll take care of the problems here, too. I won't let you down a second time."

Pop did not respond before Camille's bedroom door opened and Doc emerged. Wiping his eyeglasses wearily, his shoulders stooped and his gray hair slightly askew, the rotund doctor said, "She hit her head hard. She'll be a little groggy for a few days, but she ain't got no broken bones and she ain't going to have a scar from the cut. She'll be fine."

"Fine, huh?" Pop's relief was obvious. "Can I talk to her for a few minutes?"

"All right, but she might not be too clear. Just make it short. She needs to rest."

Relieved at Doc's proclamation, Ryder remained in the hall after Pop left. Doc turned toward him to say unexpectedly, "Your name's Ryder, ain't it?" Ryder nodded, and Doc continued, "That young woman in there is upset and confused. She said your name over and over, something about a wolf and not wanting you to go after it. I know there ain't no wolves left around here. Pop and the boys took care of that a while back. I guess she'll make more sense later, but in the meantime, I figure it's best that you don't do nothing to agitate her."

Ryder looked at Camille's door. He was suddenly desperate to see her, but he would not go in. She had shown how she felt about him when she ran away. Whether she blamed him or not, it was his fault that she was hurt. He wouldn't forget it.

Nodding, he backed up with a mumbled excuse and forced himself to leave the ranch house. Camille was an assault on his emotions unlike anything he had ever experienced before. He was tempted to tell Pop he was leaving the ranch forever. Yet he knew he couldn't, for more reasons than he wanted to explore.

Camille's face appeared in his mind accompanied by another unexpected howl, and Ryder took a sharp breath. He was either going crazy or—

James Ferguson stood at the desk in his study, staring at the report in front of him. He had received it in his office that afternoon. He had read it, and had then put it down incredulously. He had left the office that afternoon with the report tucked securely in his briefcase. He presently stood in his shirtsleeves, his vest unbuttoned, his thick hair rumpled by an anxious hand, and his expression tight. He was unable either to understand or deny the information that was reported in black and white.

Mason was almost bankrupt? How was that possible? Mason was a successful lawyer with a clientele that included some of the most prestigious people in the city. He managed their finances . . . their trusts . . . their futures, and they trusted him implicitly. If he were almost bankrupt as the report indicated, with a savings account that was nearly empty and a trust account that he had borrowed against heavily, how did he manage such a lavish lifestyle?

That question plagued James. The only answer he could fathom made his blood run cold. Many of his friends were Mason's clients. They had the utmost confidence in him and never questioned the way he handled their money. Where did this new information leave them?

James riffled the pages of the report. It was signed in Mr. Ephraim Johnson's flowery hand. James's office had used Ephraim's services quietly for many years. A small, middle-aged fellow whose appearance was average in every way, Ephraim had an unobtrusive, conversational manner. His casual inquiries were as deceptive as his appearance, and the results he obtained were dependable without exception.

James sat abruptly on the gold-leafed desk chair and stared at the report with unseeing eyes. It appeared that Mason's machinations went deeper than he had ever realized. Yet his puzzlement remained. How did Mason expect to *profit* from institutionalizing Letty?

James's face flushed. Beautiful Letty . . . strong, intelligent, clever Letty . . . passionate Letty . . . endearing Letty . . . *stubborn* Letty. The woman he loved was all those things, but the one thing she was *not*, was mad. She had not denied any of the statements that Mason had claimed she'd made, but unlike Mason, he did not dismiss them as disturbed ravings. Rather, they were the concerns of a woman who had survived and succeeded despite the odds. He not only believed her; he believed *in* her. He would not allow Mason's maneuvering to best her.

Looking up from the report, James rose abruptly to his feet and called out, "Willis, come in here, please."

Waiting until the aging servant appeared at the

door, James instructed, "Send a messenger to Mr. Johnson's house. Please tell him that I need to see him immediately."

"Sir . . . the hour—"

"Mr. Johnson will understand."

Nodding, Willis left the room, and James sat, suddenly weary. He owed it to his friends to discover the truth about Mason; but most of all, he owed the truth to Letty. He did not deceive himself that the revelation of Mason's dishonesty would change Letty's feelings for him, but that was unimportant at present. He loved Letty enough that he could not allow Mason to take advantage of her.

Ephraim Johnson's expression was sober when he tipped his hat and left James's study hours later. Still staring at the door that Ephraim had closed behind him, James remained unmoving. Ephraim would accomplish the task he had given him in his usual quiet, unobtrusive way. James was relatively sure of that. Yet he was positive of only one thing: Mason would not institutionalize Letty—no matter what had to be done to prevent it.

Otto Tears remained silent, mounted, and unseen as twilight faded into night on the rise behind the Double Bar C ranch. It had been a difficult morning and an even more difficult day as he had determinedly ignored the consequences of his excesses of the previous evening. It occurred to him that everything the brunette whore had told him was true. Camille Marcel was presently working at Pop Cooper's ranch. He had just finished confirming that fact when one of Pop's men rode into town in a panic to summon Doc Martin. Otto had then merely followed the two men back to the ranch.

The angry exchange he had overheard outside the bunkhouse a few minutes earlier had been unexpected. He considered it again:

"Wait a minute. I want to talk to you alone." The short, stocky young wrangler stepped out of the shadows of the bunkhouse to halt the taller wrangler before he entered. He grasped the taller man's arm roughly and turned the fellow to face him as he said, *"That story Camille told Doc don't fool me none. She wouldn't have gone running off like she did if you hadn't done something to her."*

The taller man responded with obvious restraint, *"I'll forget that you laid your hand on me this time because you're upset about Camille, Josh, but I'm telling you now that you'd better not do it again unless you're prepared to back it up."* Giving Josh only enough time to absorb his statement, the taller fellow said, *"For your information, I didn't do anything to Camille. We argued and she ran off. That's it."*

"I don't believe you."

"Whether you believe me or not doesn't make much difference to me—so long as you don't get in my way."

"I'm warning you now that I'll get in your way if you lay a hand on Camille."

"Camille is safe with me."

"That ain't the way it looks to me. If Camille—"

The sound of footsteps behind them turned both men toward an older fellow, who commented sharply, *"You at it again, Josh?"* Not allowing him time for a reply, the *old man said, "I'm getting tired of warning you, but I'll say it one more time. Butt out! I'll handle things here. I don't need you."*

"I was just warning this fella that—"

"I'll do all the warning that needs to be done. Get yourself inside that bunkhouse and cool off. Camille may be off her feet for a few days, but she's going to be all right, and you can thank Ryder for that, too."

"I ain't thanking him."

"Get inside then. I ain't going to tell you again."

Waiting only until Josh had disappeared through the doorway of the bunkhouse, the old man shook his head and said, "I'm sorry, Ryder. Josh is a nice enough fella, but he's got a thing for Camille, and he don't like having you around. It seems to me that you're probably thinking this job is more trouble than it's worth, so I'll understand if you want to ride off and forget the whole thing."

Ryder replied without hesitation, "You hired me to do a job, and I'm going to do it."

"All right, then." Appearing relieved, the old man continued hesitantly, "I expect that means you'll see to Camille and do the cooking until she's on her feet."

Ryder nodded.

"I ain't got nothing else to say, except I expect the next few days to go smoother than the first."

Ryder did not reply.

They parted without another word.

Otto's lips twitched with annoyance. He needed to confirm that Camille was Justine Fitzsimmons before he made any moves, but that wouldn't be easy with this Ryder fella in the way—or with the tensions that seemed to be developing on the ranch. There was nothing else he could do at present other than watch and wait.

The thought smarted.

Silently cursing, regretting that he had ever taken on this job, Tears faded back into the shadows.

Justine watched as Ryder loaded the stove with wood in preparation for the morning meal. The play of muscles across his back, his strong profile, that cleft in his chin—

Justine cut those thoughts short with supreme strength of will. She had been confined to her bed for two days now—two days spent recuperating while Ryder remained nearby, taking care of her chores. She hadn't wanted it that way. She had wanted to pull her own weight on the ranch, but debilitating headaches resulting from the fall were just another instance of everything going wrong with the plans that she had spent a lifetime making.

Her frustration soared. She had been hired to do a job and she wanted to do it. The fact that last night she had overheard the men saying the meals Ryder had prepared were the best they had ever tasted only added fuel to the fire inside her.

That fire was still burning when she had awakened this morning. Ignoring the doctor's warnings, she had insisted upon leaving her bed. Apparently unwilling to argue with her, Ryder had waited outside her door as she dressed with less stability than she would have wished. He had followed her into the kitchen, and had grasped her arm when a bout of weakness suddenly overwhelmed her. She had seen the concern in his expression at that moment and had decided not to argue with him when he seated her on a chair without another word and began tending to breakfast.

Now Justine looked out the kitchen window at the rapidly lightening sky. She heard the footsteps of the men as they entered the house. She prepared for their entrance into the kitchen with a bright smile. They stopped short at the first sight of her, and Pop's sincere exclamation—"Damned if you ain't a sight for sore eyes!"—set her heart winging. She glanced at Ryder to see a smile flick across his lips, too, before he turned back toward the stove.

Aware that she was not at her best . . . that her hair was hastily pulled into a bun, her clothing was wrinkled, and she was unnaturally pale, she responded, "I needed to get out of that bed for a while, Pop, but you don't have to worry. Ryder is still doing the cooking."

"That's all right with us, ain't it, boys?" When the men grunted agreeably in response, Pop hastily added, "Me and the boys are just glad to see you're feeling better, that's all."

Ryder glanced up, eliminating the need for a reply when he said, "Breakfast is ready. I'll put it on the table in a few minutes." He waited until the men had left the room before saying, "You're unsteady on your feet, Camille. Maybe you should go back to bed and rest for a while."

"I'm fine. I need to be up a bit."

Ryder did not respond. Instead, his gaze swept her

face, lingering a moment too long on her lips, and Justine's heart pounded. She insisted almost breathlessly, "Really, I'm fine."

Ryder remained silent.

"I really am."

Ryder's only response was a firm, supportive hand when she stood up.

"I can make it on my own," Justine protested.

"Can you?"

"Of course I can!"

Emotion darkening his light eyes, Ryder drew her arm so close to his side that she could feel the pounding of his heart as he whispered, "I made a mistake by letting you go once before. I don't intend to make that same mistake again."

Ryder's gaze was intent on hers, and her heartbeat escalated. Her mouth went dry. Her lips parted. Ryder's chest was heaving, his mouth was dipping slowly toward hers when the sound of a footstep in the doorway jerked both their gazes up toward Josh. Observing them, Josh said tightly, "You heard her, Knowles. She said she don't need your help. Just get the food on the table. I'll take care of Camille."

When she felt Ryder's grip stiffen, Justine managed, "I said I don't need help, Josh."

Hoping desperately that her legs would not betray her, she shook her arm free of Ryder's grip and walked into the dining room. She looked up when Ryder put a tray of flapjacks on the table. She smiled stiffly as he placed platters of eggs and ham beside it and began pouring coffee that smelled too good for words. She fixed herself a plate, ignoring

Josh's disapproving gaze at the men's grunts of approval.

Her stomach twisted. Damn that Ryder! She almost wished that the flapjacks were overcooked, the eggs runny, and—

Ryder poured her coffee and sat down beside her. The intimacy of his gaze when he turned briefly toward her drove all thought from her mind. Justine looked down at her plate and picked up her fork with a trembling hand. Something had changed between Ryder and her during those few moments in the kitchen. She couldn't identify it . . . she couldn't be sure what she was feeling, but—

Justine looked up when Ryder leaned toward her and whispered, "I meant it, you know. No matter what anyone says, I don't intend to let you run away from me again."

James accepted the written report that Ephraim Johnson handed him. He turned toward the window of his office as the man departed. He did not see the traffic that moved cautiously along the cobbled street in the pounding, late afternoon rainstorm. He did not see the well-dressed pedestrians gripping their umbrellas tightly as they struggled to lean into the wind-driven deluge. Nor did he see the few who ran along the street with newspapers clutched over their heads, hoping to escape the unanticipated downpour before they were soaked to the skin. Instead, the information Ephraim had imparted echoed incredulously in his mind.

What did Mason hope to accomplish with his underhanded dealings?

Could he possibly hope to . . . ?

No, surely that was too far-fetched.

Frowning, James turned back to his desk. He hesitated only a moment before sitting abruptly and picking up his pen.

Chapter Six

*T*wo days, and he was still waiting.

Otto Tears remained hidden, watching the men of the Double Bar C ranch finally ride out for the day's work. They had left Camille Marcel behind to be watched over with painstaking care by the fellow his eavesdropping had identified as Ryder Knowles.

Frustrated, Otto looked back at the house. He was uncertain how long this routine would go on, but he was not prepared to wait any more. He had to do something. He had to talk directly to Camille without her watchdog standing nearby—to ascertain if she was truly the Justine Fitzsimmons he was looking for. He couldn't take the chance that she was not. He did not want to return to the city with the report that the job had been successfully completed, only to discover belatedly that she was the wrong woman. Dobbs would not be fooled for a moment. Judging from his boss's cryptic wire, the men Dobbs had dispatched to take care of Letty

Wolf's other daughters had failed. He knew Dobbs's relationship with Mr. Charles depended on this particular job being "handled." He also knew that if it were not, if Dobbs suffered, he would suffer as well.

All the same, he was relatively certain that Camille Marcel was Justine Fitzsimmons. With a little coercion, it would not be difficult to make her admit that fact. Yet he needed to get her alone in order to do so, which would not be easy with Ryder Knowles always nearby.

Who was this Ryder Knowles anyway, and what interest did he have in Camille Marcel—aside from the obvious? Maybe none, but one glance at the fellow's size and obvious devotion to the young woman had made Otto certain that he didn't want to go up against him. There had to be a better way.

Otto glanced again at the Double Bar C wranglers as they rode out of sight—in time to see Josh Harter hanging back to give the ranch house a last glance.

Otto went suddenly still. Of course! Why hadn't he thought of that before? Josh was jealous of the Knowles fellow. He was the weak link in the chain of protection that so effectively surrounded Camille. All Otto needed to do was get Josh's confidence and his troubles would be over.

When and how could he do that?

Otto laughed to himself. That would be the easiest part.

"Your name's Josh Harter, ain't that right?"

Josh turned toward the sound of the voice behind him. It had been a long morning spent working under an unrelenting sun. Pop had sent him to repair fencing in the east pasture, a hot, sweaty job that he wouldn't normally have minded if he didn't think that Pop had merely wanted to get him out of his sight for a few hours.

Josh's temper simmered. For the life of him, he could not understand Pop's defense of Ryder Knowles. Josh had seen the way Knowles was looking at Camille when he walked into the kitchen doorway the other morning. Maybe Pop was too old to recognize Knowles's intentions, but he wasn't.

Josh's face flushed red-hot and his lips tightened. If anything else happened to Camille because of Knowles, he wouldn't wait for Pop's approval before setting it right. He had made that promise to himself, and whatever—

"I said, your name's Josh Harter, ain't it?"

Josh's gaze narrowed. He didn't like having somebody sneak up on him, and he liked the looks of this fellow even less. With hunched shoulders, a hawk-like nose, a thin, sweaty face covered with more than a week's stubble, and clothes that had obviously seen more than their share of wear, he was not a pleasant sight to behold—or to smell.

Josh glanced at the gun belt he had placed on a nearby boulder when he'd started to work. It was just out of reach.

The fellow countered by saying, "You won't be needing that."

Josh straightened up slowly. His voice guarded, he responded, "My name's Josh Harter, all right. What do you want?"

"A little of your time, is all."

"My time's valuable, so I'll ask you again. What do you want?"

The fellow responded unexpectedly, "My name's Otto Tears. I'm out hunting for the fella who raped and killed my sister."

Momentarily taken aback, Josh sputtered, "Well, that fella ain't me, so if that's what you're saying, you're barking up the wrong tree."

"That ain't what I'm saying." His expression darkening, the fellow continued, "I'm not from around here. I've come a long way, following the trail of this man. I think he's calling himself Ryder Knowles now."

"Knowles . . ." Josh went still before continuing in a rush, "You're telling me that Ryder Knowles raped and killed your sister?"

"No, I ain't."

"What are you saying, then?"

"I'm saying that my sister is dead, raped and killed by somebody, and that I'm going to get the fella responsible. But I ain't going to do nothing until I'm sure I've got the right man."

"Knowles is alone on the Double Bar C with a young gal right now . . . our cook. For all we know, he could be—"

"And I ain't jumping to no conclusions, neither." Tears continued softly, "If Knowles is the right fella, he's the kind who likes to play with his victims first—like my sister's friends said he did with her, making her trust him and think he cared about her. I need to talk to Knowles first . . . alone . . . to be sure he's the one. If he is, I'll take care of him myself, once and for all."

Anxious, Josh asked, "Why did you come to me?"

"I need to get Knowles alone somewhere so I can ask him a few questions. Can you do that . . . get him out of that ranch house and away from that woman so I can talk to him face-to-face?"

"Why don't you just ride up and ask him what you need to know?"

"Because if he's the right man, he'll lie." The stranger's oily face cracked in a brief smile. "I got ways of making a fella tell the truth, but I'd rather not have anybody around when I use them."

Josh slowly shook his head. "I don't want no part of this."

"That ain't the way I heard it."

"What are you talking about?"

"I heard that you're the only fella on that ranch who ain't taken in by that Knowles fella . . . that you've been suspicious of him from the first."

"Who told you that?"

"That don't make no nevermind. Are you going to help me or not? If you don't, I won't have no choice but to cause a bigger stir than I'd like."

Josh mumbled, "Camille's had enough problems since she got here."

"What?"

Josh paused, and then raised his chin determinedly. "How much time will you need?"

"An hour will do it."

"All right. I'll get Knowles out alone for you to question him, but that's all. I don't want nothing else to do with it."

"Just an hour."

Nodding in reluctant agreement, Josh strapped his gun belt around his waist and headed for his horse.

Standing in the ranch house kitchen a short time later, Josh ignored Camille's sober expression as he addressed Ryder. "Pop needs your help for an hour or so in the west pasture."

"He needs help from me?" Josh did not miss Ryder's glance in Camille's direction before replying, "I thought he wanted me to take over Camille's chores."

"I'm just the messenger. I can't read his mind. I'm going back to help him, but you can do whatever you want. I'll just tell him you're staying with Camille, instead."

"Josh—" Camille began.

Ignoring her, Josh walked abruptly out the doorway. Outside, he listened intently and heard Ryder say, "I'd better go, Camille. Pop must really need my help or he wouldn't have sent for me. I'll only be an hour, which means I'll be back in time to cook supper. I'll take you to your room so you can rest while I'm gone."

"I'm fine. I've told you that a hundred times. I don't have to rest."

"I don't have time to argue, either, Camille. Let's go."

"You are the most bossy man!"

Despite her annoyed comment, Josh heard her stand up and start toward the bedroom.

He mounted his horse and rode off at a gallop. Otto Tears would question Ryder Knowles, and that bastard would be out of the picture once and for all.

Despite his initial reluctance, Josh smiled. The thought was more than pleasant.

It wasn't the relentless Oklahoma sun, or the similarly relentless Oklahoma insects buzzing around his head that bothered Ryder as he rode toward the west pasture. He had the feeling that something was wrong.

The howl of a wolf caught his attention, and he frowned. Pop had insisted that there were no wolves in the area. If it were up to him, he would have made sure that Pop was right, but he had promised Camille that he wouldn't hunt down the animals, and he kept his promises. As far as he was concerned, the howls just proved how wrong Pop could be.

The tension in Ryder's shoulders tightened when the wolf howled again. He didn't like this. He knew Pop felt responsible for Camille. He knew Pop wanted to be sure Camille recuperated completely before resuming her job on the ranch. Which meant that Pop must be in some sort of trouble in the west pasture if he wanted Ryder to leave Camille, even for an hour.

Ryder nudged his mount to a faster pace. He had ridden due west since starting out from the ranch. He had been certain he would meet up with Josh, but he had not. It irritated him that Josh had not waited to bring him directly back to Pop's location, but he supposed he shouldn't have expected anything else. Josh didn't like him.

Ryder's thoughts halted abruptly when he caught sight of Pop, Pete, and Harry working at a water hole in the distance. Did that mean the water hole had become tainted somehow . . . that they needed help digging it out? He drew closer and noted that the men straightened up to watch his approach. It occurred to him as he drew closer that Josh was nowhere in sight.

Ryder reined his mount to a halt beside Pop a few minutes later.

"What are you doing here?" Pop asked tightly.

Ryder frowned. "What do you mean? You sent for me, didn't you?"

Pop shook his head. "I don't know what you're talking about."

"Josh said you needed help here."

"I haven't seen Josh since I sent him to cool off in the east pasture this morning."

"He said—"

Ryder stopped in mid sentence and then turned his horse abruptly back in the direction from which he had come.

Behind him, Pop shouted, "Wait a minute. What's going on?"

His expression black as a storm cloud, Ryder looked back briefly to respond, "I don't know. All I know is that Josh lied when he said you sent for me, that Camille is alone back at the ranch like he obviously wanted—and if he touched her, I'll make him wish he was never born."

Justine lifted her head from the pillow when the sound of a wolf's wail awakened her. She hadn't wanted to rest when Ryder had left earlier, but she had lain down when he firmly ushered her to her bed.

Strangely enough, she seemed to have fallen asleep the moment her head hit the pillow. That was when *he* had visited her. His thin, wizened figure was tense when he spoke to her in the guttural language that was so foreign to her ears. His lined face reflected his concern when he whispered:

Awaken now.

Beware.

Danger threatens.

Remembering his words and the urgency with which he spoke, she stood up abruptly. She took a moment to steady herself, then started toward the kitchen, only to stop short at the unexpected sight of a stranger standing there.

She froze as she viewed the fellow's narrow, rounded shoulders, the bushy brows that met over his sharp nose, and the oily sheen that covered his thin face. He was scrawny, unshaven, unclean, and he stank . . . but it was the look in his eyes that chilled her most.

"Well, if it ain't Camille Marcel, at last. Or is it Justine Fitzsimmons?" he asked.

Momentarily silent, Justine burst forward at a run. She had almost reached the yard when she felt a heavy hand clamp onto her unbound hair, jerking her backward. Gasping when the man wound his hand painfully in its length, she was forced around to face him.

"Don't run away from me, lady," he ordered. "I need to make sure who you are. Is your name Justine Fitzsimmons or not?"

She responded fearfully, "I don't know what you're talking about. Who are you?"

"You don't know my name, but I know yours, Justine."

"My name isn't Justine."

"Yes, it is."

"No, it isn't!"

"We'll see."

The stranger grasped the length of rawhide looped at his waist and wrapped it around her wrists, binding them tightly. He pushed her back toward her bedroom as he said, "I'm going to look around your room. I'm sure I'll find something there that will tell me exactly who you are."

When they reached her room, he shoved her onto the bed and began searching. He emptied out her drawers, throwing her belongings carelessly on the floor. Angry and empty-handed, he paused a moment before reaching under the bed. He smiled when he withdrew her suitcase, but ended up knocking it aside when he found nothing inside to suit him. His scowl set Justine to trembling.

"I'll give you one last chance. Is your name Justine Fitzsimmons?"

"No. It's Camille Marcel, and I—"

"Shut up."

"W-what?"

"I said, shut up!"

The fellow stood up, mumbling as he turned to glance at the yard. Looking back at her, he said, "We can't stay here. They're bound to be back soon and I'm not done with you yet."

Grasping her roughly by the arm, the stranger pulled her up off the bed and dragged her outside. She struggled as he lifted her up onto his horse with surprising strength, and then warned as she attempted awkwardly to dismount, "Do that, and I'll shoot you right now!"

It took only one moment for Justine to realize that the fellow meant what he said. As he mounted up behind her and turned the horse to gallop away, she also realized that she might never return alive.

"I didn't know. I thought . . . he said . . ." Josh's voice trailed to a halt as the men standing in the ranch-house kitchen stared at him fiercely. He said hoarsely, "I'll find her. I won't let that fella take advantage of Camille."

"Like he took advantage of you, you mean?" Pop's gaze was cold.

"Now isn't the time for recriminations." Ryder spoke tightly. They had all arrived back at the ranch house within a few minutes of each other, and no one seemed to know why the man who had identified himself as Otto Tears had gone to such extremes to kidnap Camille.

Could it be that he simply wanted a woman? Camille was beautiful . . . desirable . . . intelligent . . . everything a man could ever want. That truth had become clearer to Ryder every day as he had tended to her. He recalled her flawless beauty as she had lain silent and unmoving in her unnatural sleep. He remembered the uncertainty that had flashed in her eyes when she attempted to get up that first time . . . how she had leaned against him, her body warm and soft. She had been so vulnerable that his heart had ached. It was never far from his mind that she had been injured because of him. Tending to her had been both a privilege and a punishment that had raised his awareness of her to an unbearable level. Yet he had reveled in her temporary dependence on him. He had known only that she wanted him nearby, that she needed him, and that because she did, he was there. Then he had allowed someone to steal her away from him.

Ryder's fury soared. Something did not ring true. He was unable to dismiss the thought that Camille had been kidnapped for more than the obvious reason. Otto Tears was a stranger who seemed to have come out of nowhere just to find Camille. Ryder, too, was a stranger who had come to the ranch specifically to determine whether Camille was actually the Justine Fitzsimmons he had been seeking.

Ryder considered that thought. Could it possibly be that Otto Tears wanted to find Camille for a reason similar to his? Could this abduction possibly relate back to Letty Wolf and the possibility that Camille was her daughter?

If so, how?

Ryder unconsciously shook his head. He looked up when Josh declared, "I don't care what the rest of you are going to do, but I'm going to find Camille. This whole thing is my fault, but I ain't going to let that Tears fella get away with whatever he's trying. That fella admitted he was new to the area, which means he don't know it too well. But I do, and I'm going to hunt out every hiding place from here to Wyatt and back. I'll find Camille, and that fella won't get away from me, neither."

"That sounds like a good plan." Pop glanced at the three wranglers behind him. Seeing they were in agreement, he directed, "Harry, go to town to tell the sheriff what's happened while the rest of us go with Josh. It don't make no sense to have us criss-crossing each other on the trail and all. You can come back to join us when you're done."

Their plans made, they had all started for the kitchen door when Pop noted that Ryder had not moved. Turning toward him, he said, "What about you, Ryder? Are you coming?"

"I don't know the area very well. I won't be much help, so I'm going to stay here while I try to figure things out."

Pop responded tightly, "Suit yourself."

Watching as the four men checked their guns and rode off, Ryder remained silent. It was partially true that he would be more hindrance than help on the trail, but that wasn't the real reason he had stayed behind. He needed to think. If Josh was right, the fellow who had kidnapped Camille was a stranger. If the stranger was smart, he would realize that the wranglers on the ranch knew the country around it like the back of their hands, and he couldn't escape by hiding somewhere nearby. He obviously had plans for Camille, and he would need privacy in order to accomplish them, but he would be unable to travel far with Camille protesting all the way.

Where would a stranger to the area hide, especially if he wasn't sure where to go?

The answer was obvious. He would go to the place most familiar to him—the place where he felt safest.

Where was that?

The town of Wyatt.

His heart pounding, Ryder took only a moment to check his gun and then headed for the door.

Justine was finding it difficult to think. She was lying on a bed somewhere, waiting for her kidnapper to speak. She knew only that her kidnapper and she had ridden for a distance before he had dismounted and pulled her down from his horse. He had blindfolded and gagged her, then had waited for darkness before he'd lifted her back onto his horse. She had struggled against him violently at that point, only to suffer a blow that had stunned her into submission. In the time since, they had arrived at their destination. He had lifted her down from his horse, shoved her through a doorway, and said with irony heavy in his tone as he pushed her down onto the bed, "Home at last."

Justine gasped when her kidnapper ripped away her blindfold and gag and said coldly, "You can scream if you want, but it won't do you no good. Nobody can hear you here."

She glanced around, noting that she lay in a bedroom that revealed a woman's personal touches. This was no hunter's cabin in the woods, or even a hotel room.

Her kidnapper sneered. "Pretty room, ain't it? You didn't expect me to bring you to a place like this, but I figure nobody else will come here, neither. The fella I rented this house from was happy to let it to me while his wife and him went back East for a few months. I told him I'd been on the trail for a while, looking for just the right place to bring my wife when she arrived on the stage in a few days. He believed me."

Leering, her kidnapper walked a few steps closer. "The truth is that I ain't got no wife coming, but I like it here. It's real nice and private like. Nobody will expect us to hide in this little house. That'll give me all the time I need to find out the truth."

Justine took a breath before responding hoarsely, "What do you mean, the truth? You asked me my name, and I told you what it is. It's Camille Marcel. I don't know who this Justine Fitzpatrick is."

"Justine *Fitzsimmons* is the name, and you damned well know it, because you're Justine Fitzsimmons!"

"No, I'm not!"

"You're not fooling me with your lies." The stranger moved so close that he was looking directly down at her as he said, "But that's all right. I've got time. You'll tell me the truth, and in the meantime, we'll have some fun."

"Fun . . ."

Her kidnapper leaned close. "Yes, fun. You know what I mean, Justine."

"My name isn't Justine!"

"Right."

She swallowed tightly. What was happening? Who was this man, and why had he gone to so much trouble to find her? What did he want?

Ryder flashed before her mind, and Justine's breath caught on a sob. She remembered that his strength and support had been unfailing, and that his gaze had hinted at words unspoken. She suddenly wished that Ryder had had time to say those words. She wished it desperately . . . and she wondered if she'd ever get the chance to hear them.

Camille took firmer hold on her emotions as tears brimmed in her eyes. Ryder and the rest of the men would try to find her as soon as they realized she was missing.

Still, so many questions plagued her:

Why was this happening?

How long would she be able to hold out without telling her abductor what he wanted to know?

And—most soul shaking of all—would Ryder get there in time?

Ryder slid his mount to a halt in front of the Travelers' Hotel as the sun began dipping into the horizon. He slapped his horse's reins over the hitching rail and walked rapidly toward the clerk's desk. Looking down at the balding fellow, he said, "I'm looking for a small, hawk-nosed, unkempt fella who probably registered here a day or so ago. He might have used the name Otto Tears."

"Let me stop you there, fella." The clerk smiled pleasantly as he continued, "Nobody's registered here in the last week, much less anybody who looked like the fella you described. This is a small town. We don't have much traffic traveling through."

Ryder frowned at the unexpected reply. He couldn't be wrong. Tears had to be in town somewhere.

He demanded, "This is the place where that troupe of entertainers stayed a while back, isn't it?"

"No, that would be old Marge Heller's boarding-house, but she's a demon. There ain't many who want to go up against her."

"Where's the boardinghouse?"

"At the end of the street. You can't miss it, but I'm telling you, that fella won't be there. He—"

Turning on his heel, Ryder did not wait for the clerk to finish speaking before heading for the street.

Out on the boardwalk again after talking to Marge Heller, Ryder shook his head. The clerk had been correct every step of the way. The man he was looking for had never attempted to get a room at Marge Heller's boardinghouse, and Marge Heller *was* a demon.

Frustration tightened Ryder's throat. He couldn't have been wrong. He hated to think he'd been wasting time on a fruitless notion while Camille was in danger. But where else in town could they be?

Ryder looked around him. The sky had darkened and the town was coming to life. Raucous music from the saloon rang on the hot evening air, and the street was beginning to fill with the nightly traffic of wranglers seeking respite from the long day. His gaze focusing on the brightly lit mercantile down the street, Ryder took a breath. He remembered the whispered conversation between Pop and Winston Means. The mercantile proprietor seemed to be the confidant of everyone in town.

Ryder realized with a flash of insight that Winston Means might be his last chance of finding Camille.

"Come to think of it, a fella that looked like that did stop in here to pick up some supplies a day or so ago. He didn't say his name or nothing. As a matter of fact, he didn't say much at all except that he was staying in town. It looked to me like his head was hurting pretty bad." Means continued with a trace of puzzlement flashing across his round face, "Since you said he didn't register at the hotel or at Marge's, I got to figure that he's the fella Harvey Wilson was referring to when he told me he was going back East with his wife for a few months, and that he had rented his house to a fella who had been on the trail a long time and was waiting for his wife to arrive in town. I have to say that stranger didn't look like no family man to me, but I expect he took Harvey in. I think Harvey figured the stranger and his wife were going to stay in his house until they settled around these parts somewhere. I don't think Harvey expected that the fella would decide to sow some wild oats while waiting for his wife." Winston shook his balding head. "Harvey wouldn't approve of that. No, he wouldn't."

"Did this fella come back to town?"

"I can't rightly say. He got supplies enough for a few days when he was here."

"The house he rented, is it nearby?"

"It's at the edge of town. Harvey liked it that way . . . just enough seclusion for him. He didn't like—"

Ryder turned abruptly toward the door and Winston called after him, "Hey, where're you going?"

Ryder did not stop to reply.

Her hands still bound behind her, Justine was helpless against the man who was leaning over her.

She closed her eyes briefly at the fetid smell of his breath as he asked in a whisper, "How come you ain't screaming, Justine?"

"My name isn't Justine."

She inched away from him as the man lowered his scrawny body toward hers. She pleaded, "Stop! You have the wrong woman, I'm telling you. My name is Camille Marcel. I came to town with a troupe of actors who abandoned me here. I was working at the Double Bar C because—"

"I know all that!" Halting his intimate advance, her abductor sneered, "I heard all the stories about you that had the town talking, and I don't believe a word of it. Your name's Justine Fitzsimmons. Your mother is Letty Wolf, a rich woman as wily as you are."

"You're wrong. If I were a rich woman's daughter, what would I be doing here in a little Western town, struggling to make my way?"

"I don't know . . . and I don't care."

"Yes, you do . . . you care." Her mind raced as she attempted to keep the conversation going. "You care who I am because it's important for you to find this Justine Fitzsimmons person for some reason. The only problem is that I'm not her!"

"Yes, you are."

"No, I'm not!"

"Yes, you are, dammit!"

His face flushing a sudden hot red, her abductor grasped her shoulders and shook her hard as he shouted, "You're going to admit who you are so I can get out of this damned town tonight. You're going to tell me everything I want to know before I'm done with you, and you're going to beg for the chance to say more. I promise you that I'll—"

"You've made Camille enough promises, Tears."

Justine felt her abductor's grip abruptly stiffen. She witnessed the astonishment on his face when he turned to see Ryder standing in the doorway with his gun drawn. She gasped with relief when he stepped back from her and stood flat-footed, facing Ryder as he replied, "Look, friend. I don't know who you are or what you're doing here, but we can make a bargain, us two."

Justine saw Ryder glance at her bound wrists before he advanced into the room and said through stiff lips, "I don't make bargains with people who don't have the honor to keep them."

"That ain't me! I got honor!" Her abductor took a step forward. "I made a promise. I accepted a job, and I expect to do what I said I'd do. There don't get any better honor than that, nohow." Glancing back at the bed, he added, "And if I get to have some fun along the way, well, that ain't bad, neither. But I ain't selfish. This little lady's got enough for the two of us to share."

Ryder's expression twitched. Camille could see the rage building with every word her abductor uttered. She knew he could see it, too, yet he kept talking.

"Look at her." He was practically salivating. "I figure once she tells me what I want to know, the two of us can have all the fun we want with her. You're alone, so nobody else will find us for a while."

"Shut up!"

"Come on . . . you know you want to."

Ryder ordered, "Turn around and take a step back while I untie her."

"You're going to untie her? Hell, she'll scratch and fight us that way. No, tied is better. She—"

Springing forward in a sudden flash of movement, her abductor knocked the gun from Ryder's hand and struck him hard. Ryder staggered backward, but then stepped forward and dealt a single blow that knocked the other man onto the floor. When the fellow lay motionless, Ryder moved to Justine's side and began untying her hands. His voice was low and filled with emotion as he flicked her bonds free and whispered, "This is a nightmare, Camille. I was afraid I wouldn't find you in time. I was afraid—"

Her eyes widened when her abductor moved suddenly toward the gun still lying on the floor. "Look out!" Camille shouted.

Turning, Ryder dived for the gun at the same time as his opponent. The collision of bodies in that moment was almost as intense as the scrambling for the gun that ensued . . . the twisting and turning as the two men rolled across the limited space locked in a deadly embrace with the gun between them.

Fear choking her throat, Camille remained motionless, helpless in the face of the continuing battle.

A loud shot rang out.

All movement halted.

Camille gasped when her abductor turned suddenly toward her. She cried out Ryder's name, and saw him lift his head at the same moment her abductor's eyelids fluttered closed. Kneeling beside Ryder, she was about to speak when her abductor's eyelids again fluttered.

Turning toward him, Ryder asked gruffly, "Why did you abduct Camille? Who sent you?"

The stranger made an attempt to speak. Ryder leaned toward him. His lips moved and then went still.

When Ryder drew back, Camille asked hoarsely, "Is he . . . ?"

"He's dead."

A sob escaped Camille's throat, and Ryder slipped his arms around her. She leaned into the support of his embrace and remained there for the few moments it took for her to regain her composure. Drawing back, she wiped the tears from her cheeks and asked through trembling lips, "What did he say? Did he make any explanations at all?"

His light eyes intent, Ryder responded softly, "He didn't answer my questions, darlin'. He just said, 'Dobbs isn't going to like this.' "

He'd called her *darlin'*.

And then everything changed.

The sheriff came to the house, and her abductor's body was taken away after exhausting explanations that only raised new questions. Pop and the Double Bar C wranglers arrived and greeted her with open relief. Looking thoroughly ashamed, Josh apologized for his part in the debacle and congratulated Ryder for finding her. Ryder sobered when Camille thanked him again for saving her. He then inexplicably slipped back into his former role of caretaker, putting an unexpected distance between them.

Stunned, Justine realized that Ryder was actually trying to avoid her.

The men discussed the dramatic turn of events around the dining-room table until the wee hours, so Justine did not really expect them to awaken at the crack of dawn for work the following day as was their custom. But when morning came they rode out as if the previous day had never happened, leaving Ryder and her in silence.

When the sound of the men's horses had faded, Ryder suggested, "You should probably lie down for a while. You couldn't have gotten much sleep last night."

"I'm fine."

"I'll clean up the kitchen while you rest."

"I'm not going to rest, Ryder. You made breakfast. I didn't do anything."

Spotting the ring of bruises around her wrists, Ryder whispered a curse. He grasped her hands and scrutinized them carefully. "Those bruises are nasty, but they'll heal. I have some salve in my saddlebags that will help."

"I know. I don't need it. They'll fade."

"You need to rest. You haven't recuperated fully yet."

Ryder was right. Her wrists were bruised and her body was aching, but it was an ache of a different kind that plagued her. Lodged deep inside her, the ache caused her to step closer to Ryder as she said boldly, "You called me darlin' yesterday, Ryder."

"I know."

"Did you mean it?"

Ryder scrutinized her silently. His light eyes

burned her. His breath was sweet against her lips. His body heat consumed her. She knew she could depend on him, that she could trust him with all that went unsaid about her, and that her life was safe in his hands. His innate honesty touched her soul, yet he had awakened an emotion of another kind inside her. She only knew that she wanted to feel close to him . . . to feel his arms around her. She wanted his heat to become a part of her, and she wanted whatever would follow.

She whispered again, "Did you mean it?"

"Did I mean it when I called you darlin'?" He paused. His breathing grew uneven as he hesitated, and then said, "Yes, I meant it."

Justine trembled at the closeness of him . . . at the power he exuded so effortlessly. The masculinity that had formerly challenged her now awoke a new hunger that she knew instinctively only he could sate. The word "love" came to mind, but she refused to acknowledge it. Instead, she asked in a whisper, "Do you want me, Ryder?"

Justine felt the tremor that shook him. His voice was a rasping whisper as he responded, "Truthfully . . . I've wanted you from the first moment I saw you."

"Even when I was outrageously difficult . . . when I was stubborn and bossy?"

"Even then, because you were also beautiful, quick-minded, and all the woman any man could want."

Shuddering almost beyond control, Justine pressed herself against Ryder's hard body, feeling the proof of his passion even before she asked, "Do you still want me?"

"Yes."

"I've never wanted a man before, but I want you, too, Ryder."

Still motionless, Ryder looked down into her eyes and whispered, "You want me because I rescued you . . . because I'm the hero of the moment . . . because . . . because you feel you owe me."

"No, I want *you*."

"You're sure."

"I'll never be more sure of anything in my life."

Ryder took a breath, and then said, "That's all I needed to know."

Crushing her tight against him, Ryder closed his mouth over hers. A thrill chased up Justine's spine as he sought her response hungrily. His kiss was at first rough and demanding, but then gentled and deepened until she was wild with the joy of it . . . with the wonder of being in this man's arms. His strength enclosed her, and she welcomed it. His kisses surged deeper, and she abandoned herself to them. She returned kiss for kiss, caress for caress, until in a sweep of movement she felt the bed beneath her back at last.

Her heart pounding when Ryder pulled his mouth from hers and paused unexpectedly, Justine searched his face. His gaze was intense as he looked down at her, his breathing rapid. He whispered, "I need to be sure before this goes any further, Camille. I need to be certain that you don't feel just temporary gratitude—because once I have you, there'll be no turning back."

She whispered, "I don't really know what I feel.

All I'm sure of is that a simple thank you would suffice if what I felt were simply gratitude. This is more. This is . . . this is—"

"This is *need*."

Justine nodded as Ryder identified her emotion. He continued, "I know what you feel because I suffer the same madness every time I look at you. Only for me, I think it's even more intense. I need to show you how I feel. I need to make the way I feel so clear to you that you'll never be in doubt again."

Ryder's lovemaking began in earnest then. He touched and smoothed her aching flesh with maddening gentleness. His mouth sank deeper as his tongue swept the hollows of her mouth with increasing fervor. He worshiped her sweet flesh and she urged him on. He traced the line of her shoulders with his tongue until her senses tingled. He suckled her bared breasts until she was almost mad with wanting. His naked skin was hot against hers at last, and he kissed and fondled every inch of her virgin flesh until she could no longer think for wanting him. She moaned aloud when he reached the warm delta between her thighs at last. She gasped when he pressed his lips to the tender flesh. She cried out when he bathed her with kisses, and was suddenly unable to breathe when his tongue slipped deep into the sweet heat.

She panicked when the first quaking tremors began to overwhelm her. Quieting at Ryder's gentle reassurance, she surrendered fully to passion and soared high on diaphanous wings before falling to shuddering relief in Ryder's arms.

Her breathing still uneven, she opened her eyes to find Ryder as breathless as she when he whispered, "There's more, Camille. So much more."

Sliding back up on the bed, he then joined her body with his. He filled her, pausing only briefly to look down at her, to assess the passion in her expression before he began a gentle rocking motion inside her. The power of his lovemaking enclosed her, coaxed her to join each thrust, and then brought her again to the edge of passion. It exploded in the abrupt, tumultuous climax of mutual reward.

Breathing unevenly when they were both still once more, Justine exulted in the weight of Ryder's powerful body atop hers. She threaded her fingers through his dark hair and then slid her hands down his back, luxuriating in the feel of the powerful muscles that had brought her such pleasure. She slipped her arms around him and felt him crush her tight against him in a breathless embrace. She raised her face to his and noted the moment when passion changed to something else.

His eyes searched hers, and he asked abruptly, "Tell me once and for all—is your name Camille Marcel or Justine Fitzsimmons?"

Stunned into speechlessness, she stared at him. How could he ask her that question now after—?

A wolf's howl sounded unexpectedly, and Ryder raised his head. His expression tightened before he looked back down at her and said with a rigid smile, "There he is again . . . your friend."

"You heard that?"

"The wolf that Pop says doesn't exist? Yes, I heard him."

"Nobody else hears him, Ryder, just you and me."

"Camille, I—"

She interrupted in a whisper, "Don't say anything else. It's my turn to talk now. There's something I need to say." She paused. She took a deep breath, and then said, "I am the Justine Fitzsimmons you're looking for, and . . . I love you."

Chapter Seven

The hotel room was silent as Meredith Moore stared at the envelope in her hand. She had walked to the post office a short time earlier, her heels clicking hollowly on the board sidewalk that lined the main street of Winsome, Texas. With a hot Texas sun on her back and a leisurely breeze stroking her face, she had glanced around her, recalling her first reaction to the town: disbelief that she had actually been born in such a primitive area. She had scoffed at the road approaching Winsome because it was unpaved and dust-laden. She had considered the stagecoach an uncomfortable, cumbersome, and hardly adequate conveyance. The deeply pocked main street had looked primitive to her disapproving eye; the false-fronted buildings and small stores were nothing like the elaborate edifices and cobbled streets of the great city where she was raised.

Arrogant, sharp-tongued, and grimly determined to discover the past that her mother had steadfastly refused to discuss with her, she had scorned everything about Winsome.

As she approached the post office, Meredith mused that she was a different woman now. Admittedly still a bit arrogant and still determined to discover her past, she had begun looking at things differently since the man she loved had opened her eyes and her heart.

Trace Stringer had done that for her. Tall, dark, and with features that were a bit too uneven for him to be considered truly handsome, he was big and powerful, but gentle enough to practically stop her heart each time he touched her. Western born and bred, he was the Pinkerton who had been sent to inform her of the new stipulations in her mother's will. While on the job, he had proved his love for her in so many ways that he had completely won her heart.

When she reached the makeshift post office, she inquired with considerable apprehension whether any mail had been forwarded to her. She knew that the possibility was practically nonexistent; but Justine, her youngest sister, had chosen the most difficult road of all to her future, and Meredith hoped desperately that the dear girl had some good news to impart. The last thing in the world she had expected, however, was to receive the letter that the postmaster had placed in her hand—the letter that she presently held unopened as she stood in the hotel room with Trace beside her.

Meredith's glittering amber-eyed gaze focused on the return address boldly written on the envelope. Momentarily immobilized, she remembered a period in the not-too-distant past when her mother, the beautiful and vivacious Letty Wolf, had appeared to be truly happy. Meredith had allowed herself to believe briefly then that it was all over. She had told herself that, once truly content, Letty would come to a full realization of the disappointments she had caused her daughters from early childhood, and of the uncertainties and broken promises that they had been made to suffer. Meredith had been certain that with her mother's realization of a lasting love would come freedom from her own driving need to look out for her sisters.

She had never been more wrong.

Letty Wolf, their lovely, desirable, and enigmatic mother, had unexpectedly cast James Ferguson aside.

Silently berating herself for her stupidity, Meredith had firmed up the quiet plans she had made with her sisters to embark on a journey to find their own paths in the future. She had also renewed her personal determination to discover the past that haunted her in so many ways.

Still staring at the unopened envelope in her hand, Meredith took a trembling breath and turned toward Trace when he asked, "What's wrong, Meredith?"

Aware that she hadn't said a word since entering the hotel room, Meredith did not immediately reply. She loved the touch of Trace's hands, the warmth of his body, the true concern reflected in his gaze each time he looked at her. She loved *him*. It made no difference to him that she had refused her mother's offer of reinstatement in her will, or that with her refusal went all hope of sharing her mother's fortune. He understood that Meredith had come west with the hope of learning about her past—that she would not leave without achieving that end, no matter how difficult. He appreciated her needs without fully understanding the warning howls that only she heard, and the visits from the "Grandfather" that only she could see.

"Meredith . . ."

She swallowed and said breathlessly, "This letter is from James Ferguson."

"James Ferguson?"

Meredith pushed back an errant strand of hair as she replied, "James loved my mother. I thought for a while that he would be the answer to my prayers."

"What happened?"

"My mother didn't love him."

Trace's dark brows drew together in a frown as he asked, "What does he want with you?"

"I don't know. I don't know how he knew I'd be in Winsome, either."

A sound in the room behind them turned Meredith toward the two standing silently there. She watched the beautiful blond woman who approached her. Even with her platinum hair pulled into a severe bun, with her glorious gray eyes darkly ringed with exhaustion, and her delicate features drawn into a tight frown, Johanna was lovely. She had arrived in Winsome with the man she loved a few days earlier, and the reunion of the two sisters had been sweet beyond words. They had discussed the strange happenings that had followed them and had decided that in order to settle all questions, they needed to learn more about their mother's past.

That their mother had granted her three daughters the ambiguous gift of outstanding beauty was an obvious truth; yet all three resented the fact that their mother had told them nothing of their heritage.

Johanna said determinedly, "You don't have to read that letter, Meredith. We both refused our mother's offer by declining to go home. Her will doesn't include us. There's no reason for us to involve ourselves in her love life."

"I know," Meredith agreed.

"Throw the letter away." Johanna could not hide the trembling that had beset her delicate frame. "The only connection we have to James Ferguson is through our mother. You have no obligation to read what he has to say."

Meredith stared at her sister's adamant expression. She understood the sadness, the sense of loss, and the pain of the past that the return address had evoked in Johanna. She shared her sister's renewed anguish.

Meredith hesitated a moment longer. She looked at her sister's flushed face and then turned deliberately toward the wastebasket. In unspoken response, she dropped the unopened envelope into it, and walked away.

Mason grimaced as he glanced at the squalid New York City streets through which he traveled. He had been forced to pay the hired cab double to take him into this part of town, and he heartily resented it. Had it not been for the emergency that demanded he contact Dobbs again, he would not have risked the possibility of being seen in this area.

"Stop here, driver."

The driver leaned over with an expression of distaste and mumbled, "I'll stop here, but I ain't going to wait for you. You'll have to find your own transportation back to a safe part of town."

Mason nodded when the carriage drew to a halt. He paid the fellow without a word, noting that the driver wasted no time leaving. Mason started toward the dilapidated club, which looked seedier than ever in the bright light of day. He glanced around him and grimaced again. He supposed he should be glad that the littered street was empty of traffic. He sneered as he stepped over a snoring drunk lying across his path—the man was dirty and disheveled amidst the debris of a night of unbridled decadence. Mason noted without surprise that another fellow slept off the night's excesses in a nearby doorway. He ignored them as he walked toward the familiar entrance a few feet away.

The smell of stale beer, mold, and even more disgusting substances met Mason's nostrils as he entered, briefly nauseating him. He halted, momentarily blinded by the dark interior. He started toward the bar at last and was about to address the long-haired, unclean bartender when a door slammed.

"Busy yourself at the other end of the bar, Herman," Dobbs ordered. "I need some privacy here."

Waiting only until the droopy-eyed man complied, Dobbs turned angrily to Mason and asked, "What do you want? If it's information you're looking for, I don't have any. You'll have to wait until the job is done, whether you like it or not."

His lips twitching with annoyance, Mason responded, "For your information, I don't take orders from you, Dobbs. I give them, remember?"

"Is that so?" Dobbs's oily face creased in a humorless smile. "That ain't the way I see it."

"Whether you see it that way or not, that's the way it is." Taking a moment to regain his composure, Mason straightened up to his full height and said, "But I'm not here for the reason you think. I have another job for you."

"Another job?" Dobbs shook his head. "I may not have gone to one of them fancy schools that you went to, but I learn fast, and I ain't taking on any more jobs that will send my boys out of town."

"Don't worry about that. This job is local."

"Meaning?"

"I want you to see to it that a certain individual meets his end before the week is out. I'll pay you well when it's done."

"Who's the lucky fella?"

"His name is James Ferguson." His gaze narrowing when Dobbs reacted with a backward step, Mason demanded, "What's the matter? Do you know him?"

"Him and me don't travel in the same circles, but I heard of him."

"What do you mean, you heard of him?"

"The newspapers made a big fuss about a high-society man named James Ferguson being attacked and almost killed a while back."

"That's him." Mason sneered. "Are you trying to tell me it's going to cost me double for you to take care of him?"

"If I agree to it."

"What do you mean, 'if'? That's what you do, isn't it?"

"The job I originally agreed to do for you ain't

exactly what you talked it up to be. I lost two good men so far. I don't expect to lose any more."

"That's up to you, isn't it? You knew what the job entailed when you took it on. You assured me that you could handle it. Taking care of James Ferguson is an extension of the same job. This is a preventive measure that will eliminate the need to take any action on Letty Wolf in the future."

"Meaning?"

Mason smiled stiffly. "You don't need to be privy to that information."

Dobbs's small eyes narrowed, and Mason felt revulsion choke his throat. If the obnoxious fellow were not a necessary part of his plans—

But he was.

With that thought in mind, Mason swallowed his revulsion and said, "But I will tell you this. It's James Ferguson himself who's making this step necessary. If he has his way, your men will have died in vain—and you won't get the rest of your payment, either."

Dobbs replied tightly, "The sound of that ain't too appealing, that's for sure." He hesitated a moment and then said, "All right, I'll take care of Ferguson for you. When and where do you want it to happen?"

"The choice is yours as long as it happens soon, and as long as it appears to be an accident."

"An accident! Nobody will believe Ferguson's death was an accident after somebody already tried to kill him!"

"But nobody will be able to prove otherwise—*if* I can finally depend on you to do the job you're supposed to do."

Dobbs's expression turned deadly at Mason's denigrating comment. Aware that they had reached a critical point in an already strained relationship—that the next few minutes would determine the course of his future—Mason waited for Dobbs's response with his heart pounding.

The silence between them stretched long.

"All right, consider it done."

Mason fought to withhold a sigh of relief at Dobbs's belated reply. Instead, he said, "I'll pay you half now and half when it's done—the same price I paid for your men to take care of Letty's daughters."

"I guess that's fair."

"Fair? It's more than fair considering your performance so far!" Aware that his sudden loss of temper was inopportune, Mason added more reasonably, "But I need to warn you. I will not accept failure."

"Failure ain't an option."

"Good. Then we understand each other." Withdrawing carefully folded greenbacks from his pocket, Mason counted them out into Dobbs's unclean hand and reiterated, "When and how you want to do it is your choice, just as long as it happens before a week is out."

"Like I said, failure ain't an option."

Nodding, Mason turned on his heel and left without another word. His lips tightened when he reached the street. It galled him that he had been forced to deal with Dobbs again, but James Ferguson had become an obstacle in his path. He had made a mistake that he couldn't otherwise correct when he'd approached Ferguson in the first place.

He had misjudged Ferguson's reaction, and Letty was beginning to question his loyalty for the first time. He couldn't allow that to happen . . . not now. Letty was hearing things and seeing visions. James Ferguson's death could be just the catalyst that would send her over the edge of sanity.

Two birds with one stone.

In any case, he needed to get Ferguson out of the way so he could go forward with his plan, and Dobbs was the best man for the job.

Mason scrutinized the empty street. It occurred to him that he might have to walk several blocks in order to hail a carriage, but he wasn't too concerned. The inhabitants of the area didn't like daylight. He was relatively safe. Besides, all he had to do was mention Dobbs's name and a veil of protection would fall over him.

Mason started walking with the thought that perhaps his association with Dobbs would prove handy after all.

"How can you be sure you made the right decision?"

Johanna did not immediately respond to the question that Wade posed after they closed the door of their hotel room behind them. They had arrived in Winsome a few days earlier after an exhausting train ride from which Johanna had not yet fully recuperated. They had gone directly to the hotel and were overjoyed when they found Meredith and Trace in residence there. Wade knew he would never forget the sincere emotion between the two sisters when they greeted each other with tears and hugs, and with short, unintelligible phrases that only they appeared to understand.

He remembered looking at Trace Stringer for the first time and seeing reflected in his eyes the same feelings as must be visible in his own. He had known then, without doubt, that Trace loved Meredith with the same ferocity that he loved Johanna. Trace and he had silently bonded in that moment. He knew instinctively that bond would remain secure.

Yet after leaving Meredith and Trace, and entering the quiet of their own hotel room, Wade felt uncertainty taint his thoughts. Johanna was trembling and silent. They had both been present when Meredith returned from the post office with Ferguson's unopened letter. They had left soon after Meredith dropped it into the wastebasket, still unopened.

That simple gesture had said so much. It gave him a new understanding of the conversation with Johanna that had prompted their decision to seek Meredith's whereabouts. Wade remembered that discussion:

"None of this makes any sense. Why would a man come all the way from New York City with the intention of killing me—or both of us?"

"If that was his intention." Wade added, *"You won't find out what he intended if you stay here."*

"I'm not going back to the city, if that's what you're saying! My sisters and I decided long ago that we would go forward, not look back."

They had been on a train to Winsome when Wade said:

"You're going to have to face the fact that your sister may not still be in Winsome when we get there, Johanna."

"I know, but I need to try to find her. I need her advice about some things, and I can't wait until the date we all arranged to meet again a year from now. It's important for me to talk to her. Meredith went to Winsome to discover her past. I know her. She won't leave there easily, at least not until she finds out all there is to know about herself." She had continued, *"I used to resent it sometimes, you know, that Meredith always seemed to have all the answers."*

"But you know now that it just looked that way."

"Now I know she just tried to make it appear that she never panicked so Justine and I would have someone we could depend on. I love her even more for that."

Surprisingly, they'd had no trouble locating Meredith and Trace. The pair had become a legend of sorts in town. The hotel clerk had related the story of their dangerous escapades in detail.

Brought back to the present by Johanna's uncertain expression, Wade said softly, "I'm worried that you reacted emotionally when you saw James Ferguson's name in the return address, and that you didn't take the time to think through your decision."

"You mean when I told Meredith to throw the letter away?" Johanna raised her chin defensively. "That was the right thing to do. It was my mother's choice to lead her life without us, not ours."

"Maybe she's changed."

"I doubt that."

"Maybe James Ferguson can shed some light on what's going on."

"I doubt that, too."

"You won't know if you—"

"I won't ask Meredith to read that letter. I won't have anything to do with a mother who considered us impediments to her future and who distanced herself from us when we needed her most."

"Johanna—"

"Please, I don't want to discuss this anymore."

"Johanna—"

"Wade, do you love me?"

The obvious misery in her light eyes pained him, and Wade whispered, "You know I love you."

"Then let's not discuss the letter any more."

"But—"

"Please."

Unable to refuse her, Wade drew Johanna into his arms. Still trembling, she nestled closer, giving herself up fully to the consolation he offered.

He loved her. He loved the look of her, the feel of her, the sensation of holding her in his arms. He would always love her, but—

She had said the words *I love you* to Ryder, and she had meant every syllable. Yet with their saddlebags packed and bright morning sunlight shining through the trees outside the kitchen door, Justine faced Pop and his wranglers with the realization that it wouldn't be easy from then on.

"I hoped you would change your mind before morning. I hoped you'd realize that you ain't in no condition to travel yet," Pop said.

"Yes, I am. Pop—"

"Talk to her, Ryder." The old man turned toward

Ryder, who stood silently beside her. "Tell her she needs to wait till she feels better."

"I'm the one who convinced her it was necessary to leave now, Pop."

Momentarily at a loss for words, the aging cowman said suddenly, "I just don't understand what this is all about."

"I don't either. That's the problem." Her expression apologetic, Justine stood with her exquisite features tightly composed. She was dressed for the trail in a comfortable outfit, with her chestnut hair simply styled. "The truth is that I've been nothing but a problem to you since I came here, Pop. I seem to have brought my troubles with me . . . troubles that I don't fully understand . . . troubles that I *need* to understand."

"You're talking about that fella who came after you, ain't you?" Pop shrugged. "I told you. That's easy enough to explain. He saw you somewhere and had his eye on you. A fella who looked like him probably figured there was only one way he was going to get you."

"I wish that was all there was to it, but I don't think that's true."

Justine looked at Ryder, remembering their conversation after they had lain together . . . after she had confessed that she loved him. Still lying in Ryder's arms, their naked flesh intimately close, she had listened as he had said:

"I have something to confess, too." Hesitating, he had then continued, "My original reason for coming after you had nothing to do with emotion. I needed to repay a debt

to a fella who showed up at the door of my ranch too sick to finish a job himself. His name is Tom Monroe, and he is the Pinkerton agent hired to find Justine Fitzsimmons."

"*Hired to find me? Why?*"

"*Your mother hired the agency to find all her daughters and present them with a condition for being restored to her will, which was to visit her in New York City before her fortieth birthday.*"

"*That was a waste of everyone's time. Neither my sisters nor I would agree to her ultimatum. It's too little, too late.*"

Ryder responded, "*Doesn't it strike you as strange that this fella, Otto Tears, would come all the way from New York City to find you and make sure you don't return?*"

"*I suppose.*"

"*You suppose? Supposing isn't enough! Something is wrong, Justine, if that's what you've decided to be called.*"

"*I was Camille Marcel for a little while, but I'm Justine Fitzsimmons now. Camille Marcel doesn't seem to suit me anymore, and Justine Fitzsimmons is the name I've used most of my life, even if I don't have a true right to it.*"

Drawing her unexpectedly closer, Ryder said, "*Whoever you are . . . whoever you choose to be is all right with me, but I need to find some answers. I can't let your safety be compromised any longer. We have to go back to New York City to find out who Dobbs is and why he sent—*"

"*No.*"

"*Justine—*"

"*I won't go back.*"

"*What are you going to do, then? You can't stay here. It's not fair to put everyone on this ranch in danger.*"

"I . . . I have to talk to my sisters."

Ryder nodded soberly. "All right. We'll do that. Where are they?"

"I don't know." When Ryder did not immediately respond, she continued, "I need to go to Winsome, Texas."

"Why Texas?"

"That's where this all began. My mother was born in that area. Meredith went there to find out more about my mother's beginnings so she could find out more about herself. That's where she'll be until she learns all she wants to know."

"She may not still be there. You'd be taking a chance. She—"

Halting abruptly when he heard the undisputable howl of a wolf, Ryder gritted his teeth and said, "There it goes again, dammit! Pop said there aren't any wolves in this area. I don't know whether to believe him—"

"—or me." He had looked down at her when she finished his statement. "I told you, the howls are warnings that only you and I hear, Ryder."

"Justine—"

"You saw the wolf crouching beside me when I was unconscious. He was protecting me."

"No, he—"

"He was protecting me whether you want to believe it or not! I've heard those howls before, when I was younger and felt frightened. They consoled me, and then I saw—"

"—a wolf."

"No, I saw someone else." Haltingly, she related the story of the old man who sometimes appeared in her dreams.

"We have to get to the bottom of this," Ryder responded. "There's only one way."

"I won't go back to New York."

"All right, we won't go back." His voice growing unexpectedly hoarse, Ryder said, *"But there's something I need to say before we go any further. You said a while ago that you love me."* His voice dropped a note lower as he continued, *"I can only hope you love me as much as I love you. I know how truly precious love is. I know how easily it can be stolen, and how deep a hole it can leave in your heart. I don't intend to let that happen. I love you, Justine. I love you now, and I'll love you forever. I'll love you no matter what you intend to do, but I will not sit back and wait for someone to attack you again."*

"No one has ever loved me like that, Ryder," she said in a trembling voice.

"And no one has ever loved you as much as I do."

Unable to respond because of the emotion that choked her throat, Justine pressed herself closer and raised her lips tentatively to his. The magic that overwhelmed her when their lips touched was startling. It rapidly engulfed them in a whirlwind of feeling. Wrapped tightly in each other's arms, they joined their bodies, and their hearts fluttered at the beauty that rose between them. They reached mutual climax in a cataclysmic moment, with a release that they had not sought, but indulged lovingly.

Breathless and still at last, Ryder raised his head from hers. *"We'll leave tomorrow,"* he announced.

"I won't go back to New York City, Ryder."

"We're not going to New York, Justine. We're going to Winsome, Texas."

As she faced Pop and his wranglers in the temporary silence of the small kitchen, Justine said, "Ryder and I are going to Winsome, Texas, Pop."

"Where's Winsome, Texas?" Pop scowled.

"That's where everything that happened has its roots."

"You're sure of that?"

"To be truthful, I'm not sure of anything right now."

"Why don't you wait until you're feeling better—"

"Don't worry, Pop," Ryder interjected. "I'll take care of her."

The old man turned back toward Ryder, recognizing the solemn vow in his words. He scrutinized the big man solemnly. Then looking back at his wranglers briefly, he shrugged and said, "You'll come back when you find out what you need to know, won't you? We all want to be sure you're all right."

"That's a promise," Justine said. She added, "Besides, we need to return the mount you lent me, don't we?" She did not wait for Pop's response before stepping forward to kiss the cheek of each wrangler in turn—Pete, Harry, and the shamefaced Josh. She then turned back to Pop to add a tight hug to her platonic kiss as she repeated, "That's a promise, Pop."

Struggling against unexpected tears, Justine turned to Ryder and said quickly, "Let's go."

"You're sure, Willis?" James glanced at the mail that his elderly servant had placed in his hand as he entered the hallway of his home. It was the end of another day. He had riffled through the envelopes, hoping to find an answer to the letter he'd directed to Meredith Moore, but he was disappointed again.

"I'm sure, sir. That's all the mail the postman delivered."

James nodded, his brow furrowed. He had arrived home that evening, telling himself he couldn't really expect a reply. It was too soon, the address had been vague—he had sent it simply to "Winsome, Texas"—and his association with Letty's daughters had been brief. If he had not continued to employ the covert services of Ephraim Johnson, who had discovered that the town of Winsome, Texas, was Letty's birthplace and that Meredith had intended to go there, he would not even have risked sending the letter. But he'd had to do something. He needed to know if any of Letty's daughters were experiencing difficulties with strangers; if the dangers he feared were merely a figment of his overworked imagination; or if there was truly some sort of devious plot against the woman he loved.

Letty still believed the place of her origin was unknown to him. He supposed she would feel betrayed if she knew he had employed a detective to find out what she would not divulge; but in the end, it had been the only way.

Unable to help himself, James found his mind slipping back to the time when Letty and he had been a couple. It had not missed his notice that he had shocked his social set with their open affair. Some still considered Letty a pretender . . . an upstart . . . a woman whose social appetite was insatiable, but he knew better. The truth was that she was an intriguing, intelligent woman and an outstanding beauty who had the gumption to try making her own way in a man's world—a woman who had achieved success

beyond anyone's wildest dreams. Another truth was
that he had been lost ever since his wife's death. His
marriage to Madeline, linking two prominent fami-
lies, had been planned since they were children, but
Madeline had been a spontaneous young woman who
had understood him and loved him. He had known
her all his life, and he had loved her for all the good
things that she was. He had been happy in their marriage and would have been faithful to her for the rest
of his life if she had lived.

But she had not.

His life had lacked direction after her death. Bored,
and curious about the woman who was the talk of
the town, he had entered Letty's soiree as one of the
city's most eligible bachelors and a man who was
content to remain that way. Yet his heart had been
set afire the first time he saw her. Lovely, vivacious,
and possessed of a quick, challenging mind, Letty
was desired by most men. She had taken lovers along
the way, but she was not promiscuous. He had
known about those men, but the knowledge hadn't
bothered him because he had expected to be her last
man—the one she would marry and remain with for
the rest of their lives.

Because he loved her. He had believed she loved
him.

Wrong.

He didn't truly comprehend it even now. He had
known instinctively that the link between them
went beyond the physical. Intangible but real, that
link remained strong, even when she abruptly sent
him away, declaring that it was over between them.
But when he was attacked, she assumed his care,

demonstrating a sincere, loving concern. Once he had recuperated, she had stunned him again by reversing herself and reiterating that she would not see him anymore.

He had not believed that the emotion Letty had displayed at his sickbed was untrue. He had challenged her in every way possible when she said she didn't want to see him again, forcing her to the extreme of banning him from any contact with her.

But she could not ban him from loving her.

He had gone to Letty against her wishes after Mason approached him with his plot to institutionalize her. He had forced his way into her apartment, telling her that although he could not be her lover, he was still her friend. Whatever happened, he would not allow Mason Little's machinations to bring Letty down.

"Mr. Ferguson, sir . . ."

Brought abruptly back to the present, James looked at Willis as he said, "Your supper is ready. Helen will put it on the table for you."

"I'm not hungry, Willis. Tell Helen to put supper aside in the event that I'm hungry later."

"But, sir—"

James almost smiled. Willis had been in the employ of the family for years. The fellow doted on him, but he could not allow his servant's discomfort to affect him. Turning back toward the door, he said, "I'm going for a walk. I'll be back in a little while."

"Sir . . . it's getting dark."

"I'm not afraid of the dark, Willis."

Willis's expression indicated that he should be, but James was past that point. He had fully recuperated from his wounds. The reason for the attack was still a mystery, but the police had chalked it up to being somehow related to his well-publicized social work. They were still investigating. However, the perpetrator was dead and it would not happen again.

And walking helped him to think.

James repeated, "I'm going for a walk, Willis."

"Yes, Mr. Ferguson."

Not allowing Willis's disconcerted frown to affect him, James walked out the doorway onto the street without a backward look. Yet despite his greatest efforts, the rapidly darkening street renewed memories that set James's nerves on edge. He remembered the sound of the stranger's voice inquiring if his name was James Ferguson, his own politely curious reply, then the sensation of a blade plunging hotly into his back when he turned to walk away. He recalled the sinking sensation as he slumped to the ground when the knife plunged again and again. He did not remember much else, except awakening to the sight of Letty's face, and his hope that she was not a dream.

"Excuse me, sir." James turned rigidly toward a uniformed man who stepped up to him with a parcel in hand and said, "I'm looking for a Mr. James Ferguson. I have a package to deliver to him from a Mr. Ephraim Johnson, but there ain't no house number with the address. I'm kind of lost, 'cause this ain't my usual stomping ground. Can you tell me which house to deliver it to?"

His gaze narrowing at Johnson's name, James noted that the fellow's uniform indicated employment by one of the better courier services. He responded cautiously, "The house is over there."

"The house you just left? Are you Mr. Ferguson?" The courier smiled hopefully, showing crooked, yellowed teeth as he continued without waiting for a reply, "Maybe you can just sign for the package then and save me some time."

"No, just leave it at the house."

"All right. I'll do that, Mr. Ferguson. Thank you."

Unwilling to turn his back to the man, James watched as the fellow walked away. He shook his head at his unnecessary caution when the courier crossed the street, and then wondered what Ephraim Johnson could be sending him at that time of day. Making a mental note to open it as soon as he returned home, he resumed his walk.

Warned by a whisper of sound behind him and a sudden chill shooting up his spine, James turned back abruptly, in time to see a glint of steel descending toward his back. James sidestepped the blade and grasped the courier's arm. He marveled at the strength his opponent exerted as they fought for control of the knife. They struggled violently as mastery shifted from moment to moment; the blade neared, only to be forced away again. James realized with a touch of panic that he had not recuperated as fully as he'd believed. His strength was waning, and the street was empty. He could expect no outside help. He needed to do something.

With a sudden burst of power, James squeezed his attacker's hand, forcing him to drop the knife. The man responded with a blow to the chin that knocked James off his feet, momentarily stunning him as he hit the ground hard. Taking advantage of the moment, his attacker searched for the knife. He raised his head abruptly at the sound of running footsteps approaching. Cursing, he beat a hasty retreat.

The sound of the fellow's departing footsteps cleared James's head. He was about to draw himself up when a single shot shattered the eerie stillness, bringing his assailant down.

James turned to see a man rushing to the attacker's side with gun still drawn. Walking back toward him as James regained his feet, the man asked, "Are you all right, Mr. Ferguson?" At James's confused nod, he said, "That fellow's dead. My name is William Drinkle. I'm the Pinkerton agent assigned to protect you. I'm sorry, sir. That fellow took me by surprise, came up behind me and knocked me out. I'm glad I regained consciousness in time."

"You're a Pinkerton?"

"Yes, sir. Miss Wolf hired the agency to protect you."

"My own private investigator didn't inform me that I was being protected. I thought Pinkerton protection was terminated when I was on my feet again."

"Ms. Wolf came to our office to check on our progress the other day. When she learned that the protection she had ordered for you had lapsed, she reinstituted it immediately. As for Mr. Johnson, he is a capable detective, but you hired him for an entirely different job."

"It was Miss Wolf who arranged for my protection to be continued?"

"Yes, sir."

"And you know that Mr. Johnson is working for me?"

"Yes, sir. We've made note of all your visitors."

Their conversation abruptly halted when a shocked crowd began gathering and Willis arrived breathless at his side. James reassured the aging servant that he was all right. He noted that the police had arrived as well. He responded to their questions as best he could, but he was grateful when the police turned their attention to the Pinkerton at last. Aware that the agent made no mention of Letty Wolf in his carefully crafted explanation, James maintained his silence. He had some very serious questions of his own.

"Why did you have a Pinkerton following me, Letty?"

Dressed in simple nightclothes, with her hair loose on her shoulders and her face washed free of makeup, Letty did not immediately respond.

She had awakened after a fitful night's sleep several mornings earlier, determined to satisfy the nagging uncertainties that would allow her no rest. Disturbed by her conversations with James and Mason, she had paid a visit to the Pinkerton Agency. Stunned at her arrival in his office, Robert Pinkerton had also been taken aback to learn that she had wanted James's protection to continue. Claiming that a miscommunication had resulted in its cessation, he had promised to reinstate it immediately.

She had left Robert's office with her concern unalloyed; yet she did not approach Mason about the miscommunication that Robert claimed. She had not been able to face the possibility that James might be right about him.

The sound of James's voice in her apartment, however, had frightened her. Uncertain what to expect, she had waited breathlessly as he burst through the sitting-room door. Unprepared, Letty gasped at the sight of him. Hatless, his hair askew, James was sober and tense as he approached her. His clothing was wrinkled, his appearance was disheveled, and the warmth she was accustomed to seeing in his eyes was entirely absent.

He demanded again, "Why did you have a Pinkerton following me, Letty? Answer me!"

Letty muttered, "I don't know what you're talking about, James."

"Yes, you do." Taking her firmly by the arm, James ushered her to a nearby settee and sat beside her. His expression remained hard as he questioned again, "I need to know why you had a Pinkerton following me—why you felt I still needed protection. The man who attacked me the first time was dead. You should have believed that the threat against me was over. What do you know that I don't know?"

"Nothing, James. I swear it!" Letty's great dark eyes revealed a sudden fear when she asked, "What's happened? Did someone try to attack you again? How did you know that I had arranged—" Letty halted abruptly, realizing that she had betrayed herself.

"How did I know that you had arranged for a Pinkerton to follow me . . . to protect me? That's simple. The agent you hired saved my life tonight."

Letty gulped. "Saved your life . . ." The room momentarily whirled around her.

"Letty . . . Letty . . . I'm sorry," she heard James

say. "I shouldn't have upset you. Look at me, darling, please."

Letty took a deep breath, then another. She straightened up with sheer strength of will and said shakily, "I'm all right. I was just . . . shocked for a moment."

His touch gentling, James drew her closer. Concern replaced the former anger in his expression when he said, "You wanted to protect me from someone . . . from something. I need to know what it is."

"James, you know why I employed the Pinkertons. The howlings I hear . . . the fears that won't allow me to rest . . ." Breathing erratically, Letty continued, "I was afraid you would die just like the rest of the men who loved me."

"That's foolishness, Letty."

"No, it isn't!" She said more softly, "I know you find it all hard to believe, but I heard the warning howls again. That's the reason I went personally to the Pinkerton Agency this time, and made sure an agent would follow you."

"*This time?*"

"Mason was supposed to have arranged for your protection before you were attacked the first time. He was supposed to have arranged to have protection continue indefinitely, but . . . Robert Pinkerton said there must have been a miscommunication of some kind, because protection was terminated when you were back on your feet again."

"It wasn't miscommunication, Letty."

"What was it then, James? You can't possibly believe Mason hired that man to attack you . . . to kill you. Why would he do that? Mason may have made some mistakes, but his concern for my welfare is real. He's stood by me through many difficulties."

"Advising you all the way, I suppose, which is probably why your daughters chose to leave you."

"Sarcasm isn't necessary, James. Mason has been a true friend."

"A friend who lies to you . . . who refuses to help you when you need him . . . who wants to commit you to an insane asylum."

"Stop! He's not like that! He cares about me . . . about my daughters."

James's expression stiffened. "They're fond of him, too, I assume."

"Yes . . . no . . . I mean, they don't really know him very well."

"You said he cares about them."

"He does. He has always said they're the only cousins he has."

"But they aren't really his cousins. They're his uncle's paramour's children."

"Yes, they are—all but Justine. But I wasn't Archibald's paramour. I was his fiancée. I loved Archibald and we were going to be married. The only problem was that he died before we could marry . . . before he could legally claim Justine as his daughter. He died like all the other men who loved me."

"That was coincidence."

"No, the howling had stopped for a long time, James. The warnings began again just before Archibald was killed. I tried to warn him. I knew something was going to happen to him, but he wouldn't listen. Then he was dead, and I was alone again with no way to support my young daughters."

When James did not comment, Letty continued, "I made my own way then. I had to. I was alone."

"Until you met me."

Ignoring his comment, Letty continued, "But somewhere along the way I lost touch with my daughters."

"And you expect to get them back by bargaining with them."

"I could think of no other way to convince them to return after they left me—and I was frightened. The howlings began again—forecasting danger . . . death—and I didn't know what to do."

"The howlings—"

"I didn't want anything to happen to my daughters. I wanted them to return to New York so they'd be safe and I could explain to them that I was sorry, that I had somehow lost my way on the path to success and didn't realize it until too late."

"But you wrote them out of your will."

"I was angry when they left at first."

"Who did you name as beneficiary in their place?"

"Mason, of course. He's my only other relative." Letty stopped short before adding, "I know what you're thinking, but I explained things to Mason. I explained that I regretted cutting my daughters out of my life. I told him what I had proposed and said that I wouldn't forget him, that I'd still include him in my will if my daughters returned."

"But he would receive much less . . . a small part of the whole that he'd expected to inherit."

"Mason doesn't need my money! He's a successful lawyer with important clients."

James hesitated before replying, "He's bankrupt, Letty."

Letty turned pale. "That's impossible."

"It's true."

"How do you know that?"

"I had him investigated privately. There can be no mistake."

Her lips beginning to tremble, Letty whispered, "If so, that would mean Mason could have wanted to be sure that my daughters wouldn't return so he would retain his place in my will." Letty shook her head, her brow furrowing. "But what am I saying? A will only goes into effect at someone's death. I'm still young, only a few years older than Mason. He could wait a lifetime for an inheritance from me. I would have to die first or I would . . ."

Letty halted abruptly, her eyes widening as James continued for her: "—have to be found incompetent to handle your affairs. In which case the courts would appoint an appropriate guardian." Letty began shuddering violently, but James persisted, "Mason could easily arrange for that person to be himself—but that would only happen if your daughters refused your conditions or did not return."

"No!"

"It makes sense, Letty."

"No . . . no, it doesn't. What would be his reason for the attacks on you? Surely he could see that I had no intention of letting you back into my life."

"He could also see that I had refused to accept

that decision. He expected when he came to see me that I'd be angry enough to take the opportunity to get even with you. He didn't realize my love for you was unconditional. A man like him could never realize that I would accept whatever place you made for me in your life, rather than lose you. He understood too late that I'd die before I'd let him commit you to a mental institution."

"You'd die first? Oh, James." Her eyes heavy with tears, Letty whispered, "How many more times does your life have to be threatened before you accept the fact that to love me is to take on the curse that follows me?"

"There is no curse, Letty—but if there were, it would be the fact that you won't let me love you."

Letty sobbed, "I can't . . . I can't do that to you, don't you understand?"

"Because you care about me."

"Listen to me, James, please, and try to understand. Everyone who loves me suffers. It doesn't matter if I care about them. I care about my daughters, despite my unintended neglect of them, and they suffered because of me. Now—if you're right—they're threatened because of me. Two of my daughters are relatively safe—at least I think they are—but there's been no word of Justine. I don't even know where any of them are right now."

"I do."

"What?"

"I know where Meredith is—at least I believe I do. I hired a detective to find out."

"So did I."

"But Mason knew about the detectives you hired. He didn't know that I had hired an investigator."

"Tell me where she is."

His expression tight, James whispered, "Meredith went to Winsome, Texas."

"Winsome." Letty closed her eyes as the misery of the distant past swept over her. "I knew I had made a mistake when I told Meredith about that part of my past. I can't go there. There are too many memories . . . too much pain."

"You don't have to go, Letty. No one expects it of you."

"I can't, James." Raising her tear-streaked face to his, Letty said wearily, "I've tried so hard to forget everything about those days. I just . . . can't."

James drew her closer and Letty collapsed against him. Spent, unable to think, she closed her eyes.

Chapter Eight

*T*he blue expanse of the sky was beginning to dim as a brilliant sun dipped into a broad horizon streaked with pink and gold. The intermittent breeze that had been a warm bath of air throughout the day had turned cool and refreshing. The terrain was level, the surface sporadically marked with drifts of wildflowers that were a riot of color and a visual delight. The trail was dusty but well packed, making easy going for the horses.

So . . . why was she so uncomfortable?

Justine's breathing was clipped. The hair underneath her straw hat was plastered to her head in a most unladylike manner, her dress adhered to her back with sweat, pearls of perspiration lined her forehead and upper lip, and her underwear was uncomfortably bunched.

And she was tired. Dammit . . . she was tired!

"This looks like as good a place as any to stop for the night."

Startled, she looked around her. There was no

sign of civilization. She turned toward Ryder and said, "We're going to stop here?"

Appearing surprised at her comment, Ryder replied, "You don't want to go any farther tonight, do you? We have to eat yet and we—"

"I don't see any sign of a rest stop."

Ryder looked at her strangely and responded, "There's no rest stop and no town around here, Justine, just wide-open spaces. We're going to camp for the night."

"Camp?" She took another breath. "You mean cook over a fire and sleep on the ground?" The flicker of a smile that touched Ryder's lips infuriated her. "What's so funny, Ryder? What are you laughing at?"

Turning his mount so that he faced her fully, Ryder responded, "Sometimes I forget what a tenderfoot you are."

"I'm not a tenderfoot!" Pulling herself up self-righteously, she responded, "Just because I was born in New York City, that doesn't mean I'm a tenderfoot. I just wasn't expecting . . . I didn't think . . ." Justine paused and attempted to regain her composure. This was the man she loved, and he loved her, too. She was sure of it.

So why was he torturing her?

She began again in a more patient tone, "I thought we would reach a town by nightfall."

Ryder urged his horse closer. She could not imagine why his broad shoulders were still erect and his powerful body showed no sign of fatigue, as if he had not suffered the same rigors of the trail as she. His incredibly light eyes searched her face as he continued more seriously, "I don't know what gave you that idea. I asked you what you wanted to do before we started out. You said you wanted to get to Winsome, Texas, as quickly as possible. Pop said he'd never heard of Winsome, but Harry had. I asked him the best route to take because he's more familiar with the area. He said this trail is the fastest way. The only transportation we could take from Wyatt would have been a stagecoach to the nearest town or the nearest railhead. Since Winsome doesn't have rail service, we'd need to find out what the closest stop to Winsome would be and what the schedule was. That might mean more delays before we found the transportation we were looking for. We'd have to stable our horses somewhere along the way. I figured that might be a problem—"

"That's enough. I understand." Justine's voice was clipped. "This is the shortest route to Winsome—wherever that is."

Ryder looked at her a moment longer, and then swept her unexpectedly off her horse. Seating her across his saddle so she could lean on him, he whispered against her cheek, "If you don't feel well and want to go back—"

"No!" Justine took a breath. Ryder was so close. The hard wall of his body supported her. She sagged slightly against him and felt the concern in his touch as she admitted reluctantly, "I'm . . . I'm just out of sorts. I guess I'm more of a tenderfoot than I thought."

Ryder pressed his lips lightly to hers and stroked a strand of hair back from her damp cheek. The brush of his sweet breath was comforting as he said,

"See that stream over there? That's good, fresh water. After you clean up a bit, you'll feel better." She looked in the direction he pointed and saw ripples glittering in the setting sun as he continued, "When you're done, we can make ourselves something to eat." At the knitting of her brow, a smile flickered across his lips and he corrected, "*I'll* make us something to eat."

Justine felt her heart begin a slow pounding despite herself as she returned his gaze. His eyes were so light as to be almost transparent. She supposed the thing that had annoyed her most about him at first was her thought that those eyes could see right through to the uncertainty she hid underneath her arrogance. Could they read the way she felt now, so disheartened that she just wanted to wrap herself in Ryder's arms and let the misery of the day fade from her mind?

Yet he was only doing what she had asked him to. She needed to get to Winsome as fast as she could. She needed to talk to Meredith if her sister was still there. She needed . . .

Ryder nudged his mount abruptly forward, interrupting her thoughts. Lowering her to the ground minutes later, he dismounted beside her and said, "You can freshen up in the stream while I make camp and get supper ready."

Ryder unbuckled his saddlebag and withdrew the spare clothing folded inside. "You can put these on when you're done. You'll feel cooler. They're clean, and they're more suited to the trail than the clothes you're wearing."

Justine looked at the wrinkled pants and shirt

Ryder held out. In New York City she would have been offended by his offer, but here, with Ryder's deep voice providing consolation, she said simply, "Thanks."

She thought she heard Ryder's sigh of relief when she turned away.

At the stream, Justine undressed slowly. Her muscles ached. She had not imagined that riding a horse for an extended period could be so . . . so taxing. She could feel the heat that the sun had burned into her fair complexion, and she shuddered at the thought. She splashed the cool water against her face, neck, and shoulders—shoulders so stiff that she could barely brush her hair when she released it from its conservative bun. She allowed the cooling breeze to dry her skin as she brushed the tangles free, and impulsively dispensed with the underwear that had tormented her, pulled on Ryder's shirt and pants, and breathed freely at last.

The sudden growling of her stomach alerted her to the aroma wafting from the campfire that Ryder had lit. Not taking the time to tie back her hair, she started toward him. She suddenly realized that walking wasn't as easy as it had previously been, and that her normally smooth step had changed to an awkward limping gait.

Justine fought to restrain tears. She was a mess—sunburned, dressed like a beggar, and limping like an old soldier! How could anyone want to help her . . . and most of all, how could Ryder love her?

Ryder turned toward the stream at the sound of approaching footsteps. He stood up slowly, hardly believing his eyes as Justine approached. His clothes hung on her loosely. She had rolled up the pants and shirt to fit her petite proportions, which only served to emphasize her slenderness while hinting at the womanly softness underneath. Her unbound tresses, brushed into a shimmering sheen, hung loose over her shoulders, displaying brilliant streaks of red and gold highlighted by the sun. The fair skin of her face was washed clean of the dust of the trail and was a golden color, drawing attention to the doe-shaped, glittering green of her eyes.

Ryder did not immediately speak. The sight of her awoke yearnings inside him that had no place on the trail. This trip was obviously taking more out of Justine than either of them had anticipated. Yet she was so beautiful that he caught his breath.

Pausing as tears unexpectedly filled her eyes, Justine said, "I'm sorry, Ryder. I'm hungry, and everything smells good . . . but I'm so stiff that I can't take another step."

Ryder saw the lone tear that trailed down her cheek. She brushed it away angrily as he curved his arm around her and said, "I'm the one who should be sorry, Justine. I forgot what a long day on the trail can do to a person who isn't used to it." Urging her forward, he said, "Come on. You'll feel better after you eat."

But Justine balked. He saw the short breath she took before she said, "You don't understand. My muscles are frozen. They don't seem to work anymore. I *can't* take another step."

Ryder went still. He knew what it meant to her to admit she was incapable of anything, much less as simple a task as walking. He also knew she would not have made that admission if the situation were not dire. Scooping her up into his arms, he said, "I can fix that. I have some—"

She said with a hiccupping sound between laughter and tears, "I know. You have some salve in your saddlebags."

"Liniment, darlin'. The cowboy's answer to the ailments of the trail."

But Justine did not smile. Instead, she frowned as he placed her gently on the blanket he had stretched out beside his. She asked tentatively, "Are you sure this will work?"

She was smiling now, but he wasn't.

Ryder felt perspiration dot his brow as he glanced at the half-empty bottle of liniment. Taking a deep breath, he poured more of the soothing liquid into his hand and then looked back down at Justine. He had asked her to roll over so that he could massage her back. He had asked her to remove the shirt he had lent her, and when she threw it aside—allowing only a peek of the rounded breasts that had been so sweet to his taste—he had straddled her slender hips and proceeded to uncork the bottle. He had begun rubbing the liniment into her back while smoothing and massaging the knotted muscles underneath his hands. He was uncertain when he became conscious of the silky texture of Justine's skin beneath his palms, of the way her muscles gradually relaxed into womanly ripples as he coaxed the stiffness from them. He noticed that her arms lay at an awkward angle—the arms that had held the reins of her horse all day. She whimpered, then groaned when he massaged her biceps, her inner arms, her hands, and then the space between each and every finger that he longed to bring to his lips.

Aware that his feelings were growing out of control, he was about to move away when Justine whispered, "My legs, Ryder. The muscles are so tight."

Her legs . . .

Ryder took a breath and said gruffly, "If you want me to rub your legs with liniment, you'll have to take off your trousers."

"But I—"

His chest beginning to heave with the emotions running riot inside him, Ryder managed, "I can't do it any other way."

"All right."

Her hands were still so stiff, she had difficulty undoing the button at her waist.

"I'll do it," Ryder muttered.

He caught his breath as he pulled her trousers down. The bare, smooth contours of her hips were more than he wanted to see at that moment. There were no undergarments to impede his view as he continued slipping the trousers down and the rounded curves of her buttocks were gradually revealed to him—perfect and unmarked by her ordeal. He swallowed tightly and pulled the trousers down the rest of the way, off the long, slender legs she had wrapped around him so tightly when they made love.

But his ordeal was not over yet. Touching, smoothing, massaging every inch of those long legs, he then moved to her feet—rubbing the arches, caressing the heels, torturing himself with every perfect toe before he sat back abruptly and said, "All right, that should do it."

Turning her head to look back at him, she protested, "You're not done yet, are you?"

"You should be able to move more easily now."

"But . . . but . . ." Swallowing visibly, she managed, "I spent so many hours sitting on that hard saddle. I thought . . . I hoped . . ."

"All right."

Clutching the bottle firmly, Ryder poured more liniment into his palms and began massaging her buttocks. They were so smooth, so warm to his touch. He kneaded them with his palms, caressed them with his cupped hands, gave them ease with his fingertips. He was uncertain when his touch slipped to the inner juncture of her thighs, where he stroked the tender flesh sprinkled with clean, silky hair.

He was lost in the feel of her, caressing her boldly, when Justine turned over unexpectedly, her slender womanliness exposed fully to his view. "Stop, Ryder. Stop this minute!"

Halting abruptly, he heard her say in a shaky voice, "If you don't finish what you started right now, I'll go mad with wanting you."

Barely maintaining control, Ryder managed, "You're sure . . . ?"

Her response was a trembling, "Yes."

Within minutes they were flesh-to-flesh, heart-to-heart, heat-to-heat. Too far gone for preliminaries, Ryder entered her hotly and found her wet with desire. Plunging deep, he discovered she was ready to receive him. Beginning the dance of love, he brought them to swift, crushing climax, exulting in Justine's soft groan of completion when they lay silent and still at last.

The first to raise his head, Ryder said softly, "Are you all right, Justine? I didn't intend for things to end up this way tonight."

In silent response, she slipped her arms around his neck and pressed her mouth to his for a long, lingering kiss that left him breathless. As breathless as he, she whispered, "Maybe you didn't have that intention. Maybe I didn't, either, Ryder—but maybe that was the way it was supposed to be."

"The stiffness . . . is it gone?"

"It's bearable."

"Then maybe we can take it more slowly this time, so we can enjoy every moment."

The green of her eyes took on an entirely different hue as she said, "Not too slowly, Ryder . . . please."

His mouth descended toward hers as he muttered, "That's a promise."

Twilight had faded into night. Justine and Ryder had finished their belated supper and had not complained that the meat was stringy, the beans burned, and the coffee so strong that it almost walked away. They had settled the horses and the camp for the night, and presently lay in each other's arms with the fire burning low and the sky lit by a brilliant moon and endless stars.

Strangely, the ground didn't seem so hard to Justine with Ryder's arms around her. The night sounds weren't frightening with Ryder's muscled warmth pressed against her. The future didn't look so dim in the silence devoid of the familiar howls of warning.

Yes . . . sweet silence.

As sleep neared, her questions about the appearance of Otto Tears in their lives seemed far away, her uncertainties about Meredith and Johanna dimmed, and thoughts of Letty's part in the mystery gradually faded.

Moving subtly as her eyes closed, Justine said, "How much longer do you think it will be until we reach Winsome?"

Ryder's eyelids stirred. They opened into narrow slits as he replied, "I don't know. That depends."

"Depends on what?"

"On a lot of things."

"Like?"

"On things like . . . how much liniment I have left."

"Oh."

A smile flitted across Justine's lips before she moved closer and quietly fell asleep.

Ryder opened his eyes, taking a moment to study her motionless face as she slept. Her heavily lashed eyelids were motionless, her skin smooth and clear, her features so perfect that they seemed almost unreal. Her response to him tonight had been more complete than he had ever dreamed possible. Ryder was in awe that this loving woman was now his. He would not let anyone or anything separate them.

He whispered against her warm lips, "I love you, Justine."

She did not respond. She was sleeping and couldn't hear him, but he had known that. He had just needed to say the words.

Justine opened her eyes with a start. She saw a dark sky above her lit only by the moon and stars, and Ryder's powerful body turned toward hers in sleep. She felt a familiar tingling inside her and sat up as a vision gradually appeared in the darkness, becoming clearer as it neared. A bright sun shone at his back, muting his features, yet she could see clearly the unbound strands of graying hair that brushed his narrow shoulders, and the new determination in his shuffling walk. His small, dark eyes seemed to glow within his weathered face as he began speaking in the guttural tongue she knew so well. She was uncertain, but she thought she saw a flash of approval as he said:

Take care.
Do not dismiss easily.
Remember all.
It is almost over.

She waited for him to speak again, but the image turned and walked back into the bright light of the sun. She gasped when she saw the wolf that bounded suddenly into sight.

The wolf . . . her friend.

She reached out to stroke the gray fur, but the animal moved out of reach as it loped to the old man's side. They disappeared together as the vision gradually faded.

Justine was still breathing heavily and trembling

when Ryder sat up abruptly, his hand going to the gun he had placed beside him. "You're trembling. Did you hear something?" he asked.

Almost unwilling to speak, she whispered, "*He* was here. Did you see him?"

"*Him?*"

"The old man, and the wolf."

Ryder frowned.

"You didn't, did you? But he was here, Ryder! He told me to be careful and that it would be over soon. He said not to dismiss easily, and to remember everything."

"Remember what?"

"I don't know."

"Justine—"

"I saw him, Ryder. I saw the wolf, too, and I know they're both my friends."

Ryder slid his arms around her and drew her close.

Justine whispered against his shoulder, "You don't believe me, do you?"

"Maybe it was a dream. Maybe it was your mind's way of making peace with all that has happened."

Drawing back, she said, "The howling has stopped, hasn't it?"

Ryder paused, then nodded.

"I haven't heard it any more, either. I think that means there is no danger when I'm with you. But *he* came to tell me not to dismiss the warning and to remember, although it will be over soon."

Ryder's eyes scrutinized her face. She could feel their power even in the semilight and she said softly, "It's all true, Ryder."

"I don't know what to believe . . . but there's one thing I do know. I believe in you."

Her throat suddenly tight, Justine kissed Ryder's parted lips and said softly, "That's all I need to know."

Lying back down, she closed her eyes and fell immediately asleep.

"Don't belabor your decision, Letty. You know you have no choice."

Letty returned James's gaze solemnly in the early morning silence of her sitting room. Conservatively dressed in a dark jacket and pants, James scrutinized her modest gray traveling dress. The lines were simple and the color quiet. The small hat she'd chosen sat securely on her upswept dark hair and she wore no makeup.

James frowned at the single bag beside her. "Are you sure you've packed enough? We're not certain how long we'll be gone."

"Because I have just one suitcase?" Letty's sober expression cracked in a brief smile. "It's my guess that you have only one suitcase in the carriage downstairs. What makes you think I'll need more baggage than you?" Her smile fading, she answered her own question by continuing, "I'm not really the clotheshorse I appear to be, James. I've managed before with less clothing than is in that bag. I have enough."

"If it rains . . . if the nights are cold . . ."

"I was born near Winsome and lived there a good part of my life, remember? I know what to expect from the weather this time of year."

About to speak again, James thought better of it, took her arm, and said, "All right, then. Let's go."

Letty studied James as their carriage drove to the station and the train that would soon arrive to carry them to Texas. She wanted to say so much. She wanted to tell him that she knew he loved her even though he believed she didn't love him. She wanted to tell him that she wished things had worked out differently, and that she were free to express her love, but fear sealed that secret in her heart.

Instead, she said, "When we find my daughters . . . *if* we find them . . . I'm not really sure what I should say. How can I explain away all the years that turned them against me?"

His gaze understanding and his response familiar, James replied, "Take it a day at a time, Letty."

Lowering his mouth to hers, he brushed her lips with a platonic kiss as he repeated, "That's all anyone can ask . . . just a day at a time."

A day at a time . . .
Those words resounded in his ears as James extended his hand to help Letty down from the carriage. He glanced around them, noting the confusion at the train station as passengers rushed toward their destinations or milled about, awaiting later trains. Uniformed employees pushed carts of baggage, weaving their way through the crowd. James nodded when a porter picked up their bags. He told him the car number to put them in before turning back toward Letty. She stood there silently, her expression filled with trepidation. She was beau-

tiful in her demure costume. She caught every male eye without any effort at all, but he saw only that the woman he loved was in distress.

Sliding his arm around her shoulders, James drew her lightly against his side as he whispered encouragingly, "Smile, Letty. This journey will mark the end of a nightmare and the beginning of a new life. Think of it that way, and remember that I'm here to help."

Surprising him, Letty straightened up and replied, "You're right, you know. I have no choice if I want this nightmare to end, and only I can make it happen."

A train whistle shrieked above the noisy pandemonium. Doing her best to smile, Letty continued, "I just have to remember that I'm not the poor, desperate young woman who left Texas so many years ago. I need to keep in mind that I'm a mature woman now, hoping to find an explanation for her daughters that will allow them to forgive her. You helped make that clear to me, James. Thank you for that."

James did not reply. Instead, he escorted Letty silently through the crowd until he found their train at last, ushered her to their luxury car, and opened the door to her stateroom. He watched as she settled her things and turned toward him. He loved her. He wanted to stay with her, to console and support her in any way that she needed, and to hold her in his arms through the long nights that would follow, but she was determined to keep them apart. He had said he'd be satisfied with any role in her life that she chose to give him, but maintaining that promise was proving more difficult than he had imagined.

James paused with his hand on the doorknob, ready to allow Letty the privacy she desired. He needed to remember how important this visit to her birthplace was for her; it was up to him to help her find the right direction.

Waiting only a moment longer, he made an excuse and pulled the door closed between them. She had whispered her thanks, touching his heart with her sincere gratitude. As he left her to her thoughts, he replied belatedly, "You're welcome."

Mason slapped the newspaper down on his breakfast table and stood up abruptly. He was seething. Dobbs's man had failed again! The newspapers were filled with the story of the attempt on James Ferguson's life from which he had escaped unscathed. Stories were beginning to hint at a plot against him.

The fool that Dobbs had dispatched to take care of Ferguson was dead. The newspapers reported that a Pinkerton detective's bullet had brought him down.

How could that be?

There could only be one answer to Mason's silent question.

Letty.

James must have instilled enough doubt about him in Letty's mind that she'd gone to Pinkerton herself to see if he had ordered continued protection for James as she had asked.

It was all Dobbs's fault! The man was inept, unworthy of his reputation as an underworld figure who could be depended upon when a job needed to be done. Two of the men Dobbs had sent to follow Letty's daughters had been killed in the performance of what was supposed to have been an easy assignment. There had been no news of the third, which led Mason to believe he had suffered the same fate. Were it not for the fact that both Meredith and Johanna had refused Letty's offer to reinstate them in her will, his plans would already have failed. He could only hope that Justine would feel the same as her sisters and would refuse their mother's offer also.

He would not allow Dobbs to get away with his ineptitude! He had warned him, and he would now go over his head as he had threatened. He would make Dobbs suffer for the series of mistakes he had made. He would approach Mr. Charles directly.

"Barton!" Turning toward the doorway when there was no immediate response to his summons, Mason called out more loudly, "Barton, come in here!"

Mason looked at the short, slender, gray-haired servant who rushed to respond. The man had been a butler, a dresser, and an employee of his family for as many years as he could remember. Still, he had never developed a personal relationship with the man because the fellow was beneath him in every way. Barton was presently old and dependent on his goodwill, and Mason liked it that way. It gave him power.

Mason snapped, "Get my clothes ready. I'm going out, and I want to dress to impress, do you hear?

Not a crease, not a button, not a string out of place. That's important."

"Yes, sir."

"Hurry up. I don't have time to waste."

Impeccably dressed in expensive clothing that reflected his station in life, Mason stood in Mr. Charles's outer office later that morning. Three thugs had met him the moment he entered, when he declared imperiously, "My name is Mason Little. Mr. Charles knows me. I want to see him now."

A dark fellow almost as tall as he was wide responded, "Mr. Charles is a serious businessman. He don't see nobody without an appointment."

"He'll see me."

The hulking fellow took a step closer. His odoriferous breath was hot on Mason's face as he repeated, "I said, Mr. Charles don't see nobody without an appointment."

"Let him in, Ham."

Ham's head snapped up toward the voice emanating from the inner room. He shouted back, "He don't have an appointment, Mr. Charles."

"Let him in."

A small smile on his face, Mason followed the massive fellow as he led the way, but his heart was pounding despite his confident demeanor.

It was obvious that Mr. Charles had made an attempt to appear legitimate. The office was furnished with a grand desk, an imported rug, and lavish furniture. Original oil paintings decorated the walls, but the costly draperies and blinds only partially shielded a glimpse of the dirty street outside the window.

As for Mr. Charles himself, Mason was surprised to see that despite expensive clothing and a ring on his finger that probably cost more than his clerk's yearly salary, the man could not hide the seediness within. His aura raised the hackles on Mason's spine as Mr. Charles inquired flatly, "What do you want?"

Mason raised his chin and responded, "My name is Mason Little. You know who I am, and you know why I'm here."

"No, I don't, so why don't you tell me?"

"I owe you gambling debts—a greater sum than I can presently afford to pay."

"You do?"

"I had no doubt of being able to repay the money until unexpected circumstances altered my hopes of an inheritance. I hired Humphrey Dobbs to rectify the problem."

"What has this Dobbs to do with me?"

"You know the answer to that question. He's your man, and I want you also to know that Dobbs failed to do the job I paid him for. He failed—not once, but three times, and possibly a fourth, after guaranteeing me satisfaction."

"I don't know what you're talking about."

"Yes, you do," Mason insisted. "You know that Letty Wolf is the wealthy woman who wrote me into her will because of her disenchantment with her daughters. I don't deny that was an unexpected windfall. My plans included collecting that inheritance sooner than my dear Aunt Letty expected so I could pay my debts to you, but she changed her will in an attempt to get her daughters back. That was when I hired Dobbs to find her daughters and make sure that they did not accept the conditions of re-instatement. Two of Dobbs's men failed in that mission, but I was not immediately concerned because both daughters refused Letty's conditions. We still do not know the disposition of the third man Dobbs sent. Without word from him of any sort, however, I can only assume that man has failed also."

Mason continued, "Yet I proceeded with my plans to collect my inheritance ahead of time when my aunt provided me with the unanticipated opportunity to have her confined in a mental institution. It was my intention to get power of attorney over her finances. When one of Aunt Letty's lovers interfered, I hired Dobbs to see that he was taken care of, but Dobbs failed me again. Dobbs's man was killed in the attempt, and James Ferguson survived."

"James Ferguson . . . ?"

Mason nodded, nothing the brief frown of recognition that flitted across Mr. Charles's face at Ferguson's name.

Mr. Charles went on emotionlessly, "I still don't know what this has to do with me."

"I came here because Dobbs is your second in command."

"No, he isn't."

"Whether you deny it or not, everyone knows he is. I came here to make sure you know that he's not the person you believe him to be. He's inept, unable to do his job, which is a reflection on you and a detriment to your organization."

"Like I said, I don't know this Dobbs fella."

"I demand that you take action! It's Dobbs's fault

that my plans have gone awry, and it's his fault that I'll have to scramble now to get them back on track!"

"That has nothing to do with me."

"I expect you to handle it, do you hear? I expect you to see that Dobbs is punished for his failures, and I expect you to give me more time to settle the mess that he's made."

Mr. Charles replied slowly, "If I were a different man, I might resent the fact that you're giving me orders. The only thing I will say is that I'm not the man you're looking for. This Dobbs person doesn't work for me."

"I know that you—"

"I told you, you came to the wrong man." Not waiting for Mason's reply, Mr. Charles stood up behind his massive desk, revealing a diminutive size that in no way lessened the threat he exuded as he called out, "This man has completed his business, Ham. It's time for him to leave."

Perspiring profusely, Mason said, "I haven't finished what I came to say. Nothing has been settled here."

The office door opened abruptly. The big man filled the opening before entering and seizing Mason's arm with a grip of steel. Protesting as he was dragged out through the doorway, Mason shouted, "You're making a mistake! Dobbs is the person who's at fault here, not me. He's the one who forced me to come here."

The office door slammed shut behind them, and Mason glanced up at the man who still gripped his arm. He did not speak as the hulking fellow led him to the door and thrust him out into the hallway with the warning, "Don't come back."

The door slammed in his face. Mumbling under his breath, Mason turned on his heel and started back down the hallway. He had wasted his time.

Mason's mind returned to his dear Aunt Letty. She had always trusted him. Although she was finished with James Ferguson, she didn't want to see him hurt—but she wanted even less to sever the association with Uncle Archibald's family that was her only link to social legitimacy. Mason needed to find out what Letty had learned so he could manufacture a believable excuse for his actions. He would plead with his dear aunt for her patient understanding of his lapse. He would claim business pressures. He would remind her that he had stood beside her even when her future was uncertain. He would tell her that her daughters and she were the only *family* he had left, and he valued them more than she knew.

Mason was suddenly elated. Yes, he had hit on just the right approach. Letty's true family had deserted her, and his claim to cherish her as *his* family was the key to her forgiveness.

Suddenly aware that he was on the street in a very rough area of town, Mason looked around him suspiciously. He could not understand a man like Mr. Charles. The fellow had the money to make any change in his lifestyle that he desired, but despite the power he possessed, he made only a poor attempt at the appearance of legitimacy. Despite the expensive trappings he surrounded himself with, the man still wallowed in the city's gutter.

Mason considered that thought. Perhaps the difference between Mr. Charles and him was that Mr.

Charles had been born in this area, and it was home to him. Whereas he had been born to better things, and he intended to keep them.

With that determination firm, Mason started walking.

Humphrey Dobbs strolled down the familiar street, his leisurely pace belying his inner trepidation. He scrutinized the run-down buildings, the littered thoroughfare, and the remnants of the previous night's revelry that still marked the gutters. Contrarily, he liked what he saw. The well-kept street where Mason Little's office was located had left him feeling cold. There was no sign of human habitation there; people traveled to and fro without leaving their mark. He liked a place bearing obvious signs of those that had passed through. He liked being deferred to in simple ways, and he enjoyed knowing that people admired his ruthlessness. He took pleasure in their respect, and he was addicted to the feeling of being above the law.

It also pleased him that his appearance had no effect on how he was treated. He knew what people said about him . . . that being short and thin, with narrow, pointed features and large ears, he put some in mind of the rodents that filled the streets. He had suffered taunts and beatings when he was younger that he would never forget . . . until he coldly killed his tormentors and found respect. The rest was easy. He became known as a fellow who got the job done, whatever it entailed, and he had risen to a spot just below the man who had done him one better. He was proud of the position he had achieved, knowing that in the end, when someone wanted something important taken care of, he was the man to approach.

But he didn't like being called into the office of Mr. Charles, the man who "had done him one better." Small in size, standing eye level with Dobbs, Mr. Charles's proportions did not match the power he wielded over rich and poor alike in the city. Dobbs was not a man to forget it. For that reason he paused, his sharp features twitching nervously before he pushed open the door of the office and entered.

Ham, Wally, and Jiggs, the only names the massive fellows were known by, hardly blinked when he entered. Not bothering to extend a greeting, he waited until a voice from the inner office said, "Come inside, Dobbs."

Dobbs approached the massive desk. He was aware that the carpet underneath his feet was probably worth more than his entire wardrobe and he resisted the inclination to see if he had tracked the grime of the streets in with him. He resisted because he knew Mr. Charles hated weakness, and Dobbs had no desire to display it.

Standing unexpectedly, Mr. Charles said, "I want an explanation."

"I don't know what you mean."

"Don't play dumb!" His voice suddenly booming, Mr. Charles walked around his desk to face him squarely. "Mason Little was here. I don't like complaints. I don't like visits from people who pretend to be something they aren't and look down on me for what I am. I don't like having to call you in here to demand an explanation for all the failures Little claimed you were responsible for."

His gaze narrowing, Mr. Charles said, "On second thought, I don't want any explanations. I just want you to fix it. Take care of the man's complaints. I know they're legitimate, because he wouldn't have dared to come here otherwise. Whatever his plans are, I expect you to do your part without a problem—because *my* reputation depends on it. And I tell you now, Dobbs, if *my* reputation suffers, *you* will suffer, too."

"Mr. Little misrepresented—"

"No excuses! Take care of it! I don't care how, but I do care when. Make it *soon*, because I don't want to hear about any of this again. I don't have to tell you what it'll mean if I do."

His color apoplectic, Mr. Charles walked back behind his desk, sat down, and resumed his work. Still standing there, Dobbs was not immediately aware that he had been dismissed. A few moments later, he turned and exited the office quietly . . . without speaking another word.

"What do you mean, she went on a trip?" Mason began to tremble as he looked at Letty's maid. "Where did she go? When did she go?"

"I'm not sure, sir. She left early this morning. She just told me that she would return when her business was done, but she didn't say how long that would take."

"What business would take her out of the city?"

"I don't know, sir."

Doing his best to maintain his patience, Mason

forced a smile and said, "You know how close Aunt Letty and I are, Millie. You know how she confides in me. We had a brief spat over a foolish matter. I didn't want it to come between us, so I came here to apologize, but I admit to surprise at learning that she left without telling me. You're sure you didn't overhear what direction she headed in?"

"Oh, I know her direction, all right. I just don't know exactly where she went."

"Her direction . . . north or south?"

"South, to Texas."

"Texas!" Mason's color darkened as he pressed with pretended innocence, "Why would she want to go to Texas?"

"I believe I heard Mr. Ferguson say she was born there."

"Mr. Ferguson?"

"He went with her."

Mason's momentary speechlessness allowed Millie to continue, "Mr. Ferguson is such a lovely man and such a comfort to Miss Letty. I know he'll take care of her every step of the way. Even if she insists that they're only friends now, I remember how happy she was when . . . well . . . when they were closer. I never did understand why she sent him packing." Leaning forward, Millie whispered confidentially, "Mr. Ferguson's still over the moon about her, you know, and I'm hoping she'll change her mind. She deserves somebody like him. She's worked hard, and she—"

"You say they left early this morning?"

Mason's rude interruption snapped Millie out of her burst of confidentiality and she replied simply, "Yes, sir."

"For Texas."

"Yes, sir."

"You don't know where in Texas?"

"No, sir."

Mason pressed impatiently, "You can't recall the name of the town, or you just don't know it?"

"Miss Letty just asked me to pack her bag. Mr. Ferguson was in charge of the tickets."

"He purchased them ahead of time?"

"I don't know."

"What do you know?"

Regretting that yet another outburst of temper had caused Millie's narrow lips to snap shut, Mason said with an attempt at congeniality, "You'll tell Aunt Letty that I was here to see her when she returns, of course?"

"Yes, sir."

Forcing a smile, Mason said, "I hope I haven't offended you with my questions. I am concerned about dear Aunt Letty, you know."

"Then you needn't worry. As I said, I'm sure Mr. Ferguson will take good care of her."

Her final comment more than he could bear, Mason turned away from the startled maid and strode back down the hallway without responding.

He knew what he had to do.

"I want to see Mr. Charles."

Furious that Letty was on her way to Texas, and even more furious to learn that James Ferguson had accompanied her, Mason had left Letty's apartment in a fit of temper. His anger soaring, he had brushed past fellow pedestrians roughly, uncaring of the need to apologize when his haste knocked a fellow back against the glass window of an impressive emporium. His mind had been racing: it was all Dobbs's fault! The collapse of his plans could be put right at his door, and he'd be damned if he'd let the fellow get away with it. He didn't care how much Mr. Charles denied the affiliation between them. He knew how things stood. Dobbs was Mr. Charles's right-hand man, and he was useless. He promised much but delivered nothing. Justine's reaction to her mother's offer was still uncertain, but her sisters had already signed papers signifying that they wanted no part of Letty's inheritance. If Justine didn't conform, Mr. Charles would have to see to it that she didn't come back. It was up to Mr. Charles to set things right this time.

His anger had been so encompassing that Mason had flagged down a carriage, hardly noticing when the driver reacted with surprise that the destination he gave was in an undesirable part of town. He knew only one thing. Mr. Charles needed to make things right because Dobbs hadn't.

Presently standing in Mr. Charles's outer office as the sun began its descent in the sky, Mason did not bother to wipe the perspiration from his brow or glance at the stains that marked the underarms of his jacket when he shouted at the beefy fellows barring entrance to the inner sanctum, "I told you, I want to see Mr. Charles."

"You ain't got an appointment." Ham's response was emotionless.

"I didn't have an appointment earlier today, but

Mr. Charles saw me anyway. Just tell him I'm here."

"Come back when you have an appointment."

"I don't have time for that! I have to talk to Mr. Charles. Because of Dobbs, my future hangs in the balance. Mr. Charles needs to fix it."

"Mr. Charles don't need to fix nothing. He told you, he don't know that Dobbs fella."

His anger jumping up another notch, Mason ordered, "Get out of my way."

"Go home."

"I want to see Mr. Charles now."

Ham's florid complexion grew even redder. "That ain't going to happen."

"Yes, it is. Get out of my way!"

In a flash of movement so quick that he did not have time for protest, Mason felt himself lifted up bodily and tossed out into the hallway with a force that dropped him against the floor with a crash. The office door slammed closed behind him as he lay momentarily disoriented, only aware that the thugs inside had not even blinked an eye when they tossed him out.

Suddenly aware of the embarrassment the situation could cause a man of his stature, Mason stood up, dusted himself off, and started toward the street door. A surreptitious glance around him revealed that no one had witnessed the humiliating episode, and he was resolved not to admit it had ever happened. Instead, he would find Dobbs and make sure that he fulfilled his part of the bargain they had struck—because if he suffered in any way as a result of the fiasco Dobbs had caused, he would take all of them down with him.

He'd be sure to tell Dobbs that, too.

"Your boss refuses to acknowledge you, so the responsibility for concluding this job is all yours."

Twilight shadows filled the alleyway beside the run-down club where Dobbs made his headquarters. Flushed with fury, Mason faced him in the narrow corridor, ignoring the open garbage cans overflowing with refuse that fed an army of flies. The smell permeating the area was pungent—almost overwhelming—but Mason was too angry to acknowledge it or the menace in Dobbs's expression. Nor had he given a thought to Dobbs's harsh demand that they discuss the matter in the alleyway where they would have more privacy. Mason was also too enraged to see that Dobbs was as angry as he.

"You went to Mr. Charles to complain about me, didn't you?" Dobbs accused. "You said enough to make him warn me to do my job so you wouldn't bother him anymore."

"He said that, did he?" Mason's short laugh was harsh. "So you have your orders directly from your boss. That should put you in your place."

"What place is that, *Mr. Little?*" Dobbs took an aggressive step toward him. "You pretend to be better than all of us in this part of town, but here you are in a back alley, begging me to help you."

"I'm not begging you! I paid you well for services that you didn't perform!"

"*Services* that you misrepresented to me and my men!"

"I misrepresented nothing! You're the one who promised what you did not deliver. The fact that Letty's two daughters refused to return to New York and turned down the inheritance she offered them was to your advantage, but your men weren't responsible for it. They're dead, both of them, which is also probably the fate of the fellow you sent after Letty's youngest daughter."

"You can believe that if you want, but I don't."

"It doesn't make any difference now. Because of you, James Ferguson regained Letty's confidence and took her with him to Texas, where she'll probably do her best to reconcile with her daughters. If it were not for your incompetence, that same James Ferguson would be lying dead in his grave right now—where he should be! Because of you, my beautiful, *simple* plan has gone awry, and it's up to you to fix it!"

"What?"

"You heard me . . . fix it, just like Mr. Charles told you to do."

"I'm curious." Too caught up in his anger to see the deadly curve of Dobbs's smile, Mason raised his chin as Dobbs asked, "How do you expect me to accomplish that?"

"I expect you to send another man to Texas to follow Ferguson and Letty, and to gun them down on the street if necessary. I want them dead . . . do you hear me? I want them dead!"

Dobbs responded sarcastically, "That sounds easy enough."

"I don't care if it's easy. Just do it. Everything else has fallen apart, but I will not lose the opportunity to inherit my dear Aunt Letty's fortune—the money that would have come to me from Uncle Archibald in the first place if she hadn't seduced him."

"She got no part of the money your uncle left behind."

"Neither did I! But she profited from her liaison with him. My uncle introduced her to society . . . made all the men that she flirted with believe she was worthy of association. Well, she isn't. Every dollar she *earned* was as a result of seducing a man three times her senior—a man who should have been looking to me in his old age, relying on me until he died, when he would have left the whole of his fortune to me in gratitude. She took that opportunity away from me, and I'm going to make her pay."

Mason corrected himself with a harsh laugh. "No, I misspoke. *You're* going to make her pay."

"I am, huh?"

"That's right, because if I lose because of you, then you and your precious Mr. Charles will lose, too. I'll bring you all you down, and I'll enjoy every minute of it!"

"You're scaring me."

The sarcasm in Dobbs's voice turned Mason's complexion purple. "Laugh if you like, but if you don't come up with a plan to reverse your failures by tomorrow, I'll make you the sorriest man alive."

When Dobbs did not reply, Mason rasped, "Tomorrow, do you hear me? I'm warning you now, and I won't say it again."

Allowing only a moment for the import of his statement to sink in, Mason strode out of the alleyway with a heavy step.

Dobbs remained unmoving behind him, transfixed by Mason's sheer audacity. To come to his part of town and threaten him . . . to actually believe that he would allow anyone to get away with talking to him that way, as if he were a stupid ingrate hired to wash the floor.

Dobbs unconsciously shook his head. He was more than that. He had worked long and hard to prove himself to Mr. Charles and to a community that respected him. He had come up from dirt, but he would not return there.

Dobbs smiled coldly. The papers would carry an obituary of the socially distinguished Mason Little when he was found dead on the street in a day or so, a victim of random robbery. The article would extol his virtues and praise his name, but only Dobbs would know the truth—that Mason Little had no virtue, that the robbery had not been random, and that Mason was dead because Dobbs had made it happen.

Dobbs started back toward the nightclub door. He'd arrange it immediately. Mr. Charles would be pleased, and confidence in him would be restored. Then, just for the fun of it, he'd take care of Letty Wolf, and maybe James Ferguson, who was the reason another of his men had been killed, and—

But . . . what was that sound?

Dobbs's steps came to a halt when a low growling caught his ear. He turned to see yellow eyes shining at him from the shadows. He stared, mesmerized as a form gradually took shape in the semidarkness.

It was a dog. No, it wasn't. Could it possibly be—?

The growl changed abruptly into a snarling attack

as a furred body knocked Dobbs to the ground and powerful jaws locked on his throat.

Dobbs fought . . . punching and struggling against the relentless animal, straining to free himself as the vicious jaws tightened, holding him fast. He felt himself gradually weakening. He could not speak. He could not breathe. He choked on the warm taste of his own gushing blood.

He felt himself going limp.

Darkness threatened—a darkness that abruptly consumed him.

"I don't think even liniment will help me this time, Ryder."

Doing her best to hide her discomfort, Justine turned toward Ryder as he lifted her down from her horse after a long day in the saddle. Despite her greatest effort, she could manage no more than a stumbling gait toward the forested glade where they had stopped for the night. Flopping down to sit on the nearest log, she said softly, "I'm sorry."

Ryder saw her desperation. No, he was the sorry one.

Crouching beside her, he realized that even the sheen of perspiration could not mar the perfection of her suntanned skin, but she was clearly in pain. The fact that she had made no effort to seek the nearby stream to wash away the dust of the trail spoke volumes.

"I've been thinking we ought to alter our plan slightly," he said. "According to Harry's directions, we should soon be reaching a small town that's also a railhead. We could stable the horses there and wait for the next stage to Winsome."

"How often do the stagecoaches travel to Winsome?"

"I don't rightly know. Probably a few times a week."

"That might hold us up for days, Ryder!"

"I don't think so." He added as he took her hands in his, "We've already saved ourselves time by traveling on horseback this far. A day or so more won't make much difference, and you need the rest."

"But you don't."

"I'm accustomed to spending all day on horseback."

"But you're not accustomed to shepherding a tenderfoot who's proving to be more trouble than she's worth." When Ryder started to protest, Justine shook her head. "Let's face it, I'm more of a tenderfoot than I was prepared to admit—but, dammit, I'm not going to remain a tenderfoot! As soon as all this is settled with Meredith and Johanna, I'm going to make sure that I'm as accustomed to the trail as you are. I won't drag you down then, not even for a minute. I'll pull my weight just like I should, and you won't have to be ashamed of me anymore."

"Is that what you think? That I'm ashamed of you?" Ryder cupped her cheek. He said softly, "I love you, Justine. I figure I'm the luckiest man in the world to hear you say you love me, too. It doesn't make any difference to me whether you can ride like a trail hand or cook food that makes everybody's mouth water. Those things will come with time, and you're the fastest learner I know."

Justine's perfect, sun-kissed features pulled into a frown as she said, "But right now I'm holding you back."

"Everybody's a beginner at something, Justine. We made good progress today, but you can't go on in this condition."

"Maybe not now," She admitted, "but I'll be better tomorrow."

Ryder's smile was halfhearted as he whispered, "Darlin', liniment can only do so much."

The fleeting spark in her eyes faded with her sigh. She attempted to get up and fell back. Finally standing with Ryder's help, she repeated his admonition of the previous day. "I'll feel better once I wash off the dust of the trail."

Watching as Justine limped painfully toward the stream, Ryder forced himself to remain still. He knew her. She was independent to a fault. She wouldn't appreciate having him follow behind her as if she were an invalid.

But, dammit, the long ride had effectively crippled her. It was up to him to see that they took a sensible alternative.

Wincing when he heard her stumble, holding himself back when she seated herself beside the stream with a loud *whoosh*, Ryder started to gather twigs for a campfire. After she had cleaned up, he would make sure that she had a good meal and a good rest, and then—

Ryder winced again at Justine's soft groan.

Tomorrow they'd head for Barstow, Texas.

The steady click-clacking of the tracks was a lulling sound that somehow had the reverse effect on Letty as she looked out the window of her private car. The sun had set, night had fallen, and she sat alone on the way toward her destiny. She had told herself that James's abrupt departure from her room after they boarded the train had been due to his need to settle himself in his lodgings; but when his absence became extended, she had begun to think differently. Uncertainties had assaulted her mind: James was rethinking his part in their journey . . . he regretted accompanying her . . . he wanted to distance himself from her so that she would not rely on him too heavily.

Letty prepared herself for bed by dressing in a nightgown that displayed slender proportions unaffected by age, by washing her face until it glowed, and by loosening the upward sweep of her hair so she might brush it free of tangles. Strangely, she had avoided thinking of her daughters during the day, of the adversities they might have faced, of the men they had chosen to be with, and of her fears for Justine.

A day at a time. She had accepted that advice from James as the only way to handle a situation she could not control . . . but had James regretted giving it?

Lying back on the spotless bed that the steward had arranged for her, Letty realized suddenly that except for the rattling of the rails, the noisy swaying of the car, and the clattering of the train's wheels against the metal tracks, the room was silent. The howling that had given her no rest appeared to have ceased. She was startled that she hadn't realized it before, but what did the silence mean? Had she made the right choice by deciding to follow James's advice, or was this merely a temporary cessation?

The answer to her question awoke her from a restless sleep hours later. Letty sat upright as a familiar vision began taking shape before her. She smiled, tears filling her eyes at the gradual appearance of the familiar image. Her smile broadened as the figure became clearer, as she saw again the setting sun behind the wizened, bare-chested man she called Grandfather; the long, unbound strands of hair that brushed his narrow shoulders; the direct gaze that held hers as he spoke in a tongue that was foreign, yet familiar:

Take care.

Remember all and dismiss nothing.

Seek and you will find.

Have no regrets for what is past.

Your path is true.

She extended her hand toward the image, but he turned away to walk back toward the setting sun. She gasped when a wolf appeared suddenly, its jaws dripping with a substance that she did not immediately recognize. She watched as the animal looked at her with keen deliberation, and then followed the old man into the sunset.

The vision was rapidly disappearing when she called out, "Grandfather, wait, please!" Yet she knew even as she said his name that her entreaty was useless.

It was long moments before she realized that the substance dripping from the wolf's jaws had been red . . . like blood. Shuddering, she sobbed softly. What did it mean? Did the blood belong to her daughters? Were they dead or injured in some way? Was she too late?

A sound at the doorway raised her tear-streaked face. James stood there in his shirtsleeves, his clothing wrinkled, his hair disheveled, his expression worried. He walked toward her, pushing the door closed behind him as he said, "I thought I heard you crying. What's wrong, Letty?"

"I'm fine." Letty brushed away her tears and attempted to regain control, but a moment later she collapsed against him and said, "No, I'm not fine. I saw Grandfather again, James . . . and I saw the wolf."

"The wolf whose howls haunt you?"

"I don't know. All I know is that its jaws were dripping with something that looked like blood." Letty rasped, "I don't know whose blood it was, James . . . my daughers' or a warning that it might eventually be mine . . . or even worse, that it might be yours!"

Allowing enough distance between them so he could look directly into her eyes, James said, "What did Grandfather say?"

"He told me to take care. He said to remember everything and dismiss nothing. He told me to seek and I would find, and to have no regrets about what is past. He said my path is true."

"Those are all positive encouragements, Letty."

"But the wolf . . . the blood . . ."

"Are you sure it was blood?"

"I remember the look in the creature's eyes. It couldn't be anything else."

"The wolf walked with Grandfather?"

Letty nodded.

"Grandfather wouldn't have allowed that if the wolf had acted against your best interests."

"But I need to be sure."

"I don't think you can be sure, Letty."

Have no regrets.

Seek and you will find.

Your path is true.

Grandfather's words rumbled through Letty's mind as she looked up at James. Her path was true and she should have no regrets. Did that include James and the fact that she wanted him to stay with her . . . to comfort her . . . to love her? Did that mean she could lie in his arms without fear for his safety? Did that mean if she sought what had eluded her all her life, she would find it? Or was she merely deluding herself by telling herself what she wanted to believe?

Letty allowed her gaze to study James's concerned expression as he held her close. He loved her. He had risked his life for her in so many ways despite all warnings. He would not desert her now. He would stay with her no matter how difficult it might be to deny the passion of the past.

With sudden candor, Letty admitted to herself that she needed the passion that had raged between them, as much as she needed air to breathe—but would it be fair to James?

Your path is true.

Was that what Grandfather was trying to tell her?

Suddenly realizing she could not be sure, Letty knew only that the need between James and herself was mutual and real.

Taking a breath, Letty whispered, "I don't want you to leave, James."

She saw the frown that met her words. She saw him swallow as he said, "All right. I'll stay here if you feel safer that way."

"I want you to stay with me . . . to be with me, James. I want to feel your arms around me the way it was before."

Letty saw his chest heave as James responded, "You're sure about what you're saying—that it isn't just your insecurity talking? I don't want you to have regrets tomorrow."

"I'm sure." Letty pressed her mouth to James's lips. Her kiss deepened. She felt his arms tighten around her, clutching her almost painfully close.

Drawing back unexpectedly, James was breathless when he said, "You know I love you, Letty. You know I would never refuse to do anything you asked of me, but I'm telling you now that once I'm close to you again, it'll be difficult to let you go."

"One day at a time, James."

A moment of reluctance flashed across James's expression at her reply. Then drawing her close again, he whispered, "All right, Letty. One day at a time."

And the loving began.

Chapter Nine

*N*o, this couldn't be true!

Mason Little stared at the newspaper his clerk had placed in front of him. He had arrived at his office unusually early that morning, but his clerks had already been at their desks working. They had appeared surprised to see him and had begun whispering surreptitiously, but he hadn't stopped to inquire why. He had merely walked past them and slammed his office door behind him.

He was certain that Dobbs would contact him sometime that day and let him know how he intended to set his failures right. He knew Dobbs would fix things because Mr. Charles had told him to. Yet Mason needed to complete the paperwork so Letty could be institutionalized when the time was right.

It galled him that all his work to have her committed might not actually be needed if Dobbs decided to make sure neither Letty nor Ferguson came back from Texas alive. Yet he dared *not* be ready if Dobbs decided to work things out another way.

With those thoughts in mind, Mason had gone straight to his work and had been unprepared for the knock on the door and Sutter's entrance with a newspaper in his hand. Nor had he been prepared when Sutter placed the newspaper in front of him and said, "We thought you might like to see this, Mr. Little."

A picture of Humphrey Dobbs stared back at him. The picture was blurred and unclear, but Dobbs was immediately recognizable.

The caption stated that Humphrey Dobbs had been found dead.

Mason looked up at his clerk with a narrowed gaze. He noted that the bespectacled fellow took a step back at his reaction.

"We all remembered that was the fellow who came into this office to see you once," Sutter explained.

Mason responded slowly, "I don't recall."

"You sent him away, telling him that you didn't handle cases for individuals like him, but none of us forgot him. Nobody could forget somebody who looked like that."

When Mason did not immediately reply, Sutter took another backward step and said, "All the major newspapers have picked up the story because it's a mystery."

"A mystery?"

"The newspaper says that Dobbs went out into the alleyway behind a club in an undesirable part of town. When he didn't come back in, the bartender went to check on him and found Dobbs's body." Sutter paused before adding, "His throat was ripped out."

"What?"

"Some kind of animal did it—a big animal. There's a massive search in the area to find the animal before it kills somebody else."

"Is that so?"

His clerk nodded, and Mason managed, "Leave the newspaper here, Sutter. I'll read the article if I get a chance." He added by way of dismissal, "And make sure you close the door behind you."

Waiting only until his office door had snapped closed, Mason grabbed the newspaper with a mumbled curse. He cursed again as he read the article from beginning to end. There was no doubt that the victim was Humphrey Dobbs. The fellow had obviously met up with something immediately following Mason's departure the previous day.

Mason frowned at the realization that the animal had probably been there all the time while Dobbs and he had argued and exchanged threats. It occurred to him with a start that if he hadn't been the first to leave, the face now staring back from the newspaper might have been his own. He dismissed the possibility of being identified as the reason for Dobbs's venture into the alleyway. Everyone in that area of town was deaf, dumb, and blind where the law was concerned, and those afflictions would serve him well. The irrefutable result of the affair was, however, that Dobbs was dead, and the answer to Mason's problems had died with him.

Mason sat back in his chair, his expression tightening with irritation. His plan had been so simple, but everything had gone wrong. Letty was estranged from him and had gone to find her daughters with a man who had proved to be Mason's worst enemy. He needed to turn the situation around. He was in dire need of the inheritance his Aunt Letty had bequeathed him in her will. His creditors would soon begin harassing him, and it would become public knowledge that he was bankrupt. All those rich, pretentious individuals who had hired him because of his relationship to his wealthy, socially prominent uncle, and who had trusted the handling of their trusts to him without a second thought, would begin checking. They would then discover that he had systematically drawn funds from them for his personal use.

The gambling debts owed to Mr. Charles were also a problem. They must be paid.

Beads of nervous perspiration appeared on his forehead as Mason looked down again at the newspaper in front of him. Because Dobbs had been at the wrong place at the wrong time, he was dead, and a widespread police investigation had resulted. He hadn't even been able to do that right! Mr. Charles had made it plain that he wanted nothing to do with the problems Dobbs had caused, so Mason was now left with a situation that appeared unsolvable.

After a moment's pause, he sat slowly forward. He had told Dobbs that he wanted him to fix things, even if Dobbs had to send someone down to Texas to make sure that neither Letty nor Ferguson returned.

Mason stood up abruptly, folded the newspaper

so his snooping clerks would not become aware of his interest, and slipped on his jacket. He snatched up his hat as he opened his office door and said to the clerks, "I'm going out. If anyone calls, I'll be back sometime this afternoon."

Mason closed the outer door quietly behind him and started toward the building entrance. A visit to the train station, a little detective work on his own, and he would discover exactly where his dear Aunt Letty and James had gone. Certainly the number of couples heading for Texas, especially a couple as attractive as they, would be few in number. He'd then find out when the next train was scheduled to leave, would go back to the office to make a plausible excuse for a few days' absence, and follow them. He wouldn't waste words when he saw them. He'd find the quickest way to take care of them and then return home.

He was absolutely sure of three things. He wouldn't make the same mistakes that had been made before, he wouldn't hesitate to do what he had to do, and . . . he would come home a wealthy man.

James helped Letty down the railcar steps, took her arm, and looked around him. The Texas train depot where the first leg of their journey had delivered them was shabby in every detail.

James realized that he should probably be grateful that at least part of their rail journey to Winsome had been completed, but he found he was not. He knew he would never forget the nights that Letty and he had passed together in the elaborate railcar. He remembered looking down at her after she asked him to stay. He knew it wasn't only her beauty that continued to attract him from the first moment he saw her. It was her will, the determination to see things through, the total person that she was—a woman who achieved her goals without sparing herself effort of any kind; a woman who, despite it all, had no realization how truly wonderful she was.

A warm spark of remembrance caused a fleeting smile to curve his lips as he remembered the hours they had spent in each other's arms. The rocking of the railcar had mimicked his movements as he joined his body with Letty's. Deep inside her, he had paused briefly to look into her eyes, hardly believing the reality of the moment. The warmth of her still filled him, the taste of her was still on his lips, and his need . . . his love for her was a living, breathing part of him that had been resurrected during those recent hours.

Letty's response to him had been spontaneous. Her mouth had welcomed his; her slender body had received his with joy. She had blossomed under his touch, returning every kiss and caress until he was wild with the rapture of it. When all was still at last, she had been content to lie in his arms. Yet Letty had never said she loved him.

That thought was not far from James's mind when he drew Letty's arm closer and looked at the Texas passenger cars that would serve as their next connection. He had made her a promise that he would remain beside her whatever she wanted to do. He intended to keep that promise.

They had not walked more than a few feet toward the terminal building when James noted that Letty was turning heads as they passed—and grizzly, uncivilized-looking male heads, at that. James stopped, his eyes narrowing and his fists balling when they were approached by a burly, bearded fellow wearing spotted trousers and a worn shirt. The fellow stopped beside them, doffed his hat unexpectedly, and said with a heavy Western twang, "Ma'am, I feel a need to tell you that it's a pleasure to set eyes on you in this place where there ain't much else to raise a man's spirits. You're a flower among thorns, and just looking at you has made my day."

Letty turned toward the man. Instead of the chilly response James expected to hear from a sophisticated woman accustomed to formal accolades and persistent homage from some of New York society's most prominent men, she paused to search the fellow's sincere expression before responding, "Thank you. In so many ways, you've made my day, too."

As if that were not enough, the fellow extended his large, callused hand toward James and said with equal sincerity, "I need to shake your hand, partner, because you're a damned lucky man."

The fellow's grip was crushing and his gaze was direct. James returned both.

He was frowning when he and Letty walked on. Looking up at him, she replied to his unspoken question, "I know it sounds strange, but I was uncertain of my welcome when I stepped down here. This is a small Western town, but it's been so many years. That man's simple sincerity made me realize that in many ways, I'm indeed a different woman from the one who left here years ago. That woman was downtrodden and unsure of herself . . . beaten by the world. Despite her physical beauty, she didn't believe in herself or her ability to care for her two daughters. That was the way everyone perceived her. No one would have noticed *her* return. The person I am today is stronger. I have achieved success against all odds. Despite the many mistakes I made along the way, I realize now that I should be proud of the person I've made of myself and what I've accomplished." Pausing, Letty said more softly, "I wouldn't have been capable of coming to that realization alone, James. Because you were beside me . . . loving me . . . I had the courage to take that first step. I have much to make up for, but . . . somehow . . . the admiration I read in that fellow's eyes just now was a bountiful welcome home."

James replied honestly, "I suppose what surprised me most—after my initial reservations about his appearance and his direct approach—is that he saw right through to the simple truth that I'm a lucky man."

Letty's smile faded. "I'm not so sure about that."

"I am."

Their conversation came to an end when they reached the station house. Entering, he purchased their tickets. James glanced around them as they entered the railcar, noticing that the seats were covered with a fine layer of soot and grime. As he sat beside her, he also noticed that Letty was attracting attention from the bearded, tobacco-chewing, buckskin-clad men surrounding them. Despite himself, he stared intently when one of the fellows stood up and approached them. When the man was about to speak, James interjected, "I know what you're going to say. I'm a lucky man."

The fellow's spontaneous guffaw was loud and accompanied by a hearty slap on the back, but James did not join him. He knew that whatever happened from that point on, truer words were never spoken.

Mason stepped down from the carriage, paid the driver, and glanced both ways as he prepared to cross the street in front of the train station. Strangely enough, he was feeling good. He had more confidence in his own handling of the situation than he would have had in Dobbs's plan to correct the debacle he had caused. He supposed the old adage was true after all: If a man wanted something done right, he had to do it himself.

Admittedly, he was starting out with information that made things easier. He knew what Letty and James looked like, and he knew where they were going. Texas was a big place, but he did not expect to have any problem finding a ticket clerk who would remember selling them tickets or finding someone who had seen Letty and James boarding a car the previous day. No one who had ever seen his dear Aunt Letty had ever forgotten her. She wouldn't be difficult to follow.

Beauty . . . Mason's expression turned sour. Letty had used her beauty as a trap to snare his elderly uncle, but she wouldn't be able to work her wiles on him. He knew her for what she was.

Frowning at the traffic that crowded the street, Mason hesitated. It appeared that morning was the wrong time to come to the station; the area was a confusion of arriving and departing passengers. Goodbye tears were liberally mixed with random shouts of welcome; stacks of baggage were being unloaded and collected by porters who seemed to be everywhere at once; and carriages blocked the street as passengers unloaded their bags. Grateful that he had left his carriage before reaching the center of the disorder, Mason began weaving his way across the chaotic street. He heard a policeman's whistle and saw the aggravated officer signal a carriage to move out of the way of the flow of traffic. Reacting to the shrill whistle, the carriage horse reared without warning, causing the driver to scramble to regain control as pedestrians fell back cautiously.

The driver had almost regained control when a strange howl set the horse to rearing again. Caught in the middle of the street as other carriage horses snorted wildly, neighing and straining at their reins, Mason darted breathlessly between carriages to avoid being trampled. Relieved that the drivers appeared to have regained control, he made another attempt to cross, but the eerie howl sounded again, this time louder and closer. Turning, Mason saw the carriage behind him lurch out into the street. The horse's eyes bulged in panic as the driver drew back on the reins. Mason saw the whites of the animal's eyes as the carriage bore down on him. He saw the fear reflected there the moment before the animal knocked him down onto the pavement.

In a moment of excruciating pain, the carriage rolled over him.

Strangely numb in the aftermath, Mason opened his eyes. The faces of the carriage driver and the policeman were looking down at him. Pedestrians gaped, and he heard the driver protest that it wasn't his fault, that something the horse heard had scared it.

Something?

Mason wanted to cry out at their stupidity. The animal that had killed Dobbs in a dark alleyway the previous day was obviously now hunting again. They were fools . . . imbeciles!

Yet Mason was unable to speak. A blanket of quiet descended over him. A man knelt at his side and began working on him feverishly. Mason's breathing was short and labored. The bitter taste of blood filled his mouth. Sights and sounds grew dimmer—until he heard it again. The eerie howl was loud and clear, sending nearby carriage horses into another panic.

As his sight faded, Mason wondered, had he really heard the call of a wolf, or—?

The question went unanswered; darkness devoured him.

Ryder controlled his mount with an ease that Justine could only envy as she rode beside him. The sun had begun its descent toward the horizon when the town of Barstow came into view. He noted that Justine turned her head in order to avoid his concerned expression. He knew what that meant. She was obviously feeling stiffer with every moment spent on the trail. It was only stubborn determination that kept her from complaining.

Ryder stared at her a moment longer. She continued to avoid his gaze, and his heart did a flip-flop in his chest. Damn, he loved her! He loved the look of her, the innate self-confidence that allowed her to believe that with honest effort, she could accomplish anything she set out to do. He supposed the fact that her body temporarily refused to cooperate was a shock to her, but he loved her even more for refusing to accept defeat.

The rest was up to him. He understood this hard Western world where some things took more time than others. He would not remain silent while Justine suffered crippling discomfort, not when he knew that a comfortable night's sleep and a change of travel plans could do more than any pep talk he could offer her.

His hope was that she would acknowledge her temporary debility by agreeing to the change of plans. To that end, he said, "That's Barstow over there. We should be able to find a hotel room where we can rest."

"I told you, I'm fine now. I'm stiff, but I can make it."

Ryder didn't have the heart to counter with the argument that if they didn't find comfortable accommodations now, they'd lose time when they finally arrived in Winsome because she'd be in even worse condition. Instead he said, "I know, but it's better this way."

Still avoiding his gaze, Justine trailed behind when they reached town. He waited until she was again riding beside him on the rutted main street, then said with deceiving casualness, "After I drop you off at the hotel, I'll find a stable where I can leave the horses. Then I'll go to the stagecoach office and find out when the next stage leaves for Winsome."

"I'll go with you."

"No, you can get us settled at the hotel while I—"

"I know what you're trying to do, Ryder." Justine's eyes were green points of light that pinned him when she said, "You want me to rest while you take care of all the details."

Slowing his mount's gait when he saw a hotel in the distance, Ryder said unexpectedly, "You're right, Justine. I do want you to rest. I figure that makes more sense than both of us taking care of details that I'm accustomed to handling by myself."

"But this is my problem! I'm the reason we're going to Winsome. I should be doing the work."

"You forget." His gaze linking with hers, Ryder replied, "You don't have any problems that I don't share through my own choice. I want you to get things settled in your life so our future can begin."

Justine blinked. She took a breath and said, "All right, but I'll be better in the morning. You'll see. I only hope the stagecoach schedule works out so we can get on our way without more wasted time. I need to find Meredith soon. There are so many questions I hope to clear up by talking to her."

They entered the hotel room minutes later and Ryder watched as Justine looked tentatively around them. The furnishings were spare and battered. He did not speak as she assessed the comforter on the double bed, the window shades, the surface of every piece of furniture. Her attention came to rest on the washstand with a fresh towel hanging beside it. Ryder released a relieved breath when she said, "All right. I'll wait here." He did not miss the grimace of pain she attempted to hide when she sat on the edge of the bed and said, "You're right. I should clean up a bit and take care of some necessities while you're gone."

"Ryder," Justine asked hesitantly. "You're going to stable the horses, and then you're going to find out when the next stage leaves for Winsome?"

He looked back at her, frowning. "That's right. Why, do you need something?"

"Oh, I just wondered . . ." Her face gradually reddened.

"You wondered what?"

She shrugged. "I just wondered if you were going to stop at the pharmacy. I thought you might . . . maybe . . . you might want to buy more liniment, just in case."

Ryder went perfectly still.

Just in case?

Oh, hell!

Walking back to the bed, he pulled Justine to her feet and kissed her long and deep. Their breathing was short when Ryder forced himself to draw back. He looked down into her beautiful face and promised, "I'll do that. I'll go to the pharmacy, and I'll be back as soon as I can."

Leaving before Justine could reply, Ryder would not allow himself to look back again when he pulled the door closed behind him.

His chores completed, Ryder returned to the hotel room to find Justine standing at the washstand in fresh underclothes, her glorious hair brushed out and hanging on her shoulders, and her skin pink, damp, and clean. Taking a breath, he pushed the door closed behind him and reported softly, "The horses are stabled, the stage leaves for Winsome at noon tomorrow, and I stopped off at the pharmacy to get a powder to lessen your pain . . . and another bottle of liniment."

"Oh . . . good."

Limping toward him, Justine threw her arms around his neck and kissed him full on the lips. When she drew back, she said softly, "Have I told you recently how much I appreciate everything you're doing for me, Ryder?"

"Yes . . . no . . ." Ryder went still. "Is that what this is? Gratitude?"

"It's a little more than that."

Justine began unbuttoning Ryder's shirt. She looked down to see that the bulge beneath his belt indicated he appreciated her efforts. She was surprised when he said gruffly, "I haven't had a chance to wash off the trail dust yet."

"Later."

Ryder's gaze tightened. "Later?"

"Yes."

"As long as I brought the liniment?"

Justine looked up at him and whispered, "I may be tired and sore, but I don't really need the liniment, Ryder. The truth is, I just want you."

Ryder crushed her close. He then proceeded to prove without doubt that he wanted her, too.

After a long day of traveling, Letty and James arrived at their destination as twilight began darkening into night. James had endured the countless annoying and exhausting rail stops along the way with one thought in mind, that Letty was growing more tired with each hour that passed. As he finally escorted her down Barstow's primitive main street, it amazed him that she still managed to smile despite her obviously slower pace. Nagging at him was the realization that he had kept her awake the major portion of the previous night with his loving attentions. This afternoon, neither of them had dozed, although the ride had been tedious and hot.

Instead, with all the barriers inhibiting their former conversations removed, Letty had talked confidentially, straight from the heart. James had maintained his silence while she spoke in detail about former marriages that had ended badly—all forecasted by the howling of a wolf—and about the memories of past difficulties that the return to Texas stimulated. His throat had thickened when she stopped speaking and rested her head against his shoulder as emotion briefly overwhelmed her. It was then that he had curved his arm around her. No matter how the situation turned out, he was a luckier man than even he had realized.

James gripped Letty's arm tighter, remembering their departure from the train. Admittedly, he'd lost patience when they'd stood up to leave and the gruff male passengers who had stared at Letty for the duration of the trip blocked their way, taking turns shaking his hand and paying their respects to the "most beautiful woman they had ever seen." He supposed it annoyed him even more that Letty remained gracious throughout, with a smile that was sincere.

Ushering Letty into the stagecoach office minutes

later, James asked the bespectacled clerk, "When is the next stage scheduled to leave for Winsome?"

"It leaves at noon tomorrow," the man replied, staring at Letty a moment too long.

James turned toward Letty for her nod of approval and then took out his billfold.

"You can pay me tomorrow. I'll be here." Looking at Letty again, the fellow said, "If that's all right with you, ma'am."

"It's all right with me, of course."

At Letty's response, the fellow swallowed visibly and said, "If you don't mind my saying, ma'am, you're the most—"

"I know, she's the most beautiful woman you've ever seen." James's tone was impatient, reddening the fellow's complexion as he replied, "You're a lucky man, sir."

James glared at him.

James was escorting Letty toward what was apparently the only hotel Barstow had to offer when she tugged on his arm and said, "Are you angry, James?"

"No." He looked down into Letty's pale face, and his frown softened. "No, I'm not angry. I guess I'm just annoyed."

"Don't be annoyed, either. You don't understand, James. Most of the men we saw today have led hard lives. Their pleasures are few, and not many of their experiences have been positive ones. For some of them, the last woman who treated them with courtesy and respect was their mother; and, unfortunately, not too many of the women they've met deserved much courtesy or respect, either. People on the wild frontier have no time for incidentals, James. Their lives are spent coping with survival in a country that is too beautiful for most of them to leave behind. So their pleasures are fleeting. When they see something that pleases them, they say so; and when they express their appreciation, it's mostly sincere."

"Are you saying that the inhabitants of New York City are too civilized to be truthful?"

"No, I'm saying that a man speaks his feelings more openly out here, whether it's to express appreciation or . . ." She hesitated. "Or prejudice."

"You can be sure you'll never be exposed to prejudice when I'm beside you, Letty."

"I know . . . because you wouldn't let it be any other way. Yet the woman that I am now is confident enough to handle situations here that she couldn't handle before."

James was eager to get settled as they approached the hotel, but his enthusiasm dimmed when they entered. The lobby was primitive in every detail, from its few ancient, abused chairs to the worn stairs that led to the second floor.

As if reading his mind, Letty whispered, "This is fine, James, truly it is."

He was equally disturbed when they reached their room.

Letty said soberly, "The furnishings are spartan, but the room is clean. I've suffered far worse than this." She added with a sigh as she removed her hat, "If you don't mind, I'm going to lie down for a while. I'm not hungry, but you probably are. I'm sure the restaurant that we passed on the street is open."

Letty was asleep the moment her head hit the pillow.

James sat beside her, but when his stomach began growling he realized he was indeed hungry. He'd find that restaurant while Letty napped, and make sure he was present when she awakened.

Letty woke up when he returned to the room later, just long enough to change into nightclothes and to nibble at the food he had brought for her before falling again into a deep sleep—this time curled up against James in the bed they shared.

In the silence of the room, James brushed his lips against Letty's smooth cheek. It had not missed his notice that she was totally comfortable with him. It made no difference to her that he was unfamiliar with the surroundings. She trusted him, and he was glad. Still uncertain what that signified for the future, he slipped his arms around her and drew her closer.

He wondered as sleep closed in on him what the next day would bring.

Ryder stirred. He opened his eyes into narrow slits, enough to see that the morning sun was shining against the window shade in a way that forecasted another hot day. But he didn't care. He moved subtly and drew Justine closer. Her naked back was turned against him, and he reveled in the feeling of her rounded buttocks lying tight against him, in the female scent of her, and in the womanly softness that he had explored with loving diligence the previous evening. He silently marveled that although she was stiff and uncomfortable in the saddle, she had been incredibly limber and willing in his arms.

Ryder opened his eyes further to study her sleeping face. He never ceased to marvel at the sight of her: the luxury of her dark hair, so splendidly streaked with color as it lay against the pillow; her perfect, delicate profile; the slight parting of her soft lips—lips that he had nibbled with loving hunger during the night past. She had become as important a part of him as the heart she had stolen to keep as her own. He knew that she was haunted by things he did not understand, but he had seen too much to question her claims. Instead, he drew her closer, refusing to envision a time when he would not hold her in his arms.

Justine's eyelids fluttered. Her eyes opened—great green eyes that were suddenly questioning when she asked, "Is something wrong?" Not waiting for his response, she gasped abruptly, "Did we miss the stage to Winsome?"

"It's morning. The sun is barely up. The stage doesn't leave until noon."

Sighing with relief, she turned toward him. Her ample, naked breasts brushed his chest as she said, "I'm glad we have time, because I'm hungry, Ryder."

"There's only one restaurant in town—the best restaurant in Texas, to hear the owner tell it."

"Yes, food . . . I'm hungry for breakfast." Justine inched closer. She rubbed her body against the part of him that allowed no denial as she whispered, "And if I'm not mistaken, you're hungry, too."

Ryder's expression sobered as he looked into her eyes and said honestly, "I expect you're not as hungry as I am right now."

Justine's breathing grew more labored. Her lips touched his as she replied, "I'm not so sure about that."

"I am."

Sliding himself down her body as he pressed her onto her back, Ryder circled the warm triangle between her thighs with his lips, and she gasped. He slid his tongue into the moist slit awaiting him, and she mumbled incoherently. He drew from her, savoring the taste of her as he pressed his kiss deeper. He reveled in her intimate groans, extending the pleasure until she cried out in shuddering need. Still he persisted, loving every sound, every expression, and every quiver until her delicate body quaked, bursting forth with an uncontrolled tribute to his lovemaking.

Slipping himself back up the bed when her quaking stilled at last, he whispered against her lips, "I love you, Justine. I'll never get enough of you."

He slid himself deep within her then, gasping at the moistness that awaited him. Proving the truth of his words, he brought them to swift climax and held her breathlessly tight as they shuddered to ecstatic mutual release.

He asked hoarsely as her heavily lashed eyelids lifted, "Are you still hungry?"

Justine replied with startling honesty, "I've discovered to my joy and dismay that I'm always hungry for you, Ryder."

"That's a good thing."

"I'm not so sure."

"I'm sure . . . more sure than you'll ever know."

Ryder then slid himself back inside her, and the dance of love began again.

Awakening abruptly sometime later, Ryder glanced at the window shade and mumbled softly. Lying beside him, Justine asked groggily, "Is something wrong?"

"We have to get up."

"What?"

"We have to get up and get dressed, Justine, or we're going to miss the stage."

"What!" Bolting upright without realizing that the coverlet had fallen to her waist, exposing her breasts, she exclaimed, "What time is it?"

He glanced again at the window shade and responded, "It's nearing noon."

Standing abruptly, Ryder reached for his clothes. His actions came to an abrupt halt when Justine did the same, exposing her womanly nakedness fully to his gaze. Swallowing tightly, aware that she had not intended to excite him, he forced himself to continue dressing. Justine was still struggling with her hair when he said, "I'll buy the tickets now, and make sure the driver knows we're riding with him. We may even have time to eat."

Her hands stilling in their attempts to confine her heavy dark hair into a tight bun, Justine looked up at him. She said with a brief smile, "I guess we should eat breakfast."

"Like I said, the restaurant here is touted as the best in Texas."

Ryder reached for the door. Yet he almost failed to pull it open when she mumbled with her back to him, "I was afraid that was what you meant."

Letty was as composed as she thought she would ever be as she walked beside James toward the stage to Winsome. She took a stabilizing breath of warm Texas air, glanced at the small town of Barstow, and straightened her shoulders. She looked at James as he walked beside her and smiled. They had risen early, visited the town's only restaurant, and ordered a big breakfast. She had picked at hers without appetite while James consumed every scrap. She had almost laughed when he whispered with a half smile, "I think all the bragging they do about this place is true, after all."

She had been unable to take her eyes off James at that moment. It was strange that she had never fully acknowledged how truly handsome he was. His thick brown hair was peppered with more strands of gray than when she'd first met him, and there were a few more creases around his eyes, but his shoulders were broad and erect, his chest deep, and his waist narrow. He was all man . . . every inch of him from the top of his expertly cut hair to the tips of his presently dusty, expensive shoes. He was successful and wealthy, but luxury had not spoiled him. Nor had it negated his manliness and determination, his strength of character.

Letty took a breath and blinked back unexpected tears. And he loved her. There was no doubt of that—nor any doubt that she loved him in return. The nights they had spent together had been filled with emotion that only he was able to arouse inside her—emotion that had left her breathless with a mixture of happiness and fear. She had refused to say the words that she knew he longed to hear. She had clutched that last reservation in her mind, telling herself that as long as she did not declare her love, James was safe. At his request, she had dismissed the Pinkertons she had hired to protect him. Yet she had done so with silent reservations, knowing that he was now on his own against the curse that followed her.

"Letty . . ."

She took a breath and replied, "I'm fine, James . . . just a little anxious."

James gripped her arm more tightly, and Letty accepted the strength he lent her. She needed it now when she was unsure—

Her steps came to an abrupt halt when she looked at the stagecoach awaiting them. She swallowed, incredulous as the two figures standing beside it turned toward her.

It couldn't be!

She did not move.

She did not speak.

She did not react.

Until she heard the words, "Hello, Mother."

Mother . . . ?

Ryder looked at Justine, then at the woman who had halted a short distance away. He felt Justine tremble as she waited for a response. The woman was beautiful, surely too young to be Justine's mother.

Ryder suddenly understood the hotel clerk's reaction when he'd seen Justine that morning. He remembered that a different man had been at the desk when they'd registered and that the clerk was seeing Justine for the first time. Staring wordlessly at her as they passed, the clerk had muttered with a half smile that he needed to mark that date because it was the first time two such beauties were in the hotel at the same time.

Ryder recollected that he had almost been amused at the clerk's stupefied expression.

Almost.

Ryder looked closer. Justine had told him her mother was an outstanding beauty. She had also insisted that although her sisters and she had inherited their beauty from Letty Wolf, they were nothing like her. It occurred to him as the two women stared at each other, trembling and hesitant to speak, that the unexpected meeting had shocked them both. He also realized that neither of them would take the first step, making them more alike than they realized.

Ryder slipped his arm around Justine to lend her his support. He noted that the big fellow beside Letty did the same, prompting Justine to say, "Hello, James. It's nice to see you again."

James.

Ryder did his best not to react when he saw the man's determined protection of Letty Wolf. "It's nice to see you again, too, Justine. I only wish it were under better circumstances."

Justine replied softly, "Many people have called me Camille since I left home. It's good to be called Justine again, James."

"Camille?" Letty interjected. "I don't understand."

"No, Mother. You never did."

Letty took a step back at the softly spoken retort. "Maybe you're right." She unconsciously leaned into James's support as she continued, "I wasn't sure where to find any of you, but James said his investigator discovered that Meredith had purchased a train ticket after mentioning a final destination of Winsome. I thought Winsome would be the best place to start. There are so many things that need to be faced . . . to be done . . . things I've put off too long already." She shook her head as she muttered, "The reverberations just grow louder. They allow me no peace."

Ryder saw Justine's expression whiten. He saw the way James acknowledged her reaction with a glance in Letty's direction.

"What do you mean by reverberations?" Justine asked.

"Nothing. That was just a figure of speech." Letty swallowed and briefly closed her dark eyes.

"Tell her, Letty," James insisted. "Now's the time to tell Justine the truth."

Ryder saw the fear reflected in Letty's gaze when she looked up at James and shook her head.

"It wasn't a figure of speech, was it, Mother?" Justine asked boldly. "Do you hear the wolf, too?"

Letty went still.

Justine's delicate face turned white as she rasped, "Does *he* visit you, too?"

Letty's complexion turned so gray that Ryder took a spontaneous step toward her. He was halted when James gripped her arm supportively.

Justine continued hoarsely, "No one believes that you hear what you hear, or believes you see what you see, do they, Mother?"

Letty swayed, and James said harshly, "That's enough for now, Justine."

Justine trembled as Ryder said, "The stage is

going to leave. Either we board now or we stay behind."

Her expression rigid, Justine raised her chin and replied, "I'm going to Winsome."

Ryder turned to help Justine board when he heard a female voice behind him say just as resolutely, "I'm going, too."

He did not need to hear James's reply.

Chapter Ten

Meredith's fiery hair glowed in the subtle light as Trace regarded her intently. He supposed he'd never become fully accustomed to the reality that the beautiful woman in front of him was his alone to love. Red hair that blazed in the subtle light; heavily lashed amber eyes that were mysterious and seductive while being open and loving only with him; a heart-shaped face with skin that was creamy and faultless; features that were strong, yet feminine in a way that tore at his heart; and her mouth . . .

A chill ran down Trace's spine when he thought of her mouth.

He had been dismayed when Robert Pinkerton assigned the case to him and told him the daughters of the infamous Letty Wolf were spoiled brats. The only thing that had convinced him to take the case was his realization that he'd have no other opportunity to pay a debt of gratitude that he owed Robert Pinkerton. He had accepted the assignment reluctantly, but he knew now that despite the difficulties he had encountered, it was the best decision he had ever made.

He had found the woman he loved, and she loved him. That had seemed enough until unanswered questions returned to plague him:

What was the explanation for the mysterious wolf that seemed to appear when ever Meredith needed it most?

What was the source of the danger that seemed to shadow Letty's daughters?

Trace said softly, "You need to proceed carefully, Meredith. There's more to everything that's happened than meets the eye."

Meredith responded with equal softness, "Maybe, but the decisions my sisters and I made weren't reached easily. We thought things through a thousand times, but we had to make a complete break from Mother."

"The letter from James Ferguson could shed some light on the situation."

"No."

"He wouldn't have written to you if he didn't have something important to say."

"You saw Johanna's reaction to the letter." Meredith took a shaky breath. "If I had any doubts about opening it . . . about restoring contact with my mother in any way at all, Johanna settled the question for me. Too many years have passed for us to change our feelings or to care."

"You care. Neither your sister nor you want to admit it, but you care."

"No, we don't!"

"Then why is the letter still lying unopened in your wastebasket? Why don't you either destroy it or open it and read what Ferguson has to say? If you didn't care, it wouldn't make any difference to you. Instead, you and your sister both reacted emotionally to just the sight of James Ferguson's name in the return address."

"We won't let ourselves care, don't you see?" Meredith pleaded for his understanding as she said, "Caring is what made us suffer through all those years when my mother gave nothing back in return. We won't let it happen again."

"Meredith"—Trace gripped Meredith's shoulders lightly so she could not avoid looking at him as he responded gently—"you may not have a choice."

"I have a choice!" Brushing off Trace's grip roughly, Meredith walked rigidly to the wastepaper basket where she had dropped the unopened letter days earlier. Retrieving it, her jaw tight, she tore it into shreds and dropped it back into the basket. Her complexion pale, she turned back to Trace and whispered, "I've made my choice. I hope you understand. If you don't—"

Trace closed the distance between them in a few quick strides. Not allowing Meredith to finish her statement, he took her into his arms.

Unaware that she was trembling, Meredith leaned into Trace's embrace and allowed his silent solace to comfort her. Tears streaked her cheeks when she looked up moments later and whispered, "I hope you understand, Trace. I want you to understand."

"I understand. I may not agree, but I understand."

His head hurt. Every bone in his body ached and he was nauseous.

Mason made an attempt to move, only to cry out from the pain that resulted.

He squinted through slitted eyelids at the long, narrow room where he lay abed. Cots lined the walls on either side of him. The floors were spotted, stained, and badly in need of washing, the metal cots flaked paint, and the limited furniture was battered and mismatched. Over it all hung the sound of intermittent groans and the acrid smell of urine.

Where was he?

Mason reached up tentatively to touch his head and felt the bandage there. He looked around him as a woman wearing a white apron and a white cap perched atop her tightly bound hair approached. Halting beside him, she said with an attempt at joviality, "Well, awake at last, I see. How do you feel, Mr. Little?"

A nurse. So he was obviously in a hospital—and she asked him how he felt? Stupid! He felt terrible, and he had no doubt that he looked terrible, too.

Ignoring her question, Mason mumbled, "Water . . ."

The nurse poured water into a cup on his nightstand. She held it to his lips, and he drank greedily.

"That's enough, Mr. Little. We don't want to overdo. You had a terrible accident and you've been unconscious. You're in New York Hospital, your doctor's name is Dr. DeMarco, and we need to take things slowly."

Accident . . . yes, he remembered. The carriage horse had panicked when it heard that persistent howling. He asked hoarsely, "Did they get him?"

"Did they get who?"

"The animal that was howling." He took a breath and said, "The animal that scared the horses."

"I don't know about any animal. I just know that a carriage ran you down and you're lucky you're alive. So lie quietly, please. Don't excite yourself. I'll call the doctor."

"I don't need the doctor!" Mason closed his eyes at the pain in his head that his outburst caused. He waited a few moments for it to subside and opened his eyes to repeat, "I don't need the doctor. I need to get out of here."

"You can't do that. You're injured. You'll be here for a few days, at least."

"A few days!"

Mason closed his eyes again at the thought. He couldn't afford the delay. Too many things were closing in around him. He needed to settle the situation with Letty before she could reconcile with her daughters. If by some chance her daughters were reinstated in her will, all would be lost for him.

"Very good, Mr. Little. Close your eyes and rest. I'll get the doctor."

Mason snapped his eyes open in time to see the stupid woman walk away. He reached up to still the throbbing in his head and fingered the bandage there. Wrong, wrong, wrong! He shouldn't be lying here now, as helpless as a fish out of water while Letty Wolf was free to destroy him at her whim. He should be on his way to Texas, where he would settle the direction of his future once and for all.

He gritted his teeth when a gray-haired fellow approached. Judging from the stethoscope around his neck and the concerned expression on his face, he was Dr. DeMarco.

"How do you feel, Mr. Little?"

Mason stared at the doctor, who spoke in a heavily accented voice. The fellow was an import, he thought contemptuously. His lips tightening, Mason managed, "What am I doing here?"

"You were in an accident."

"I know that. I want to know why I've been placed in a hospital ward like some . . . some indigent."

"It's only temporary. You were brought in here unidentified. Now that we know who you are—"

"Get me out of here!" Mason interrupted the fellow's halting reply with a scathing glance at the beds surrounding him. "I will not remain where I am lumped in with the refuse of the streets. I want a private room that befits a man of my stature!"

"Mr. Little—"

"A private room, do you hear me?"

"I hear you"—perspiration appeared on the doctor's upper lip as he attempted a smile—"but you'll have to wait until—"

"I will not wait!"

Suddenly coughing and holding his head when the pounding expanded, Mason heard the doctor say, "All right, Mr. Little. I'll have someone change your room immediately. Don't upset yourself. You have a concussion, broken ribs, and are severely bruised. Excitement can be your worst enemy."

"No, this place is my worst enemy." His hoarse voice growing shrill, Mason repeated, "Get me out of here now before I succumb to the stench!"

His jaw tightening, the doctor said, "All right, Mr. Little. Just as you say." He turned and called out, "Orderly, please move this patient to the nearest private room. We can settle the paperwork later."

Mason nodded, not without pain as an emaciated-looking fellow approached. Were he not nauseous from the stench, he might even have smiled when the orderly began rolling his bed into the hallway.

Mr. Charles sat at his desk, his perspiring face drawn into a frown as he looked at the blurred picture of Dobbs in the newspaper. He ignored the fact that the jacket of his costly suit was spotted, that a button was missing on his sleeve, and that dark rings of sweat outlined his underarms, marking the number of hot days he had spent wearing the garment. He was a businessman; he would not remove his jacket under any circumstances. The expensive furnishings in his office were silent proof of his success—and if he chose to remain in a section of the city that was not highly regarded, that was his prerogative.

He was a businessman who had made good, and no one survived who contradicted that claim.

Mr. Charles continued staring at the report of Dobbs's death. He had kept it on his desk because it filled him with unrest. He had learned many things during his rise to prominence in his organization, the most important of which was not to ignore that feeling of unrest when it nagged at him. It was the only intuition he heeded, and it had served him well.

He hadn't initially understood his reaction to the article. He had already made the decision that Dobbs was no longer an asset to his organization—that, in fact, Dobbs needed to be eliminated. He had been prepared to dispatch Ham to accomplish that purpose when Dobbs's image had appeared on the front page of the morning newspaper. He supposed no one would have paid Dobbs's passing any notice at all if he hadn't been killed by a mysterious, vicious animal that was apparently roaming the city streets. Every policeman in the city had been alerted to be vigilant, and extra men had been called out to participate in the massive hunt for the beast.

Mr. Charles snorted. As it turned out, Dobbs was responsible for increased police presence, damn him!

The unrest nagging at him had continued, however, and sometime in the middle of the previous night he had come to a conclusion. Dobbs had made a mistake in accepting the assignment that Mason Little had given him. He should not have gotten involved with Little's plans regarding Letty Wolf. The woman was a phenomenon. By all standards of the day, she should have been considered a pariah by the social set, yet she had become socially prominent and exceedingly successful, thanks to the power of her personality. Dobbs should have realized he was taking on more than he could handle—but he hadn't.

Letty Wolf was a personality unique to the city and to the social set that had taken her to its heart. To members of Mr. Charles's organization, however, he had decided that she was to be considered untouchable.

Yet Mason Little wasn't untouchable in any way. Mr. Charles's brief meeting with the man had shown him to be an annoyingly arrogant fellow who thought much too highly of himself. It galled him that Little had actually had the impudence to *demand* that he fix what Dobbs had mismanaged. It had not made any difference to Little that Mr. Charles had denied any connection with Dobbs and had eventually had Little thrown out. He sensed that wouldn't be enough. The man was a gambler who owed him money that he was not able to repay. Little could not be trusted. Should he be backed into a corner with the law, he would involve Mr. Charles without batting an eye if he thought it might help his own situation.

Mason Little needed to be eliminated.

Mr. Charles regarded the newspaper lying on the desk in front of him more intently. He read again the report that Mason Little, Esq., a prominent attorney, had been run down accidentally on the street in front of the train station and had nearly been killed. It reported that Little had been taken to New York Hospital, where he was expected to recuperate.

Fortunately for Little; unfortunately for him.

Mr. Charles brightened slowly. On second thought, the accident provided the perfect opportunity. It would be considered a regrettable circumstance—a result of the accident—if Little were found to have expired during the night. Keeping in mind that Ham was a strong fellow and that a pillow was an expedient device, Mr. Charles was certain such an occurrence would appear a natural death.

Mr. Charles's smile widened briefly. Satisfied that he had found the perfect solution to the problem Mason Little posed, he stood up and called out, "Ham, come in here. I need to talk to you."

Twilight had turned into night outside the hospital window as Mason glanced out onto the street and then turned back to look around the "private" room to which he had been transferred. Pathetic, that's what it was: dingy, hot, airless, and unclean. All it had to offer was the privacy he had demanded.

Mason glanced out into the hallway at the white-clad individuals who avoided looking his way as they walked briskly past. That was all right with him. He wanted as little contact with them as possible. He knew the night nurse would come in shortly to check his pulse and temperature. After dispensing whatever powders the doctor had ordered, she would then most likely leave him to his own devices.

He was fine. He had a concussion, but it was little more than a headache. He had broken ribs, but the doctor had seen to it that he was properly strapped up. He was battered and bruised, but none of the injuries were permanent.

He needed to be on his way. It did not bother him that the doctor had declared him unstable as a result of the accident and refused to sign his release. He didn't need anyone's permission to leave. It was up to himself now.

Mason looked again out the grimy window. He could hardly wait until the night nurse made her visit. He had slept most of the day and was sufficiently rested. He was certain he'd be able to dress himself and steal down the hallway and out the side door without being noticed in the darkness. He would go directly to the train station and buy a ticket for Texas—with the ultimate destination of Winsome, where Letty had undoubtedly headed. He would doze in the station until the train was ready to leave, no matter how long it took.

He was determined. He would not allow Letty to ruin the future that he had planned. That inheritance was his, and he would not let it slip away from him. When he had the money in hand, he would personally present the sum he owed to Mr. Charles, and he would make certain never to be beholden to that individual again.

He only needed to wait a little while longer.

Fairly certain that most of the patients would be asleep for the night, Ham approached the hospital. He entered the side entrance with a package in hand marked, "URGENT—DELIVER TO DR. DEMARCO."

Ham smiled. A little bit of investigation that afternoon uncovered the name of Mason Little's doctor, and he had thought it would be clever to mark the package that way. He expected that the busy doctor would not be suspicious of the new powder samples Ham had obtained through a contact at his pharmacy, especially if he included printed material about the drugs.

He had also learned that Mason Little had been transferred to a private room, and inwardly rejoiced at the ease with which he would be able to accomplish his purpose.

Ham walked down a hallway of the institution and grimaced at the smell. The odor of human waste was overwhelming. He couldn't wait to leave. It occurred to him that he might be doing Mason Little a favor after all.

Still holding the package, Ham approached Little's private room. He glanced inside and saw that Little was lying in bed. He wasn't moving and appeared to be asleep.

How considerate of him!

Ham entered the room and placed the package on the table near the door as he withdrew his knife. He'd use it if he had to, but he preferred to use a pillow as Mr. Charles had suggested. Of course, Mr. Charles had said he didn't care how it was done, as long as it was done. He knew he had earned Mr. Charles's confidence, but he appreciated the leeway his boss allowed him.

Beside the bed at last, Ham smiled. Little hadn't moved at all.

Pausing for a deep breath, Ham ripped the pillow out from underneath Little's head, but his eyes widened with shock. Blankets were merely lumped up underneath the coverlet, making it appear that there was someone in bed. Little wasn't there!

His expression confused and his heart pounding at the unanticipated situation, Ham forced himself to remain calm. He took the time to restore the pillow and coverlet to the way he had found them, and turned toward the door. He was about to leave when he remembered the package with Dr. DeMarco's name on it. Stepping back inside, he picked it up, walked back out into the hallway, and continued on with as normal a step as he could manage. He stopped abruptly when a nurse asked, "What are you doing here this time of night?"

Stone-faced, Ham replied, "This package is marked urgent, so I was sent to deliver it now."

The nurse glanced impatiently at the package he was holding and said, "I suppose no one stopped to think that Dr. DeMarco would be gone for the day and that the package would have to wait until he returned in the morning. Anyway, Dr. DeMarco's office is on the other side of the building." She added briskly, "Just follow that corridor and leave the package where he can find it as soon as he arrives."

Nodding, Ham walked in the direction she had pointed. He had no choice but to deliver the package. If he did, no one would give his presence a second thought when Little was discovered missing the next morning.

His step growing more confident, Ham nodded. That was why Mr. Charles depended on him, because he could handle things, however they turned out. But the truth was—Ham cursed—Mr. Charles wasn't going to like this at all.

A short time later, as Ham faced Mr. Charles in the elaborate study of his home, he realized that his concern had been well founded.

Mr. Charles's face reddened with anger as he said, "What do you mean, Little wasn't there?"

Ham paused in response. He had thought long and hard before going to his boss's house at such a late hour. He knew Mr. Charles didn't like his "business associates" bothering him at his private residence, especially after dark, but he'd had no choice. He had been certain Mr. Charles would only be angrier if he had waited.

Livid, Mr. Charles said, "I want to know what happened."

"Mason Little was gone, boss. At first I thought he was in his bed at the hospital, but he had wadded up sheets and things that only made it look that way. He wasn't there."

"Nobody saw him leave?"

"Nobody seemed to realize he was gone."

"How did the bastard know you were coming?"

"I don't think he did, boss." Ham frowned, deciding he'd better take a chance and say what he thought since Mr. Charles had asked him. He continued, "The place was dirty, and it smelled bad. I don't think a fella like Little would've liked it there."

"A fella like Little?"

"You know, somebody who thought he was better than everyone else, and who was so fussy about the way he looked and all."

"Really."

"That fella didn't have a hair out of place when he came to see you, boss. I figure he must've spent a lot of time getting himself to look that way, and a man like that wouldn't want to be someplace like that hospital, where it smelled bad and people were moaning with pain and all."

Mr. Charles's eyes narrowed as he said, "Where do you think he went?"

"Home, maybe."

"Home? Then what are you waiting for? Do what you started out to do!"

"In his house?"

"In his house, on the street, wherever you find him. Just get it done! Is that too much to ask?"

"No, boss. It ain't. I'll find him and I'll do what I started out to do. That's a promise."

Mason limped toward the seating provided for passengers and plopped down unceremoniously. The train station was almost deserted. A single clerk had been present to take his money when he'd bought a ticket for the next train to Texas. The fellow had looked at him strangely, but Mason was past caring that his appearance was less than presentable. He had shrugged into his clothes haphazardly in the hospital, with pain accompanying every movement. He had unwrapped his head but had not bothered to comb his hair or even look at his appearance before slapping on his hat and stealing out into the hallway. The lights had been lowered in deference to the hour, facilitating his escape, and he had slipped out the side entrance without incident. He had walked several blocks, limping every step of the way. He had been almost certain he could not make it another step when he was finally able to hail a solitary hack on its way back to the stable. He had arrived at the train station, bought a ticket, and congratulated himself on having accomplished his purpose. Yet now that he was seated, with his head throbbing and the pain in his ribs growing steadily stronger, he only wanted to sleep.

Mason glanced at the ticket clerk one last time before closing his eyes. He had told the fellow that he was going to wait there for the early morning train to make sure he didn't miss it. He had slipped the fellow a sizable sum to watch out for him. He felt confident the bespectacled clerk would not fail him. The fearful look in his eyes had said it all.

Mason drifted off to a half sleep while seated upright. Pain throbbed through every bone in his body. He silently wished he had remembered to take the packet of powder that the doctor had left at his bedside. But he hadn't. He supposed it had been the least of his concerns at the time, but now . . .

At last Mason slipped off into a restless sleep.

Ham's hulking figure twitched uncomfortably as he entered Mr. Charles's office. The sun had begun its ascent in the morning sky. It was early, but the heat that caused so much discomfort at that time of year was already building. Ham paid no attention to the weather as he approached the inner-office door apprehensively and knocked. It seemed that Mr. Charles had not gone back to his bed after last night's visit. Instead, he had gone directly to his office.

A bad sign.

Mr. Charles had apparently not even considered

sleeping after hearing of Little's escape. The news Ham had to impart now would not make Mr. Charles any happier.

"Come in!"

The tone of Mr. Charles's voice sent shivers down Ham's spine as he entered. Approaching the desk, Ham blurted, "Little didn't go home, boss. I made an excuse and woke up his servant. The old fella just said Little was in the hospital. I didn't say nothing about him not being there. I waited outside where nobody could see me until morning. I figured maybe Little would show up eventually. I figured he had nowhere else to go, being as he wasn't feeling too good, but he didn't show up at all."

"So where is he?"

"I don't know, boss." Ham swallowed nervously and added, "Maybe he collapsed somewhere and won't be found for a few hours. Maybe they'll take him back to the hospital. I'll finish him off then if that happens."

"*Maybe* . . ." Mr. Charles's gaze was cold. "It all comes down to the word *maybe*."

Ham did not reply.

"I want you to find him and take care of him, Ham. *Now!* And I don't want to hear any more excuses."

"I know, boss, but—"

"No buts!" Mr. Charles stood up. His diminutive figure was in sharp contrast with Ham's massive size, but the sight of him set Ham to quaking.

"Wait a minute." Mr. Charles's eyes narrowed.

"Did you check the train station to see if Little had gone there?"

"No."

"You should have! That's where he was going when the carriage struck him. You said yourself that a man like Little was determined enough and thought highly enough of himself to believe there was nothing he couldn't do. Maybe that's why he sneaked out of the hospital, so he could make another attempt to get where he was going. It makes sense."

"Yeah, but he had been run over by a carriage. He was hurting."

"A man like Little—"

Ham hastened to respond, "All right, boss. I'll check. If he did go there, it shouldn't be hard to find him or somebody who remembers seeing him. There couldn't have been too many fellas about at that hour who looked like he did."

Mr. Charles walked slowly around his massive desk when Ham finished speaking. Staring at him, Mr. Charles said softly, "I want you to find him, Ham. I want you to make sure you finish what you started to do, no matter where you have to go."

"Yes, boss."

Mr. Charles stepped closer. He said with an emphasis that could not be misconstrued, "No matter where that takes you. Do you understand what I'm saying, Ham?"

"I understand."

"Then do it!"

"Yes, boss."

Ham turned toward the door and pulled it closed

behind him. He'd never forget the look on Mr. Charles's face just then. It was deadly.

Dressed in Western traveling clothes, Meredith stood rigidly as the town of Winsome began coming to life behind her. She looked at Trace, who stood tall beside her. He and Wade, Johanna's husband, seemed to have formed a silent partnership as they had scrutinized a crude map of the area and finalized their plans over breakfast that morning.

They were presently in the livery stable, ready to mount up, when Meredith said unexpectedly, "I'm sorry I let you down, Johanna."

"Let me down?"

"I thought it would be easier than it's turned out to be to find somebody who remembers either our mother or grandmother."

"It's not your fault, Meredith." Similarly dressed in a recently purchased split skirt, with her platinum hair tightly confined under a broad-brimmed hat, Johanna said, "Justine and I depended on you to fix things for us all our lives, but we're adults now. We have to do things for ourselves, and this is all part of it. It's nobody's fault that finding out about our family isn't easy."

She continued, "Wade and I will go west from here and you and Trace can go east, as we planned. We'll make sure to stop at every ranch or trading post along the way, like we agreed. Somebody has to remember something. We'll return here again in three days, or sooner if we learn something. With luck, we'll be able to explain things more clearly to Justine when we see her again."

The sisters locked gazes for a moment, then stepped forward to hug each other simultaneously. Frowning as she drew back, Meredith said, "Please be careful."

"But the danger is past, isn't it? I mean . . ." Johanna paused. "The man who was hunting you is dead. The same goes for the one who was after me."

"I suppose, but the person who sent them remains," Meredith said. "I can't help thinking about Justine. What if a man was also sent to hunt her down? What if he's still looking for her?"

"If we don't know where she is, how can anyone else find her?"

"They found us, didn't they?"

Johanna responded with a tight shake of her head, "I refuse to even consider that possibility. I keep telling myself everything will be all right and we'll be able to tell Justine everything she wants to know when we meet again."

Meredith attempted a smile. "Right."

But Justine was still on their minds when they rode to the edge of town with Trace and Wade beside them. Splitting up at a juncture in the trail, Meredith waved good-bye to her sister and the man who loved her, and then turned resolutely to gallop in the opposite direction. When she eventually slowed her mount, she turned toward Trace. He was beside her when she asked in a voice tinged with uncertainty, "Do you think we're wasting our time, Trace?"

"No."

"Do you think we'll find someone who remembers my mother's family? Anyone . . . anywhere?"

"I don't know."

"Trace—"

Suddenly sweeping her from her horse, Trace positioned Meredith on his own saddle and held her close. He heard her attempt to stifle her tears and said, "None of this will change anything as far as I'm concerned, you know. I love you. I'll always love you, and I'll always protect you with my life."

"Maybe that's part of the problem. I need to know why that would be necessary—why anyone would want to hurt my sisters and me."

"Your mother's will—"

"I know, but there has to be something else. The will doesn't explain why the wolf appeared and why I heard . . ." Refusing to complete that statement, Meredith took a breath. Again in control of her emotions, she whispered, "I'm all right now, Trace. You can put me back on my horse."

"No."

"Trace—"

"I want to hold you a little longer." Trace brushed her mouth with his. He whispered, "Humor me, Meredith. It's not much to ask."

"But—"

Trace's light eyes held hers as he said, "I want to feel you close to me for a little while."

Softly, Meredith replied, "I want that, too."

Trace smiled briefly before he snatched up the reins of Meredith's horse and nudged his mount into motion.

The sun had dropped past the meridian when the stagecoach arrived in Winsome at last. The journey had been bumpy, dusty, and hot, and silence had reigned for hours in the cramped interior.

Ryder helped Justine down the coach steps and turned toward the driver as he prepared to throw their bags down. He noted that she stood rigidly, without speaking. He saw the concern with which James helped Letty down onto the street, but it was Letty's expression that stunned him. He saw fear flash in her eyes as she looked up at James.

Ryder glanced at Justine to see that although she was obviously anxious, there was no fear on her face.

Frowning, Ryder looked at James as the driver prepared to throw down Letty's bag. He knew the moment their glances met that James was aware of Letty's fear, and that whatever its cause, James would protect her with his life. Bonding in that moment, both men turned back to the women they loved and waited expectantly.

Letty fought to stabilize her emotions as she glanced around Winsome. The stagecoach journey had been difficult with Justine sitting across from her as if she were a stranger.

Her daughters, she knew, resented the years they'd spent apart, and she sincerely regretted her decision to send them away.

But she needed to do more than regret her previous choices. Now it was time to face the past, and to do her best to alter the present.

Letty glanced again at James. She knew instinctively that no matter how this encounter with her past turned out, he would stand beside her. She wished she were free to tell him how thoughts of him sustained her and how good she felt when his arms were around her. She dreamed of the moment when she could whisper the words he wanted to hear . . . but she doubted that that time would ever come to pass.

Trying to make casual conversation, she said, "This town hasn't changed very much over the years."

James looked at her cautiously. "You remember it well?"

"Yes, perhaps too well." Forcing a detached demeanor, she said, "I suppose we should get settled. If I remember correctly, the hotel—the only one Winsome has to offer—is down the street."

Letty was conscious of Justine's and Ryder's footsteps behind them as they approached the hotel. She stood back as James approached the desk. She saw him frown when the clerk stared at Letty and Justine and muttered, "Well, I'll be . . ."

She saw James's even features color with impatience as he responded, "You'll be what?"

"I'll be damned!" The clerk looked up at James with a half smile. "There I was thinking two of the most beautiful women I had ever seen had left town, when here come two more. I never thought I'd hear myself say this, but your women match those other two in every way."

Letty's head jerked up at the clerk's comment.

"Who were these two women?" James asked.

"One was pretty well known around here. She and her fella are responsible for a lot of changes in this town, but . . . well, that's another story. The other woman showed up unexpected like, but they seemed to know each other."

Approaching the desk, Letty said, "Their names . . . are they on the register?"

"Sure enough. Like I said, we know the one woman. The other one, she—"

Letty looked down at the register. The clerk continued talking, but she was no longer listening.

She heard James ask, "Are they coming back?"

"They said they was."

"When?"

"They didn't say."

"What *did* they say?"

"They said they was going to try to find out something about people who lived here a long time ago—some people named Wolf. They was asking about the same people around here, but nobody'd heard of them. I figure that's why they was going to try looking a little farther out."

Letty mumbled. "It's no wonder nobody ever heard of them."

Taking her arm without responding, James accepted the key to their room and ushered her up the stairs with her daughter following close behind. Letty turned toward Justine when they reached the privacy of the upstairs hallway.

"You knew they wouldn't find anyone who remembered the family, didn't you?" Justine asked.

Letty took a breath. "Yes."

"How did you know?"

"Because the family they're looking for never existed."

"What?"

"I adopted the name Wolf for reasons that may sound difficult to understand now, but which were important to me then. My family name was McGregor."

Justine went still. She glanced at Ryder briefly before turning back toward Letty to say incredulously, "You're telling me that my sisters and I didn't even know what your real family name was?"

Letty responded simply, "I changed my name when I changed my life. Certainly you can understand that."

"But you didn't bother to tell us—your own daughters."

"My former name didn't matter."

"It did to us!"

"It shouldn't have. It had no reflection on how I acted . . . how I pushed you and your sisters aside in my climb to success. It has no bearing on what's happened since then, either."

"If that's true, why do we both hear the howlings? Why do we both see *him?*"

Letty paled. "You mean . . . Grandfather?"

"If that's what you call him."

Letty could not respond.

"What if Johanna and Meredith hear the howlings and see Grandfather, too. What then?"

"I don't know."

"You may not know." Justine raised her chin as she continued, "But I intend to find out. There are other things I need to find out, too. I need to know why Otto Tears was hired to find me . . . to kill me."

"I never heard of him . . . I swear."

"I need to know if someone intended to do the same to my sisters, too, and I need to know if it all had anything to do with the conditions of your offer to put us back in your will."

"That was a mistake." Letty's color drained. "It was the wrong thing to do."

"And I need to know . . . who is Dobbs?"

"Dobbs?"

Letty and Justine stared at each other in the ensuing silence.

Questions without answers.

Letty hoped it was not too late to solve the mystery, once and for all.

Mason moved uncomfortably on the train seat, which seemed to grow harder by the moment. He winced when the steady rocking of the car enhanced the pain in his ribs. He groaned when the ceaseless din of metal wheels screeching against tracks raised the pounding in his head to thunder. He coughed when a loud belch from the engine smokestack emitted another fine layer of dust to settle on everyone in the car.

All he wanted to do was sleep.

Unable to find a comfortable position, Mason moved restlessly again. He consoled himself that all his suffering would be worthwhile when he accomplished his purpose and inherited his dear Aunt Letty's fortune. He would have all the time in the world to sleep then . . . in the comfort of his own room . . . in the warmth of his own bed . . . in the silence that a wealthy man could demand.

Mason opened his eyes into narrow slits when the train jerked unexpectedly, then slowed its forward motion. He shook his head, hardly able to believe they would soon be stopping. He kept himself upright with pure strength of will when the engine pulled into the depot, and then he exited, staggering every step of the way, as the last of the passengers left the car.

Unconscious of the attention he drew from other passengers, he approached the waiting railcar, and boarded. He closed his eyes. Barstow was his next stop, where he'd take a stagecoach to Winsome. He'd find Letty then. He'd do what he had to do, one way or another, and then he could rest.

Ham ran awkwardly toward the train that had begun pulling out of the New York City station. Catching it at the last minute, he pulled himself aboard and walked through the swaying car until he found a seat. It had taken him too long to find the night clerk at the station who remembered Mason. He had wasted too many hours and had just managed to catch the next train, but he was gratified to at least have learned Mason's ultimate destination.

Winsome, Texas.

Well, that was his destination, too. Mr. Charles had made it clear that he was to do whatever was necessary to eliminate Little, and if he needed to travel to another state to do it, he would. It occurred to him that it might turn out better that way, too. Communication was poor between police departments, and it could be months before Little's disappearance was explained. Ham knew that the longer notification took, the better it would be for Mr. Charles, and that was what it was all about . . . pleasing Mr. Charles.

Ham's sagging features hardened at that thought. He *would* please Mr. Charles. That was a given.

Chapter Eleven

Meredith had forgotten the intimacy that camping out on the trail afforded. She had not remembered how blissful it could feel to be wrapped in the arms of the man she loved, safe and content, with the only cover overhead the swaying trees, and the only light the silver rays of the moon.

Meredith inched closer to Trace's powerful sleeping form in her semiwakefulness. Tall, dark, with light eyes that spoke without words when they gazed into hers, Trace was masculine in a way that had stolen her heart. He had earned the trust that had come to her with such difficulty.

She had somehow known that the time spent visiting ranches and talking to old-timers about her relatives would result in negative responses. She had at first despaired that no one seemed to remember Letty Wolf or her grandmother. She had begun to lose hope that she would ever discover her roots, or that she would ever fully understand the background that had driven her mother so relentlessly. She had started to fear that without the information she was looking for, without seeing where her mother had gone wrong, she would not be able to avoid . . . *becoming like her.*

But hopelessness did not overwhelm her with Trace beside her now. Speaking little but saying much, he lent her the strength of his presence. When she lay beside him, the will to go on returned, and she—

Meredith's classic features froze as a lingering wolf's wail shattered the nighttime silence. Unaware that she had begun shuddering, she listened more closely and heard it again. She swallowed, uncertain. The constant howling . . . the visits from Grandfather . . . they had all abruptly ceased. She did not know why. She only knew that she had been relieved to be free of the uncertainty and wariness the warnings evoked.

"What's wrong, Meredith?"

Meredith responded breathlessly to Trace's question, "I should be accustomed to the sounds of the nighttime wilderness, but the sound of a wolf's howl still startles me."

"What do you mean? I don't hear a wolf."

Meredith could not respond.

"It's started again, hasn't it?"

When Meredith did not reply, Trace drew her closer. "Whatever it all means, you know you're safe with me."

"But is Johanna safe? And Justine? Johanna has Wade to protect her, but I have no idea where Justine is or what's happening to her."

"You can't be responsible for your sisters all your life, Meredith."

"But I'm all they've ever had to depend on!"

Trace studied her expression for long moments before whispering, "What do you want to do?"

"I want to see Johanna again and make sure she's all right."

"Your sister will be on the trail for another day, at least."

"I need to find her now."

"This is a big country. She could be anywhere."

"We can find her."

Trace studied Meredith's adamant expression. He was a Pinkerton who dealt with facts, but he had learned not to question the phenomenons that Meredith experienced.

Trace said simply, "We'll start out at first light."

Johanna awoke abruptly. Uncertain of the reason for her discomfort, she glanced at Wade where he slept beside her. She looked around her at the temporary camp they had made after a fruitless day of searching for some word of her mother's family. She remembered that she had been frustrated and that her distress must have been apparent, for Wade had approached her and whispered, "We may not have found what we were looking for today, but I don't intend to stop looking until you're satisfied. You have my word on that."

Johanna recalled that her frustration had eased when he had taken her into his arms for long moments of consolation that only he was able to provide. They had later eaten their meager fare and had fallen asleep in each other's arms with her sense of purpose renewed.

Yet the discomfort with which she had awakened remained.

Drawing herself up to a seated position, Johanna blinked, then stared into the distance as a familiar glow gradually materialized.

She gasped as the old man appeared with a large gray wolf at his side. The setting sun was at his back, the ragged strands of his unbound hair brushed his bare shoulders, and his weathered face was shadowed, but she recognized him immediately despite the new sense of purpose in his step. She held her breath as he halted a few feet away, the intensity in his small, dark eyes clearly visible as he whispered in the foreign tongue she had come to know so well:

Do not despair.
The time draws near.
Your family searches.
Find them.
In them there is safety.

Nodding, Johanna did not attempt to reply as the old man waited long moments for the import of his statements to settle in her mind. He then turned and walked back into the bright rays of the setting sun. She took a breath when he disappeared, then realized that Wade was sitting up beside her.

Wade said flatly, "You saw him again, didn't you?"

Johanna nodded.

"What did he say?"

"I don't know exactly. He said the time is drawing near, that I should find Meredith."

"What else did he say?"

"Nothing . . . just not to despair, and that in my family is safety."

Wade locked his dark-eyed gaze firmly with hers as he whispered, "Your family includes me now, you know that, don't you?"

"I know, but—"

"You don't have to explain."

"Wade, I have to find Meredith."

After a few moments, Wade responded simply, "We'll start out in the morning."

Mason coughed and sputtered, his eyelids heavy. The pounding in his head was ceaseless, and the pain that made him catch his breath every time he moved seemed to grow stronger by the moment. He looked at the fellow sleeping peacefully across from him in the cramped stagecoach, which had started out on the trail at first light. He had not asked when the stage would depart for Winsome when he arrived by train and went directly to the stagecoach office. He had merely paid for his ticket and sat down on the nearest bench after instructing the ticket clerk to make certain he was on the next stage.

Unsure how much time had elapsed, he remembered moaning when the ticket clerk awakened him to say the stage would be leaving shortly. He had not bothered to eat or drink, but had merely climbed aboard the stage and closed his eyes. He had not known what he was in for as the stage rocked and jolted him on the bumpy trail to Winsome and his pain became almost unbearable.

Hardly conscious, Mason lifted his head when the

stage began to slow. A glance out the window revealed that a town was coming into view. His churning stomach and staggering step were his greatest concerns when he stepped down on the street at last and stumbled toward the nearest hotel. He needed sleep. He needed to rest. He couldn't put it off any longer.

His vision blurred, Mason paid the hotel registration clerk for a week's stay with the hope that he would not be disturbed. A simple glance in the clerk's direction halted the man's protests when he did not bother to sign the register. Instead, he accepted the key the fellow handed him and dragged himself up the stairs to his room. He opened the door, and pushed it closed behind him with his strength fading fast. He fell down on the bed fully clothed as darkness closed in around him.

The sun was high in a cloudless sky when the two sisters returned to the town of Winsome. Strangely, it had not been difficult for them to find each other despite the opposite directions in which they had originally traveled. As if it were predestined, Meredith and Trace had met Johanna and Wade on the trail late the previous day. With the need for explanations minimal, they had automatically turned back to Winsome when it was morning again.

Wade and Trace dismounted when they reached the hotel. They swung Johanna and Meredith down from their horses watchfully and maintained close contact with them when they entered the hotel.

Aware of their tension, Johanna looked up at Wade. She said with an attempt at a smile, "Don't worry. We're fine."

The glances Trace and Wade exchanged said it all. They would continue their vigilance.

They had all reached the second floor of the hotel when Meredith halted abruptly. The blood drained from her face at first sight of the man who stepped out of a doorway nearby. She felt rather than saw that Johanna's reaction was the same when she managed breathlessly, "James . . . what are you doing here?"

She knew she would never forget the moment when the beautiful dark-haired woman stepped out of the room behind him. Johanna's gasp echoed her own.

"Mother . . ."

Letty went stock-still at the sight of her two daughters. She looked at the men standing close behind them in a silent wall of masculine protection. She felt their shock multiply when Justine exited the room beside hers and rushed past her to hug them close. She noted that Ryder took his place beside Justine. As one, her three daughters turned to face her, their expressions cold and emotionless.

The first to speak, Meredith asked, "What are you doing here, Mother?"

Letty looked at each of her daughters in turn. The regret inside her expanded to pain as she drew herself up to her full height. She shook off James's supportive hand gently, refusing to allow him even partial responsibility for her failures over the years as she responded, "I wish I knew the whole answer to that question, Meredith. I suppose . . . I suppose I came here to free myself from a past that I couldn't forget, as well as to find my daughters again."

Silence was the only response she received.

The sun was dropping into the horizon, signaling the end of another day. Yet no one within the quiet room appeared to notice. The silence was broken when Letty turned soberly to her daughters and said, "I know you're all expecting this to be a time of reckoning that was held years in abeyance, but the truth is that I don't have a clear-cut explanation for the things that brought us to this point in time."

Sighing, Letty continued, "What I can tell you is that I was young and uncertain when it all started—only five years old when Mother and I were rescued from a Kiowa camp. All I remember is that Mother was delirious with happiness at first, but that I didn't feel the same when we left the camp behind. I felt lost, as if a part of me had been stolen, but my mother refused to sanction those thoughts. She told me that the Kiowa had kidnapped us both and killed my father when I was an infant. She said I would suffer greatly in a 'civilized society' if it was suspected that my bloodline was 'tainted.' She ridiculed everything I had been taught and told me to forget the past—most especially the man I knew only as Grandfather. She said I should be happy to be returned to my own people."

Letty frowned when she continued, "But Mother became solemn and unresponsive when the whispers about us started. My uncle, William McGregor, did nothing to help. When we awoke one morning and discovered that he had deserted us—had left us friendless and penniless—Mother made no attempt to explain the reason for his leaving. She merely went on denying everything as if our years spent in the Kiowa camp never existed."

Turning toward Meredith, Letty continued, "Difficult times followed, and I was so young when I met your father. I remember the first time I saw Weston Moore. He was big, handsome, and all male, with copper-red hair and a broad smile that made everything right with the world. You resemble him more than you realize, Meredith. He was also loving, passionate, and protective—everything I had ever dreamed of in a man, and I loved him desperately." She paused before saying, "I'm not certain . . . but I think that's the first time I heard the warning howls."

Letty looked at James and did not see the startled glances of mutual understanding her daughters exchanged. She continued, "My mother died unexpectedly when I was sixteen. I was alone, but not for long. When Wes and I were married shortly afterwards, it was the happiest day of my life. Yet our time together was so short." She looked at Meredith and said hoarsely, "He did not even live to see you born."

Letty's glance was a silent entreaty for understanding when she turned to Johanna and said, "I met your father sometime after that. I did not believe I could ever love anyone the way I had loved Weston Moore, but John Higgins was such a good man. He was slight, blond, sincere, and wonderful in ways that were so different from Wes, but he loved me with the same fervor. He promised me protection and said that his feelings for me would never end. When the whispers about me grew to encompass my innocent child, I married him. We went to Arizona to pursue his dream of striking it rich, and I grew to love him, too. The warning howls began again just before he was killed unexpectedly, leaving me pregnant and alone again.

"I panicked and left Arizona to return to the only true home I had ever known. The only problem was that I also returned to rumors that seemed to grow with every passing day. The warning howls persisted, and when an elderly traveling couple, Archibald and Elizabeth Fitzsimmons, offered to take me back to New York City with them as their maid, I saw an avenue of escape that I couldn't refuse. They knew nothing about my two young daughters, so I left both Meredith and you in an orphanage, telling myself that you would be better off without me. I silently thought to return one day to claim you both; but, truthfully, I'm not certain I believed it would happen. I can't explain it, but the howling then abruptly ceased."

Letty took a breath. She trembled as she scrutinized her daughters and the men they loved, hoping she could make them understand. She glanced at James, praying he would not despise her as she continued, "You all know what happened when Elizabeth Fitzsimmons died." She said resolutely, "I loved both Elizabeth and Archibald—I truly did. When Elizabeth died, Archibald and I found a way to assuage our mutual grief together; you, Justine, were the result." She exclaimed in a rush as her gaze held

Justine's intently, "Archibald was so happy knowing you were to be born. We were both happy. I confessed to him that I had left my other daughters in Texas, and he insisted that I send for them. We were a happy family together, until . . ."

After a silent moment, Letty continued flatly, "I knew what was going to happen the minute I heard the first howl. I warned Archibald, but he laughed at my concerns. He was killed that same day."

Briefly unable to go on, Letty closed her eyes. She forced herself to continue, "I swore I would beat the curse that followed me. I was left with three fatherless daughters to support, and I became determined to achieve financial success so that I would never need to depend on a man again. I resolved to keep all intimate liaisons casual so that no other man would die because of me. The past had only caused me pain, so I refused to speak of it— even to my own daughters. My only acknowledgment of it was the name I adopted—a name that somehow seemed appropriate in light of all I was determined to achieve. The name was Letty *Wolf*."

Pausing, Letty continued more softly, "I worked hard to achieve success, and at some point the howlings ceased. Society, which had formerly shunned me, now opened its doors. I became somehow caught up in the unexpected glory of it. Men flocked to my side, showered me with compliments, begged me for intimacies, yet I took only occasional, casual lovers. Then, to my everlasting shame, when you— my daughters—began interfering with that life, I sent you away—again telling myself it was for the best."

Letty shook her head in silent self-condemnation as she forced herself to go on. "Still, the illegitimacy of my relationship with Archibald and the child I had borne him disturbed me. I suppose that was the reason I clung to Mason Little as I did. Even now, with almost irrefutable facts facing me, it's difficult to believe that designating him as the heir in my will caused him to send men to kill my daughters—his own cousins."

Letty smiled weakly at her daughters as she said, "But, of course, you aren't legally Mason's cousins. I suppose if I had kept that reality in mind, none of this would have happened. In any case, I made excuses for Mason's shortcomings because his relationship to Archibald offered me a form of legitimacy. I allowed him to exploit my personal weakness—but I swear to all of you that I truly, truly believed he cared."

Letty paused again. Her expression tightened as she whispered, "Time passed so quickly. Somehow I didn't expect my daughters to grow up so quickly. Nor did I expect to finally meet a man unlike the rest . . . one I would find myself unable to cast aside as I did the others." She glanced up at James before concluding, "Nor did I ever expect it all to come to this."

"What did you expect, Mother?" Justine whispered. "Did you expect that we would remain under your rule but out of your sight for the rest of our lives?"

Her voice a soft accusation, Meredith added, "Did you think that we would be only shadow figures you could call upon when you felt the need?"

Appearing confused, Johanna asked haltingly, "Did you truly expect that we would grow up to be less determined to be ourselves than you were?"

Letty took a spontaneous step backward. She looked at her daughters as they awaited her reply. Each was startlingly beautiful in her own right . . . reminiscent of the fathers she had loved so dearly. Dissimilar in physical appearance, yet alike in the women they had become, they had learned in the most difficult of ways—without any help from her at all—the true meaning of love.

Her throat suddenly tight, Letty responded softly, "I have no good response to those questions, except to say that you've overcome the obstacle of being my daughters . . . and you make me proud."

Meredith said, "If you are truly proud of the woman I am, you may take considerable credit for it. I would not have been so determined . . . so resolved to become someone my sisters could depend on if you had not sent us away from you."

"I resented your secrecy about the past," Johanna interjected. "I felt I deserved to know more than the little you had told me about my father in a weak moment. That was the reason I was driven to finish what he started. That was also the reason I met Wade."

Justine offered reluctantly, "I have little to say . . . little to thank you for, except for the difficult memory of learning that the name Fitzsimmons, which I had used all my life, wasn't really mine at all." Justine paused and then added, "Without my realization, I chose a path that you had already followed by changing my name. I used an alias until I realized that there is no way to escape the past or who we really are."

Briefly silent in the wake of her daughters' responses to her revelations, Letty summoned her last spark of courage and said, "I'm sorry for all the heartache I caused you. None of you will ever realize how sincerely I mean those words. I hope you will believe me when I say that I never meant to drive you away."

"We know," Meredith replied softly. "You just didn't care."

Her expression pained, Letty stiffened her shoulders and said, "My only excuse is that whatever I did was the best I was capable of at the time. All that's left for me now is to face something that I should have faced long ago."

Meredith's hair blazed in the meager light of the room as she asked quietly, "And that is?"

"I need to visit Grandfather."

Realization hit Letty with the force of a blow when her daughters suddenly paled. She stumbled back against the hard wall of James's body as she mumbled incredulously, "It can't be . . . that you all see him, too."

"Grandfather . . ."

"The old man . . ."

"*Him* . . ."

Letty's breathing accelerated. "So you all see him! That means you all hear the wolf's howls, too." Tears streamed down her cheeks as she rasped, "I brought this down on you . . . this curse . . . this unrelenting phenomenon that allows no peace."

"He wasn't a curse!" Meredith countered.

"He was my consolation."

"He was there when I needed him."

Letty nodded stiffly. "And the howling?"

"I didn't understand it."

"I grew to expect it."

"It was a sign that someone cared."

Letty did not immediately respond. Then raising her chin, she said quietly, "I'm going to see *Grandfather*."

"Where?"

"How will you find him after all these years?"

After a moment's silence, Justine asked quietly, "Is he really our grandfather?"

Justine's question struck Letty to the heart. She gave the only response she could.

"I don't know."

The silence that followed was deafening.

Mason woke up slowly. His mind was unclear as pain struck simultaneously in his head and ribs; he glanced around him. Yes, he remembered. He was in a shabby Winsome hotel room and his final reckoning with Letty Wolf was at hand.

Staggering to his feet, Mason walked to the mottled mirror above the washstand and drank greedily from the pitcher there. Then looking up, he stared at his reflection. The image he saw was gaunt, dirty, and bearded with a growth of several days. His thinning hair was uncombed, and the expensive clothes hanging on him loosely were wrinkled and spotted. He had a look about him of total desperation. The reflection was so unfamiliar that Mason was momentarily startled—before he laughed aloud. No one would recognize him as the meticulous Mason Little—which suited him fine. He was anonymous.

Mason took a few moments to splash water on his face. He needed to wake up . . . to be of clear mind if he was to accomplish his purpose. Waiting only a few moments more, he searched out his hat and headed for the door.

At the lobby desk, he was about to speak when the clerk said hesitantly, "So you're all right after all. I was beginning to think I needed to check up on you. I hadn't seen you in a few days."

"A few days!" Mason's eyes widened. "You're telling me I slept that long?"

"If that's what you were doing up there, you did." The clerk hesitated before adding, "I figured you wanted to be alone, which is why I didn't interfere. You looked so bad and all when you got here."

"Did I?" Withholding his anger at the clerk's comment, Mason said stiffly, "I came here looking for someone . . . a very beautiful woman and her escort. I think they—"

Interrupting, the clerk said with a smile, "You'll have to be more specific. We've got a bevy of beautiful women registered here all of a sudden. I ain't seen the like of it before, neither."

Mason inquired gruffly, "What do you mean? The woman I'm talking about is older . . . dark-haired and dark-eyed . . . very beautiful to hear some describe her. Her escort is a big, well-built, middle-aged man with brown hair that's gray at the temples."

"That woman would be the mother."

"The mother?"

"That's right." The clerk tapped his finger on the

ledger as he said, "She came in with a fella named James Ferguson. Her daughters were already registered here."

"Her daughters!"

The clerk frowned. "I thought you said you knew her."

Mason did not deign to reply. He demanded, "Where are they?"

"They left early this morning . . . the whole bunch of them."

Mason took a backward step before the clerk continued, "They asked me to direct them to the Kiowa village that used to be around these parts, but I told them there wasn't no village left, that them Indians disappeared—or was killed off. Whatever, they ain't around no more."

The clerk stopped talking. Irritated, Mason urged, "And?"

"They was surprised. The older woman—she was a beauty who didn't even look like she could be their mother—said she wanted to go there anyway. She didn't remember where it was, so I told her how she could find what was left of it. Her daughters and the fellas they was with didn't say much."

"The fellows they were with?"

The clerk frowned as he said, "Yes, the fellas they was with—real fine-looking Westerners, too. They looked like they knew what they was doing."

"When did they leave?"

"You just missed them."

Mason asked with limited patience, "How long ago?"

"About an hour."

"How can I find that village?"

The clerk frowned. "You ain't expecting to go there, too, are you? I mean, you don't look like you're in any shape to make the trip."

"Don't I?" Mason inwardly sneered. He had just been served the opportunity of a lifetime. He said, "Just tell me how to find it."

"You're making a mistake. They all said to keep their rooms for them, that they'd be back. You can see them then."

"I said . . . tell me how to find it."

The clerk shrugged. "If that's what you want. The place ain't hard to find when you know where it is, but it's not the easiest ride getting there."

"That's my problem."

The clerk did not comment.

Leaving minutes later with the route committed to memory, Mason smiled. What could be better? A deserted Indian village.

It was the perfect place for Letty Wolf to die.

Spotting a gun shop, Mason entered and slapped down the price of a rifle, congratulating himself that he always kept his wallet full. He smiled at the recollection of allowing a wealthy client to talk him into joining a gun club with him, then a riding club, and into taking numerous other *lessons* that he had thought ridiculous at the time. He had not realized those lessons would come in handy for the task of making him a rich man.

The sun was setting and Letty's heart was pounding. Dressed for the trail in a split skirt, shirt, and wide-brimmed Western hat similar to the ones her daughters had purchased, she appeared more their sister than their mother as the silent entourage proceeded toward the abandoned Kiowa village. Their progress had been slow, steady, and silent. Strangely, although her daughters had not said they would accompany James and her, Letty had known they would be waiting when it was time to leave. She supposed it was as important to them as it was to her to settle the events of the past.

Memories of a time long gone paraded across her mind as she drew closer—memories that her mother had bullied her into forgetting. The wooded trail they presently traveled was overgrown, but she recalled a time when it had been beaten down by the feet of hunting parties. Happy, carefree days spent in the sun returned to mind, as well as lessons taught over the flames of a fire pit—unusual lessons that she had been forced to forget—taught by a grandfather who sang and stamped his feet against the ground to the rhythm of mystical, mesmerizing chants. She remembered the shadows she'd seen in the flames as Grandfather scattered powders that raised the fire to a roaring blaze. She recalled the words of his chants, words meant for her ears alone. She recollected the respect Grandfather received when he walked down long lines of tepees with her at his side, and the reverence given his words when he spoke at gatherings attended only by elders of the tribe . . . and her. Through it all, she recalled that her mother had sat stone-faced and silent.

The trail became uncertain and Letty dismounted to continue on foot. She was deaf to the sound of her daughters walking behind her, and to James's footsteps as he followed cautiously with the other men beside him. Scrambling, growing more anxious by the moment, Letty finally stood at a point where she could see the remains of the village, and pain stole her breath. Gone were the sturdy tepees that had housed the friends of her youth, the curving paths where she had raced like the wind, and the large remudas of horses where warriors had mounted with inborn grace. She remembered the horsemanship that seemed so much a part of the people's heritage, the reverence with which they had met each day, and the sense of purpose that accompanied each task, no matter how humble the chore.

All gone.

Only the skeletons of proud tepees remained standing lopsided in the shadows.

Tears filled her eyes, blurring the terrain. She was about to turn away when she heard her daughters gasp and looked back to see the light that had begun glowing a short distance away. Incredulous, she watched as it expanded. A sob of joy escaped her lips at the image that gradually approached her.

She remembered him now! The setting sun was at his back as it had been in the visions. His face, although weathered and lined, restored memories of her childhood; and the hair that had once been gray now streamed a snowy white onto his bare, bony shoulders. The ragged strands lifted in the slight breeze as she met those small, dark eyes that had not lost their intensity or their joy. She had no trouble understanding the formerly foreign, guttural sounds that rolled off his tongue as he stopped a few yards away.

Mason crouched in a thicket a distance from the remains of the Kiowa village. He'd had no trouble catching up with the entourage. They had traveled slowly, as if they had been almost reluctant to find what they were seeking, but he had not even stopped to eat. He witnessed Letty's dismay as she viewed the skeletal outlines of tepees visible in the setting sun, the overgrown paths that had once felt the steady beat of moccasined feet, the devastation that reigned. He barely controlled his laughter.

This was what she had come so many miles to find? This was the fulfillment of a dream that had made her tremble through long, empty nights? This was the memory that had ruled her life and forced him into the incredibly painful journey he had just endured—that she was a *half-breed*?

Mason's satisfaction at the thought was complete. Letty Wolf's blood was tainted, and his uncle had been seduced into producing a daughter with tainted blood as well!

The answer to the present situation was clearer to him than it had ever been before. Letty Wolf did not deserve the success she had attained, and her *half-breed* daughters did not deserve to inherit her wealth. He was the only one of them whose blood was true. It would be up to him to put the proper ending to the story . . . to settle in personal triumph the difficulties that had begun the first day his aging uncle had set eyes on Letty Wolf.

Sending an impatient glance toward his mount when it stirred behind him, Mason raised his rifle to his eye. Letty made a clear target where she stood looking at the burial ground that the Kiowa village had become. Her daughters stood behind her, vividly outlined against the brilliant red and gold of the horizon, but he wasn't interested in them. He knew he needed to bring Letty down with his first shot, and that he needed to immediately follow with a second to finish her off. He was only too aware that James stood behind her, and that James would give chase as soon as incredulity left his mind. But Mason had the advantage, and he had not come so far and endured so much to accept failure now.

Mason focused through the sights of his rifle. A swift, subtle twitch of the finger, a sudden, quick report, and it would all be his.

With that thought in mind, he concentrated intently, his finger on the trigger.

Mason gasped at the unexpected, searing pain that struck his back! He spun around, the rifle falling from his grasp as a knife plunged again and again into his chest.

Unable to speak as his blood pulsed forth, Mason stared. His eyes widened at the sight of Ham's grin. He was not dreaming. Grim reality made the sky darken although it was not yet night.

It wasn't fair! One more moment and he would have been a wealthy man! One more second and he would have been at the top of the world!

Yet as another moment passed, Mason's life ended

in a wilderness totally foreign to the city where he had expected to become a king.

Standing over Mason's bloody body, Ham could not control his widening grin. He had done it! He would be well rewarded for his effort, but it was not the money he would receive for doing his job that elated him. He had proven that Mr. Charles's faith in him was not unfounded. He had confirmed the truth that he was the most dependable of Mr. Charles's men, and his prestige within the organization would grow.

Ham sneered at Mason's lifeless body. It had not been difficult to follow him and to accomplish his purpose because he was determined. He had never really liked the fellow either, and—

Ham went suddenly still at a sound behind him.

The menacing growl sounded again. Ham turned toward it as a form gradually took shape in the shadowed glade. He gasped when it drew closer and he saw saliva dripping from its powerful jaws. He took a step backward, his hand clenching tight on the knife he still held. The animal sprang toward him, hitting him with the full force of its weight and knocking him to the ground. The knife was struck from his hand as Ham fought to keep the powerful jaws from locking on his throat, but the effort was wasted.

The animal's attack was overpowering. Even as he struggled to free himself, Ham felt his hot blood streaming freely. A yellow-eyed, feral gaze glared into his, and the fetid scent of death grew strong as his life crashed to its end.

* * *

Letty trembled as Grandfather stood before them, his voice carrying clearly in the charred village that had once been their home. He held Letty's gaze with his as he said:

"Welcome home, daughter. The earth that bore you awaited your return. My time is short and my words are now few, but the blood that flows inside you assures me that you will comprehend all I have to say.

"I cherished you from the day you were born. I recognized in you a gift that would be your torment and your joy. You were taken from me against my wishes, but I did my best to protect you through the years. I asked the spirits to follow you so that you would not suffer unduly at the hands of the people who claimed to be your own. But that was not enough. I could not defend you against the whispers that followed you, against the baseless prejudices that raged, against the memories your mother harbored while she would not allow your own recollections to survive. I cherished the fruit of your loins even when despair forced you to abandon your daughters. I held them close in my mind, knowing that they carried in them all that remained of the son I held dear . . . your father . . . who died defending his woman and child. I gloried in the triumph of your spirit—one that had been beaten and nearly crushed by an angry world. I celebrated when it survived, knowing that the blood of my son survived with it. I did not lose faith, even when my people were driven from the land you knew.

"I called you back, just as the land called you. I embedded in you a knowledge that you must return . . . that you must remember if you were to regain your daughters once again. I spoke to the Great Spirit and asked his help in order that my people might survive in this way."

Letty watched as a large gray wolf bounded to Grandfather's side while he continued, *"I protected you, and all who belonged to you in any way I could, and you have returned. You have remembered, and it is good, for my time is short and my strength wanes."*

Letty listened as Grandfather's voice grew fainter and he said, *"I have only one thing to ask of you . . . that you do not allow yourself to forget. As the memories return, you will feel the need to share them with those who are dearest to you. They will understand. They will cherish all that you cherish. They will never forget what was, and through you . . . through them . . . our people will never die."*

Pausing, Grandfather raised a rawhide rattle toward her. He shook it as he chanted loudly. He turned and repeated his chant for each daughter in turn as they stepped forward solemnly to receive his blessing.

Letty knew she would never forget the sound of Grandfather's sigh or his fading voice as he said, *"I am tired now. It is time for me to say farewell. I have remained here only to bring you home, so that you will know that you and yours are forever cherished in the hearts of the many who have gone before you, and that you are esteemed by those who know that through you, our people live on."* Pausing to look at each in turn, Grandfather said, *"This is my final farewell."*

Turning, Grandfather walked slowly back into the light of the setting sun with the large gray wolf at his side.

Letty was not certain when she first heard light footsteps approaching her from behind. She felt her throat fill with emotion when Meredith touched her shoulder, and she turned to see that her daughter's amber-eyed gaze was moist. She bit her lip when Johanna placed her hand on her arm, and she closed her eyes at the sweet consolation of Justine's arm slipping around her shoulders. With a mumbled phrase, Letty gathered her daughters into her arms.

Freeing herself at last, she walked back soberly into James's waiting embrace. She looked at her daughters as they also stepped into the comfort of their men's arms. She saw the looks they exchanged and the new understanding in their eyes when they glanced briefly at her. They did not hear her finally whisper without fear the words James had waited to hear her say. The words "I love you" trailed from her lips as James crushed her closer and her daughters' tears fell freely.

In the purity of that moment, none of them realized fully what had just happened.

They would never see Grandfather again.

They would never again hear the sounds that were meant for their ears alone . . . the howls that both warned and consoled them.

Finally, in their bittersweet joy, they did not realize that they were free, and that the cry of the wolf was silenced forevermore.

EPILOGUE

Mr. Charles glanced again at the headline on the society page of the morning newspaper. He looked at the blurred photograph of Letty Wolf with a smiling James Ferguson standing beside her.

The couple had returned from their unexpected trip west to the welcome of the many who had sorely missed Letty at her thrice-weekly soirees. But there was a surprise in store for some when Letty announced that her marriage to James Ferguson was imminent, and that her daughters would return briefly from their new homes in Texas to attend the ceremony.

Mr. Charles snickered. The untouchable Letty Wolf. He admired her gumption almost as much as the beauty with which she had bewitched so many. There were not many women like her.

Mr. Charles's smile faded. He was pleased when Mason's body was found not far from Winsome, Texas. It bothered him that Ham was found a few yards away, the victim of an animal attack. He would have liked to tell Ham he approved of his decision to follow Mason to Texas in order to finish the job he had started—but it was too late for that, and there were many waiting to fill Ham's shoes. He knew he would not suffer any true loss in the long run.

Mr. Charles locked the office door behind him as he left. He had been delayed in attempting to reconcile his accounts and it was getting dark. The street was empty, yet he had no fear. He knew that however dark and empty the street appeared to be, however alone he presently was, he was safe in this portion of town that he had made his own. Like Letty Wolf, he was untouchable in his domain.

Mr. Charles walked confidently, but he halted abruptly at a sound in the shadows. Turning, he strained to peer into the semidarkness as the light shifted and a shape gradually emerged. He recognized the growl when it grew suddenly louder, yet he was unprepared when an animal leaped at him out of the shadows. The weight of the creature knocked him down against the hard pavement as jaws fastened on his throat.

Stunned and helpless, he struggled wildly.

His blood flowed and he weakened, but the animal did not.

When fatal darkness overwhelmed the sound of his last, gurgling breath, he did not see the animal release him to slink back into the shadows . . . never to be seen again.

Read on for an exciting preview of
TUMBLEWEED
by award-winning author
JANE CANDIA COLEMAN

Allie Earp always said the West was no place for sissies. And that held especially true for a woman married to one of the wild Earp brothers. She had no fear of cussing a blue streak if someone crossed her, patching up a bullet wound, or defending her home against rustlers. Every day was a new adventure—from the rough streets of Deadwood to the infamous OK Corral in Tombstone. But through it all one thing remained constant: her deep and abiding love for one of the most formidable lawmen of the West.

Chapter One

I was too young to know that nothing ever stays the same, that sooner or later the world finds you. I was four, maybe five, when the Kansas-Nebraska Act brought trouble right to our doorstep. All of a sudden there was death in the air and folks shouting words I didn't understand—Abolition, state's rights, slavery—and Mum kept the shotgun by the door when Pa was out in the field. We didn't get the shooting and hanging Kansas did, but wagons headed there went through Omaha, some even through our pasture, and always there was night riders up to no good.

"It'll come to war," Pa said one night when we was at supper. The light in the lamp flickered when he spoke, and all of a sudden he looked old.

It scared me. Like I was seeing the future, seeing change, and helpless to stop it.

Mum sighed. "Seems it's already war here. All these folks coming and ready to fight. What'll happen to us?"

"I don't know. I wish I did. But the day anybody brings slaves to Nebraska is the day I start my own fight."

"What's slaves?" I asked, although us kids weren't supposed to interrupt our parents.

Pa stared across the table at me. "It's one man ownin' another. Or a lot of others. And it's wrong."

I thought about that. "Like we own Sally?" Sally was our cow.

"You might say that. 'Cept men ain't animals, and Sally's treated better than some of the slaves I heard about."

By the time us kids crawled into bed, my five-year-old mind was running off in all directions. "I don't want nobody ownin' me," I whispered to Melissa.

She giggled. "You will one day. When you're grown."

"I won't, either." Growing up to me meant trouble.

"Anyhow"—she gave a big yawn—"folks like us ain't slaves, and we sure don't own any. Now go to sleep."

"What if there's a war? Will we get to fight, too?"

"It's men who do the fightin'. Women stay home and worry."

"I bet I could fight good as a man," I said. "Even if I am a girl."

"And if you don't hush talkin', you'll be a sorry one." She turned over, her back to me.

"You ain't my boss," I mumbled, but she didn't answer, and I lay there, hearing all the night sounds—Pa snoring on the other side of the quilt that divided the rooms, the wind in the leaves of the big cottonwood, an owl calling from the creek bottom.

One thing I knew for sure. I didn't want anybody bossing me. Not then, not ever. What I didn't understand was that, when you love somebody, there's no question of who owns who or who gives orders.

That's what I was thinking when Virge found me later that night, a long ways from camp. My feet had taken me up the big wash to where the hills turned rocky, and the trees thinned out.

"I thought you'd got lost." He put his good arm around me, and I leaned up against him.

"Lost!" I said. "All you men can think of is a woman who can't find her way in the dark. I was just rememberin' back."

He shook his head. "Seems we never stop talking about that place. We're marked. Like Cain. I wish we'd never left the farm. Or stayed in Prescott. Had a family instead of followin' some pipe dream." He sounded bone-tired.

"Spilt milk," I told him.

"I'm not cryin'."

"I know that."

The Earp men didn't waste time on tears. That was left to us women, but, if we cried, we did it alone where no one could see. The faces we showed were masks, but I reckon everybody does that—hide behind a smile or a pokerface. You're safest that way.

I put my arm around Virge's waist. "Let's go on back. Let's go to bed."

His laugh began down low. I could feel it moving up into his chest. "You got somethin' in mind, Allie?"

"How'd you guess?"

The laugh spilled out, big and jolly, Virge's laugh. "Because I know you down to your toes."

And that's a comfort. Being understood and no need to play games. But being me, I had to have the last word. "That's what you think," I said.

✂ ☐ **YES!**

Sign me up for the Historical Romance Book Club and send my FREE BOOKS! If I choose to stay in the club, I will pay only $8.50* each month, a savings of $6.48!

NAME: _____

ADDRESS: _____

TELEPHONE: _____

EMAIL: _____

☐ I want to pay by credit card.

☐ **VISA**   ☐ MasterCard   ☐ DISCOVER

ACCOUNT #: _____

EXPIRATION DATE: _____

SIGNATURE: _____

Mail this page along with $2.00 shipping and handling to:

Historical Romance Book Club
PO Box 6640
Wayne, PA 19087

Or fax (must include credit card information) to:

610-995-9274

You can also sign up online at **www.dorchesterpub.com**.

*Plus $2.00 for shipping. Offer open to residents of the U.S. and Canada only. Canadian residents please call 1-800-481-9191 for pricing information.

If under 18, a parent or guardian must sign. Terms, prices and conditions subject to change. Subscription subject to acceptance. Dorchester Publishing reserves the right to reject any order or cancel any subscription.